LYOVITALIS

DEDICATION

In memory of my most beloved grandmother,
Ruth Kirtón

Lyovitalis (dissolution of the soul) Source unknown—Victims are stricken with complete, sudden paralysis of the body producing a lifeless state that endures three to five days before complete system failure occurs. Eyes may remain open even after death. There is no cure. There is no understanding. There is only uncertainty—and fear.

PROLOGUE

APRIL 3, 1913

"Audrianna, you know how I loved her, don't you?"

Dr. Audrianna Foster lifted her weary head from her father's bedside, where it had been resting for the past two days. Two pairs of cyan eyes met.

"Yes, Father, I do," she said.

It was a cruel twist of irony that a hospital stay now brought father and daughter together. Dr. Foster's long clinic hours when Audrianna was a child, and too many overnights in the hospital, had robbed them both of walks in the park together or family trips to the beach. "A doctor's life is not his own," he would remind her then. Even in his final moments, Dr. Foster's life was still not his own; the obsession still possessed him.

The obsession was Audrianna's mother, of whom he now spoke. After she unexpectedly contracted a rare and poorly understood disease called lyovitalis, her father had given up his private practice to devote all his energy to studying the disease. Lyovitalis had consumed not only her mother, but also her father in the years following her death and continued to be the object of his obsession even here on his deathbed. To Audrianna, it always seemed like she had lost both of her parents to lyovitalis. Now, however, terminal pneumonia was killing off all that was physically left of her father.

Audrianna's mother had been the joy for both her and her father—conjuring birthday parties, leading Christmas shopping ventures in New York, being the perpetual provider of hugs and kisses and visits from the tooth fairy. Rather than trying to continue her legacy in life, Audrianna's father had, instead, chased after her into the grave. "She was my angel," he continued. "My sanity."

Audrianna's life took a different direction following her mother's death. She wanted to move on with her life and broke ties with the sole link to her dead mother—her obsessive father. In the three years since her mother's death, Audrianna had not followed her father's progress. She had heard, through various channels, that he had spent time abroad researching in Switzerland. Occasionally, when they did write to each other (and this was rare), he had mentioned his partner, Dr. Gustav Adler, a professor of medicine at the University of Zurich, but she was not very interested. It was only a week ago that Audrianna had received the call about her father's condition while at her internship at the Women's Medical College of Pennsylvania. She had not seen her father since her mother's funeral.

"Three years! Christ, what have I done?" she thought to herself as she stroked his unkempt silver hair.

She longed to find closeness with him in his final hour. Pale wrinkled skin exaggerated his true age, intensified by sleepless nights and regrets that would go unresolved. She wished she had paid more attention to his deteriorating condition.

"When she was taken from me," he continued, "I vowed to avenge her death through the eradication of that dreadful disease. But I have failed her, as I have failed you."

His voice was faint from dry, sticky lips, and Audrianna's throat tightened. She closed her moistening eyes, speaking to him as the child she tried to remember being. "You never failed me, Daddy," she whispered.

"Yes, I have. I never gave you the love or affection you deserved, never took the time to help your mother with your upbringing. You were such a beautiful little girl." He smiled faintly. "You are still so much like your mother."

His breathing became raspy and labored; he choked back secretions. Audrianna observed him as a physician, rather than a daughter, as she was far more comfortable with the science of death than the emotion of it. "Calm your breathing," she coached him. "Don't waste your air."

"No! There are things I have to tell you, Audrianna. For pity's sake, let me finish while I still have the strength."

Audrianna bowed her head. If listening to his deathbed confessions might help him achieve a peaceful transition, then that is what she would do. It was her obligation, not only as his daughter but also as a human being.

"I want to tell you how very proud I am of you," he began. "It's no small task to undertake a career as a physician, especially as a woman. I know you'll be an asset to the community. I'm happy to call you both my daughter and my colleague."

A coughing fit shook his frail body. "My life is coming to an end. I've accepted this. I embrace the wonders the hereafter may bring. However, I must admit I am unhappy to be leaving this world with so much unaccomplished. Audrianna, you must promise—"

Again he stopped, gasping for the air required to finish his thoughts. Audrianna winced at the sight. She leaned closer to him, pressing her ear to his lips, alleviating the need for him to speak above a whisper.

"What promise do you need from me, Father?" she asked him. "I'm listening."

"My work," he panted. "You must continue my work."

Audrianna jolted awake. Surely she had misunderstood what he just said! How could he ask this of her? The thought was absurd. Abandon a budding career in obstetrics for a foray into pathology, halfway through her residency? It would be professional suicide. No. She would not do it.

Audrianna took a breath and released it as she spoke. "Father, I can't," she said softly, but sternly.

His blue skeleton-fingers, frigid from inadequate blood flow, snatched up her hands with sudden zeal. They worked their way up her arms to her face and dramatized his demand. "You! Must! Promise!" His voice was strangled but commanding; his eyes blazed like a tormented soul desperate for reprieve from killer angels.

"Father, no!" Audrianna then cowered from him as she regained control of her emotions. "I mean—I'm not. I'm not you!" She threw out her hands. "My strength is not research."

Of course, this statement was untrue. Audrianna was a champion of exploration within her discipline. She helped lay the groundwork for the social hygiene movement and was a pioneer in the field of modern contraception. The Comstock Act of 1873 banned contraceptives in the United States and the distribution of any information related to them, but Audrianna did not care. Unwanted pregnancies yielded orphaned children. Botched abortions brought death. She had seen far too many of both already. She worried about the legal ramifications, of course, but not enough to sway her vocation. Her father did not know that, though. He had never shown interest in her medical aspirations or achievements before this moment. That realization made her dishonesty seem less despicable.

"Audrianna, please," he pleaded with her. "Think of your mother. Remember how she was taken from you. Remember how it felt to be so helpless. If not for me, do it for her and the countless other mothers, fathers, sons, and daughters who will lose what you have already lost if a cure is not found."

Audrianna stood up from the bed and turned away, annoyed by this untimely manipulation. What a reckless, impossible fantasy! She was an accomplished, well-educated, and well-adjusted young American woman. Of course she loved her mother, but to what lengths? To give up her own life, as her father had, chasing the great unknown. She did not want to become another victim of obsession with lyovitalis.

Stop!

Audrianna cut into her own internal rant with a silent scream. She dredged the fingers of both hands through her hair and left them there while she considered his plea rationally. She wanted him to see her consternation. There were a thousand reasons why making such a promise did not make sense. She knew it and believed he knew it, too. If he had impressed her with anything during his lifetime, it was that he had maintained incredible focus in the presence of emotionally charged circumstances—but this situation was clearly different.

"Wasn't it?" she almost whispered audibly to herself.

Audrianna was not sure how or why, but there was another principle at hand: one she did not know how to fight. And one she was not sure she *should* fight. But she, too, had unanswered questions regarding her mother's death.

"All right, Father. I will." Audrianna heard herself make the promise with a voice not entirely her own. She lowered her hands to her hips and turned around.

Her father leaned back onto his funeral bed. The corners of his mouth were turned slightly upward, taunting death with a fearlessness that only comes when destiny is in play. "Safe, my child," he murmured.

"Yes, Father, I'll be safe." Audrianna's annoyance piqued again. She went to him and sat on the edge of his bed. He seemed to be trying to speak, but had exhausted his energy. His hands moved up to his neck where he fished a leather pouch from beneath his undershirt. Finally, he unearthed a metal key and offered it to her.

Audrianna took it. "What's this?" she asked, momentarily transfixed.

He did not respond.

"Father, what is this to?"

She shook his shoulders gently; he did not respond. His eyes were open, but now seemed vacant. Their sea-foam hue had been extinguished.

"Father!" Audrianna succumbed to the same childish tears she had imposed upon him years before. Then, as now, they did not reach him in his realm of vestigial loneliness. She embraced the self-pity a minute more and then, gradually, the awareness crept in. She cried for something that was never really there, had never been there, and which she, therefore, had not lost at all.

"Goodbye, Daddy," she whispered.

CHAPTER 1

"*Est-ce qu'il y a un docteur ici?*"

Ears buzzing, Audrianna bolted upright from a restless night. Burning oil in her nostrils and steam clouds billowing past her window reacclimated her to her seat on the locomotive. The station outside told her they were temporarily stopped. It was dark, the station largely deserted.

Out on the dimly lit platform, a young man sprinted from the darkness, shouting at the station attendant. "*Est-ce qu'il y a un docteur ici?*"

French. They must still be in France. The young man seemed to be asking a question, not making a declaration. Either way, Audrianna did not understand. She had studied German in school, not French. And for this trip, not anticipating spending more than twenty-four hours in France, she had only memorized what she considered to be the most important

French phrases—*Where is the washroom? I am hungry. I am lost,* and *I don't speak French*—none of which contained this word.

The station attendant granted the young man access to the train with a wave of the hand, and he quickly ascended the stairs, repeating his question to the passengers in Audrianna's boxcar. *"Est-ce qu'il y a un docteur ici?"*

Audrianna peeped up and over the seat in front of her. The young man appeared to be eighteen, maybe nineteen years old. His skin was much too flawless for him to be any older than that. He was tall, with a slim, muscular build, handsome although not yet a full-grown man. The crowd dismissed the young man, returning almost instantly to their reading or sleeping—everyone except Audrianna.

Curiosity overrode her sensibilities, directing her eyes to announce her interest. She studied him, intrigued by his presence and touched by his distress, although she did not understand what he was saying. The young man caught her stare and came down the aisle to crouch at her feet.

"Est-ce qu'il y a un docteur ici?" He asked her in a normal speaking voice, repeating his question slowly and looking only to her for the answer.

Audrianna licked her lips, feeling the need to reply, but not knowing how. The rhythm of her heartbeat thumped beneath her shirt, driving adrenalin into her already shaky hands. It was impossible to know for sure, but she thought she heard a word that sounded like *doctor* in the obviously urgent question.

"Are you English?" he asked her, discerning that she had been completely clueless as to his first inquiry.

Audrianna shook her head. "No. American."

"Are you a nurse?" Again, he looked hopeful. He seized one of her hands and clutched it between his own. Audrianna shook her head again, amazed at his directness and now scared for what must be a dire predicament. She felt like she should clarify her position to him, but found herself fixated on the physical connection of her hand in his. Instead of wondering why he needed a doctor, she felt herself unable to look away from his strong, sculpted jaw line, high prominent cheekbones, and beautiful olive skin. But what riveted her and rendered her speechless were his eyes, his brilliant emerald-green eyes. They were mesmerizing.

"I'm sorry." Audrianna forced herself to look away from him to reorient her thoughts. She rubbed her fingers across her forehead like a crystal ball, summoning the ghosts of the words she had misplaced. "I'm a d-doctor," she stuttered, flustered by her sudden inability to communicate and also by the sudden rush of blood to her face. Her clothes stuck to her skin with a nervous adhesive secreted by her pores, making them tighter and heavier than they had been just minutes earlier. She plucked the fabric of her shirt to cool herself.

"I need your help," the young man told her, ignoring her obvious discomfort. He spoke with an unusual accent, flaccid and carefully enunciated. "There is no time to give you the reasons you must require in order to come with me," he continued, "but I'm afraid that you must. I promise you will not be harmed."

He grabbed her overnight bag with one of his hands and curled the fingers of his other hand through hers like a weed sprouting roots. Audrianna opened her mouth to utter a refusal, but found herself unable to talk—not like before when she just could not find the right words, but physically unable to talk. Her lips were numb, her tongue was numb, and strangely, her vocal chords seemed to be paralyzed. She was prone to panic attacks, but never as severe as this.

A rush of warmth flooded her arm, pulsating from the young man's fingertips like blazing flares. He pulled her to her feet and tugged her out into the aisle as the heat made its way up and throughout her body. Her spatial perceptions became inaccurate, subverted so severely by his mind-altering fire fingers that Audrianna was not even sure she was attached to her body. Her arms were too heavy to lift, her legs unresponsive to her demands; it was clear she was going with him whether she liked it or not.

"Help me!" she screamed with her mind alone. She beseeched the porter with her eyes to intercede on her behalf. Surely the porter would not let this depraved kidnapper remove her from the train against her will. The train porter, however, hardly glanced as the young man, with Audrianna in catatonic tow, rushed by and neared one of the train's exits. Before Audrianna knew what was happening, she was outside on the train platform, coughing and shivering in the wake of steam.

"*Regarde que les sacs de Madame soient livres a Zurich,*" the young man told the station attendant. He pulled a large wad of bills from his pocket and stuffed a couple of them into the man's hands.

The station attendant eyed them both suspiciously, but Audrianna was frozen inside her mind, non-vocal and motionless, with nothing more than a meaningless mental rebellion raging inside her. Either her seeming complacence or the bills in his hand convinced the station attendant of her security.

He scribbled out a baggage-claim ticket on a timeworn pad, separated the check, and handed a portion of each to the train porter and to her captor. The whistle sounded from the front of the locomotive, announcing its departure with a malicious heckle seemingly meant only for Audrianna. She then watched with dread as it pulled away, leaving her in a most precarious predicament.

———•◦•———

The night was lit with the glow of an almost perfectly rounded moon. Only the shroud of the occasional passing cloud dimmed its light. Audrianna began to regain her senses with each passing step, although she was still unable to speak. She watched her escort closely as he pulled her forward by the hand. He did not talk at all. His focus was on streets, on lanes and landmarks, but not on her.

Audrianna oscillated between playing out murderous scenarios in her mind and focusing on whom her abductor might be. He was trying to pass himself off as a common laborer with his heavy khaki trousers and oversized tweed newsboy cap, but Audrianna was not buying it. He had to be a professional. The amount of money he carried, his bilingual education, and dressy slide buckles on his suspenders gave him away. He was like an actor in costume, and he had recruited her to perform some role in his sordid theatrical production.

Above the noise of her own frantic thoughts, Audrianna heard the sound of music carried through the darkness by the wind. Nearby lamplight cast the pair's linked shadow against distant buildings bathed in red. Maybe they were not headed for the woods after all! Maybe he was not going to hang her from a tree or drown her in a river. Maybe this was all some kind of misunderstanding. After all, he was headed toward civilization, not away. A murderer would surely want to avoid that kind of public place, right?

Multiple lilts of high-pitched laughter assaulted her ears. The vocal fireworks exploded from an intersection ahead. The young man slowed his pace with caution, and then ducked against a ramshackle building, dragging Audrianna behind like a small dog on a tether. He peered around the corner of the wall, examining the scene on the street. Audrianna spied mobs of French-speaking soldiers and lewdly dressed women cluttering porches and spilling into the road. Piano music invigorated the drunken revelry in a manner so pronounced it would take an act of God to clear the area. This was not a place of sanctuary after all! He had brought her to a red-light district.

Certain now that her own tortuous rape and death awaited, Audrianna finally wrestled herself away from the stranger and attempted to run. The momentum of her willpower carried her forward a good five steps before she succumbed to the same debilitating numbness that had plagued her since the train. She fell to the ground and screamed, not once, not twice, but over and over again until she felt dizzy from the exertion. But it was no use. Nothing came out of her mouth except the natural sounds of forceful exhalations and small globules of spit.

The young man stepped up behind her and folded his arms underneath hers. He pulled her straight up and into him with minimal effort and backed them both into the same wall that they had been hiding behind. Audrianna did not struggle, choosing instead to conserve her energy so when she was able to run again, she could. She thought about crying, but did not. Tears would be useless in this situation anyway. Her kidnapper was obviously immune to the indecency of his exploits, and if anything, he might be perversely excited by a visible exhibition of emotion like crying. She had read about criminals like him in school and was not about to give him that kind of leverage. No. This circumstance called for quick thought and decisive action. Even if she had lost the use of her body, she still had her brain; that is exactly what she would have to employ to get herself out of this.

Sedately, Audrianna rested in his arms, moving only her mind and her eyes in search of an ally. She would have to take a chance on the crowd. Surely someone out there on the street would help her if she could only communicate her distress. She just had to find the right person and wait for the right time.

"Listen to me carefully," the young man said, cutting into her budding scheme. "There is no one out there who would be interested in helping you. If anything, they'd be more likely to take advantage of you in the same way that you're imagining I will."

Audrianna stopped short. It was as if he knew what she was thinking. She looked around for their reflection in a window. He must have been watching her eyes. Her eyes had betrayed her.

The young man breathed with a controlled rate into the air near her ear. "Be at ease," he whispered, striking a nerve in her that had lain dormant until then. "I mean you no harm. I am not a rapist, nor am I a murderer. I've brought you here because I need your help, nothing more."

Audrianna took a deep breath. There *was* something tender and nonthreatening in his voice. It was languid and compelling, containing sympathy for a woman who was clearly on the verge of a breakdown. The tender feeling of his arms around her validated his statement, allowing her some time to take in what he said. After ten seconds, she dropped her head against his shoulder in an outward show of compliance and felt, with a little uneasiness, his slow, regular heart beating against her back. Maybe it was just this, his composed presence, which Audrianna found persuasive. Or maybe it was just that she needed to believe him in order to free herself from the worry of death. Either way, calmness gradually overcame her. Her heartbeat slowed to match his, almost as if he had commanded it to do so, and she began to abandon her plots of escape for a position of faith in his sincerity. By the time he spoke again, she was open to what he had to say.

"You are in Mullhouse, France," he began. "Earlier today, the French launched an attack on the Sixth German Army about five miles from here. Tonight, the French soldiers are celebrating their victory all around us. Do you see?"

The Great War! One month ago, Bosnian nationalists assassinated Austria's archduke and Europe descended into hellish battle almost immediately. The American consulate advised against travel in Europe until negotiations were complete, but Audrianna considered their warning to be excessive. She could not fathom war as a response to such a random act of violence. Obviously, she was wrong. She lifted her head and looked around. The landscape was littered with men wearing long, blue-gray overcoats and bright red trousers. They laughed and drank together in groups, congratulating each other for being conquerors. To them, it was probably a most magnificent victory. They survived a day of shelling and gunfire, long enough to drink one more pint of ale with their brothers, perhaps to make love to a woman one last time. In war, days held death, while nights spent drinking and carousing meant another day survived—token victory in the midst of so much loss for a solider. The war for them had to end at this moment, for tomorrow death and mayhem would continue, possibly silencing them forever. Yes, she saw them. It was sad, though. As far as she was concerned, wars were never worth celebrating.

"I'm going to turn you loose now," he continued. "For both of our sakes, you mustn't draw attention our way. Do you understand?"

Audrianna nodded her head, and he released her from his hold. He retained his position against the wall but encouraged her to stand firmly on her own, away from him. As soon as she did, sensation returned to her vocal chords and her extremities instantly strengthened, leaving her solid and perfectly able to run. But she did not.

What had just happened to her? Had her panic triggered some sort of psychosomatic episode in which she was unable to control even the basic functions of her body, her voice, and her movements? She did not know. Furthermore, she was still unsure of what to do. Any attempt to flee would be futile because she did not know where the hell she was. And who knew what else she might run into? At least this young man had not tried to hurt her in any way—at least not yet.

"How did I get here?" Audrianna asked without looking at him.

"You walked with me from the train."

Audrianna sneered at his answer. "Yes, I realize that. What I mean is—" She threw her hands into the air, frustrated. This was pointless. He had not forced her. She never even said no. She may have wanted to, but she did not, or had not been able to. Yes, that's right, she *had not* been able to. Something had prevented her from refusing; she was just not sure what it was.

"What do you want from me?" She turned to the young man with a sudden, assertive force of suspicion.

"I need your expertise," he replied. "My friend is very sick and I need to get him home. Alive." His face was hidden in a shadowy silhouette requiring Audrianna to analyze his answer without visual cues.

"You're joking, right?" She laughed out loud.

Her reaction drew nothing but silence.

"I'm supposed to believe you're a simple French boy who pulled me off the train, into this deplorable area of God knows where, because you have a 'sick friend,' and there are no doctors anywhere in this, this *civilized* town?" She gestured at the hookers and revelers. Anger sharpened her voice, squashing other emotions. "Even if you are telling me the truth, what do you expect me to do? I have no facilities, only basic equipment and very few medicines. What kind of lunatic are you?"

The young man stepped out of the darkness, offering her a full look at his face for the first time since the train. His eyes were large and bright—so bright they fought the shadow off of his skin with a kind of piercing green luster. The color was so penetrating that Audrianna found it difficult to maintain eye contact. She took a step back as a reflex, then scolded herself for not standing firm. It did not matter. He did not pursue her as she thought he might. He was cool and unruffled, with his hands at his sides and his eyes locked on her in a way she could not explain. It was as though he knew her angry outburst was not a regular part of her character; he had no intention of taking her insults to heart.

"I've caused you much distress," he acknowledged humbly. "Forgive me. But I have no one else to turn to. Will you help me? Please?" He handed her the overnight bag he had carried with them from the train, and Audrianna seized it from him in a superficial demonstration of hostility.

"And where is my other luggage?!" She started toward the train indignantly, but stopped, finding she could not hold onto her rage. It was vexing to see him standing there in such a restrained, mild manner; not begging, not pleading, not even making excuses or trying to prevent her from leaving—just asking for help, as a stranger might ask for a drink of water or a coat to keep away the cold.

She surveyed the location, watching the people as they carried on their frivolities. She was far less frightened now than she had been, and, in fact, found it oddly amusing that she was in the midst of an experience, something, and someplace that should have always remained a fairy tale to her—the French countryside. But what was she supposed to do? If she said no to the young man, would he abandon her there on the street? And if he did, what were her chances of making it safely back to the train station on her own? And how long before the next train stopped? Perhaps if she made an effort to help him, at least he might feel obligated to take her back. Yes. That was it. She had to do it. She had to get back to that station. It was her only way out of this dilemma. And the only way to get out of this dilemma was to accede to this stranger's requests.

"Are we going into one of those *establishments*?" Audrianna asked, knowing full well what the answer was going to be.

"I'm afraid so," he said. "I'm sorry."

Audrianna scoffed. She bowed her head in silent prayer, remembering the sacred oath she had taken upon graduating medical school and asked God to consider the circumstances of her decision to follow this stranger into a whorehouse before damning her to hell. She never understood the qualifications for eternal damnation, but decided she should cover her bases in case she did not make it out alive.

"Well then, I guess if I'm to accompany you into a brothel, we should at least be introduced, don't you think?" she said.

The young man grinned at her and looked away, allowing a small crack in the impenetrable façade that Audrianna believed he possessed. For the next several seconds he was quiet and thoughtful, as though he was not sure of what to say or do next. Anxious to proceed with her plan before she changed her mind, Audrianna presented her hand to him. "My name is Dr. Audrianna Foster."

The young man accepted her hand into his and then pressed it to his lips. He bent his head forward in a modified bow. "You may call me Devon."

Audrianna nodded at him, but that was it. She considered adding "nice to meet you" or "my pleasure," but the truth was, she would have been happy to have ridden out her already regrettable European adventure without ever having made his acquaintance. She did not see the point in pretending differently. Besides, she was determined to remain as detached and objective as possible. This was still a dangerous situation, and just because she had come to a sort of agreement with this individual did not mean she trusted him.

"Are you are ready to come with me?" Devon asked.

Audrianna sorted through her arsenal of snarky responses, but found in the end that a simple "yes" was the most suitable. It was imperative for her to present herself as the detached, unbiased physician, calm and courageous in her line of servitude. That should be easy enough. Tempering emotion was not her strong suit, but it nearly always disappeared in the presence of medical practice.

"Stay close to me," Devon warned, wrapping his arm around her shoulders. Audrianna tried to shrink away from him but was held in place. "I apologize, but I must hold you like this if we are to be successful in carrying out this charade. It is important that we blend in. You are my consort, interested in showing me a good time, and I am the drunken patron who will pay your fee. If we are confronted, say nothing. Let me do the talking. And please try to remember, this is a celebration. If we are not participating, then why are we here?"

He spoke perfect English, his words delivered so formally and almost without inflection that he seemed to read from a translation book. Audrianna contorted her lips into an artificial smile, and they maneuvered through a dozen sets of pawing soldier hands. Devon pulled her from his side to his front, fending off the pack of hungry wolves and their groping, pointing, laughing, grabbing paws. He placed his face along the side of her head and spoke into her ear. "Do you understand what they are saying to you?" he asked.

Audrianna shook her head. Of course she did not know. She did not want to know either—but she got the gist. Did they not have mothers? Sisters?

"War knows no civility, Dr. Foster," said Devon. "The only other women here are prostitutes. These men assume you are for hire and that is why they are treating you this way. Try not to let it trouble you." He helped her up onto the porch of one of the hotels while Audrianna critiqued her own performance as his bought-and-paid-for mistress.

Maybe she had shuddered. Why else would he have found it necessary to assuage her angst? She needed to be more careful, to be mindful not only of what she was saying, but also of what she was not saying lest he discover more about her than she wanted to reveal.

The wood on the porch creaked and groaned with the weight of their two additional bodies, threatening to cave from movements too swift or footsteps too heavy. Audrianna clenched her teeth in expectation of complete structural collapse. They edged toward a shambled staircase. No one was ever going to believe this tale, she thought, testing the first stair before entrusting her entire weight to it. She was heading into a sex house with a stranger she had just met, in a country where speaking English was a liability. She felt like a character in one of those dark and dirty romance novels, the type that could only be purchased from the avant-garde vendors of the underground—the type that combined innocence, immorality, and exotic location with explicit sexual detail for the purpose of lascivious entertainment. The difference was her own situation was hardly entertaining, and while this place could definitely qualify as exotic, it was almost certainly an unsavory stage for romance.

As they climbed the stairs, Audrianna heard erotic moans behind curtains and doors. Heat surged into her cheeks. Her knowledge of physical love was limited to what she had learned via books in school, and nothing she had read in a textbook prepared her for this.

They exited the staircase at the second floor, stepping over the progressive trail of vagrants that were sleeping in the stairwell. A paltry spattering of moonlight lit the way. Audrianna found it necessary to feel her way along the squalid walls just to keep from tripping over the obstacle course of bodies. The stench of stale urine scorched her nasal passages as it seeped up from the floor. She wiped her forearm underneath her nose, deflecting the smell from her face with the scent of her own skin, comforted, if by nothing else, the darkness. She needed to be invisible, if only for a moment, to everyone but herself—to calm her jitters, to compose and restore the confident persona she knew she must portray.

Devon followed silently. Perhaps he, too, was grateful for the darkness and escape from the awkward sexuality on display. Maybe he was accustomed to this sort of lifestyle, although

Audrianna thought not. There was something refined in him, something she could not put her finger on but which did not seem to endorse houses of ill repute.

"We are here." He pulled a key from his pocket and opened one of the doors. Audrianna felt butterfly wings swat the insides of her stomach with a cruel, crippling tickle.

At the encouragement of Devon's hands, she stepped into the pitch-black room and then listened as the telltale "thunk" of a deadbolt seemed to pronounce a finality to her deal with fate. Why in the world had she thought coming in here was a better decision than running away when she'd had the chance to?

A crisp breeze swept through the dark apartment, infused with the scent of freshly smoked tobacco, cherries, chocolate, licorice, and one more scent that Audrianna did not readily recognize. What was it? She leaned into the unidentified smell, flaring her nostrils to accommodate and identify the pungency: blood. It was blood. She had smelled blood a thousand times before, although this was different. This was not the normal blood odor associated with female disorders or birthing babies. This was the perfume of suffering, like eau d' rotting flesh or the essence of gangrene, either of which were unmistakable vectors for slow, painful deaths.

Oh God! *Stay calm, stay calm.* One hard kick to the groin would stall him long enough for her to escape. Why in the world had she not thought of that earlier while out in the street?

"Everything is fine, Dr. Foster," Devon reassured her. "It must be the darkness that is frightening you. Let me find some light so you can see you have nothing to fear here." Again, he seemed to read her mind. Either she was an extremely poor actress or he was some kind of gypsy-warlock mind reader. She was not sure which idea discomforted her the most.

"Lorna?" A pitiful voice called from somewhere deep inside the room followed by the noise of urgent, shuffling feet.

"Dr. Foster. Over here!" Devon called to her.

Audrianna crept down and around the outside wall, bracing her body against the furniture as she felt it come and go. She made a sharp turn toward the sound of whimpering, knocking her knees against a single wooden bed in the middle of the room. The shadow of the wall engulfed the entire length of the bed, keeping its occupant shrouded. Moans of agony identified his position; stink foretold the severity of his condition.

"I can't see a thing!" Audrianna hissed. "Is there a lamp? A candle? Something?" She moved around the bed, reaching forward with her hands and then retracting them quickly each time she felt a cold, immovable mass. Devon finally brought forth a lamp. He lit the wick and adjusted the flame, hanging it on a hook above their heads to expose the sweaty, swollen face of a young man in soldier's uniform. His shirt bore bloodstains in various stages of congealment, from the crusty outer tails to the oozing volcano of macerated flesh on the right side of his chest. His skin was pale and his lips were gray, emitting shallow and strained respirations.

"This man isn't sick—he's been shot!" Audrianna exclaimed, leaning deep into the boundary of the injured soldier's personal space to examine the wound. She pried one of his eyelids open with her thumb and forefinger, finding a pupil so large it nearly covered the entire circumference of his eye. "He's in shock!" she cried. "We've got to get him to a hospital! Go and get some help. I'll do what I can until you get back."

She pulled her stethoscope and the newly invented pocket sphygmomanometer from her bag along with a few cloth bandages. The porous material was meant for cuts and scrapes, not gunshot wounds, but she had nothing else to stop the man from bleeding to death.

"Devon, did you hear me?" Audrianna asked him. She rolled all the bandages into one large compress and pressed it into the soldier's wound. Devon had made no move toward summoning assistance; in fact, he gave no indication he even heard her, so she repeated the command more aggressively. She grabbed his shirt with her free hand and pulled him to her, jiggling him until he looked into her eyes. "He will die without help," she said sternly. "Go and get someone *now*."

Devon took two steps back from the bed and covered his face with his hands. He did not snap from his stupor and bolt for the door as she expected him to. Instead, his shoulders sank sheepishly inward, telling of regret. He sat on a wooden chair next to the bed, without making further eye contact, and shook his head, muttering, "I can't."

"Why in God's name not?" Audrianna asked, confused. He moved heaven and earth to bring her from the train to see this man but was now unwilling to take additional steps to save his life? Was this just a ploy? Had this all been an elaborate scheme to get her into the hotel without a fuss? Was he about to carry out all the crimes she initially suspected of him?

"No!" Devon shouted. He stood up from his seat and opened his arms out, palms upward. "You are safe with me. I won't hurt you."

Audrianna stared at him, bewildered. She had not said any of that out loud. Her body language must have cued him. His intuitive perceptions were incredible. But—he had not been looking at her. What in the world was going on here?

"My friend is a German officer!" Devon blurted, then stopped himself as though he knew he said something he should not have, or could have been heard outside the door. "Nobody here will help him. He would be better off dead than in the hands of the enemy."

Audrianna shelved her wariness for a moment and attacked his excuse on the level of humanistic sensibilities. "Devon, I don't care who he is, and no serious doctor would. We have to find a surgeon. If his shock is from blood loss, there is nothing I can do. Do you understand what I'm telling you? He needs someone with battlefield medicine experience—not me!"

The physiological aspects of shock were still unknown in the world of medicine. Recovery was difficult, even under the best conditions. Yet despite her attempts at reasoning with him, Devon still stood unmoved. What did he expect her to do, fix the poor man with a magic wand and her bag of tricks?

"This is insane," Audrianna muttered. She turned back to the wounded young man and felt for a pulse on the side of his neck. She donned her stethoscope and listened to all areas of his chest and abdomen. There was no appreciable air movement in the right side of his chest; his trachea deviated away from the side of his wound; his neck veins were distended. She surmised the most life-threatening condition arose from a pneumothorax—an air collection in the pleural space resulting in the compression of the heart and shock. She had already plugged the hole in his chest. Now, if she could find a way to release the trapped air, the pressure on his heart would be lessened; the shock might be corrected. Far removed from her field of practice, Audrianna turned to what she knew. She spun around. "Do you have a condom?" she asked.

Devon's eyes widened. "I beg your pardon."

"A condom," Audrianna repeated. She made an oscillating hand gesture. "It's a … I mean, it's a …" She had spoken of condoms to women a hundred times before, but never a man. She was suddenly embarrassed.

"I know what a condom is, Dr. Foster," Devon said. "I don't have one. Why do you need one?"

Audrianna dropped her hand. "You're not in a strong position to judge my methods," she responded with a little eye roll. "Go and get me one now—a new condom, not a used one. I need it in less than ten minutes or you've most certainly sealed your friend's fate."

Devon's footsteps thumped out the door and Audrianna rolled the soldier's sleeve up to his armpit; she placed the blood-pressure cuff directly against his bare skin. It was the habit of physicians to carry their instruments with them when they traveled, in case of emergency, and Audrianna was no different. Had she known this was the emergency she would encounter, she would have chosen other tools. As it was, an accurate blood pressure would at least give her some idea how close to the brink of death he was. She inflated and released the cuff slowly, listening through her stethoscope for the sign of life. *Thump, thump, thump*—it was still there! His blood pressure was low, but she heard it!

Shock meant poor perfusion. He was not getting enough blood to his brain and his brain was the control center of his body. What else could she do to help him with that while she waited for Devon to bring her the condom. *Heat!* Heat dilated the vessels, making it easier to perfuse tissue. She must get him warm.

There was only one tiny blanket to be found in the room. It was made of linen, not wool, and thus not ideal for insulating, but Audrianna wrapped the soldier in it anyway, tucking the edges beneath his body to contain what little body heat he possessed. She had brought two vials of morphine with her, which had been useful to her in the past for treating women with strenuous labors, but for now she hoped the drug would also act as a dilatory agent, expanding his blood vessels and raising his body temperature. Or the morphine might have too much effect, completely wipe out what little blood pressure he had and send him into a cardiac standstill. That was a chance she was going to have to take. She knew of nothing else to do.

Her hands were completely still as she withdrew the medicine into a hypodermic syringe, She injected the morphine deeply into the shoulder muscle of the man's arm. The soldier's eyes flew open at the sting of the medicine and he looked at her, licking his lips repeatedly and ineffectively. He finally spoke to her in German.

"Lorna? Is that you?" he asked through terrified eyes.

"No. I'm a friend—a doctor," Audrianna replied in her own basic German. She had no idea who Lorna might be—a wife or girlfriend perhaps—but she was definitely someone of great significance to him, and someone he needed a connection with in order to calm his state of mind. "I was asked to look after you while you're sick," Audrianna continued. "It won't be long before you see her again." She felt certain that false encouragement was important; that keeping his hopes alive might keep him alive as well.

"Lorna, I'm so thirsty," the soldier whispered. "Will you get me something to drink?"

Audrianna took his hand. Clearly he wanted her to be some-one else. Maybe, in his mind, he needed her to be someone else so he could rest, whether it was for a few minutes, a few hours, or forever. She was taught never to encourage hallucinations, but she also understood this man needed the comfort of a lover now, not a stranger, and since she could not provide him with much else, she would provide him with that.

"Everything is going to be all right," she said soothingly, stroking his mud-caked hair down to his scalp. There was very little else she could do for him, the poor thing. His freckles cap-tured her attention, individualizing him in a way she would rather not happen. She wondered what set of unfortunate circumstances had brought him here, to this place so far from home and to this point so close to death. Had he been part of the battle Devon had spoken of earlier? It was crazy and self-absorbed, she knew, but she felt as though she could identify with him—trapped in a foreign land, relying on a stranger for help, unsure of what the very next hour might bring.

Audrianna pulled her hand away from his head. She did not want to humanize him. She did not want to think about his mother, his friends, his Lorna. He was dying, and she was power-less to prevent it. She wanted to think about Devon and how he could have prevented all of this. Anger was easier than regret.

Rage festered inside her like a ferocious cloud of smoke, choking the memory of Devon's image with imaginary hands. She would be close to Switzerland by now if not for him—close to her true mission of fulfilling her father's dying wish. Why would her legs not sneak her out the back door while he was gone so she could leave this nightmare here where it belonged? She folded her face into her hands. Outside, sounds of cheering and laughter mocked her feeble attempts at scorn. She was no more capable of scorn than she was of abandoning someone who needed her help. The only thing she could do was wait for Devon to return—or for the Angel of Death to come. She did not know who would arrive first.

CHAPTER 2

The door banged open against the wall.

"I've got it!" Devon said as he rushed forward with a flat rectangular box. "Is he any better?"

Audrianna took the box out of his hands and dropped the lid on the floor. "No," she said. She picked up the empty morphine syringe and severed the condom in half with the needle's edge, tossing away the top half. "Why should he be better?" she scoffed. She inserted the syringe into the remaining half of the condom so the needle poked through the bottom. She counted three rib spaces down from the man's clavicle on his injured side. "He's not better because you're an imbecile—but that isn't his fault." She inserted the needle into the man's chest and an immediate "hiss" was heard.

"What are you doing?" Devon rushed forward to stop her, but she brushed him back with her shoulder.

"His lung is collapsed," Audrianna said as she unscrewed the syringe, leaving the needle buried in the soldier's chest cavity. "I've just created a one-way valve: air can escape, but none can re-enter." The rubber flap opened when the man exhaled and closed when he inhaled. Devon took a step back and Audrianna continued, "This should correct the immediate problem, but he still needs help with perfusion to the brain. I need lots of blankets and hot water bottles, Devon, and I need them quickly. Bring hot coffee or tea back with you, and if you can't get that, just bring hot water suitable for drinking." Devon was halfway to the door when Audrianna felt compelled to make another snarky remark. She looked over her shoulder. "Devon, since you thought me capable of saving this man, I wish you'd let me do it. I would never willingly hurt someone, despite his foolish acquaintances."

Devon nodded. He made his exit with a slam of the door and returned an hour later with hot water and blankets. "This is all I could get. Coffee is not the drink of choice tonight, it seems," he said.

It was well after midnight. Audrianna had started to think he might not return at all, that he left her there with this dying man to ease the guilt of his own desertion. But that obviously was not the case.

She rose from her seat and met him halfway across the room, taking the three corked bottles of hot water one by one before returning to the bedside. She felt like giving him another piece of her mind, telling him everything she had been think-ing and feeling since he left, and forcing him to confirm the carelessness of his actions that night. But she lost her chance. He disappeared back into the hallway to retrieve blankets he had left there, and by the time he returned, she had changed her mind about arguing with him.

Audrianna placed the hot water bottles strategically against the soldier's armpits and groin. She worked the warmth into his skin with her hands, moving from one arm to the next, and then one leg to another. It would not be long before the water would chill, and she needed to take full advantage of the heat while she could.

It was a given that the man had long since fallen under the influence of the morphine, but his unresponsiveness frightened her. What if she had made a mistake in giving him morphine? What if the dilatory effect was too much for his body to handle and he never woke up? She would have to live with her blunder the rest of her life.

Audrianna stared at the red heap of sodden bandages covering the wound. The bleeding had stopped, but not before it had drained another several cups of crimson gush into the compress. If she removed it now, it would invariably dislodge any clot that had formed between the wound and the material, resulting in a torrential, deadly rush of blood; air would be reintroduced, negating the efficiency of the valve. As much as it pained her, she had to leave it alone and focus on his circulatory complications. Infection could always be cut out later, but a heart stopped would not beat again.

"How is he doing?" Devon asked, stepping close enough that she felt the humidity from his perspiration violating the surface of her skin. He piled the blankets on the table and leaned into the bed, watching her as she worked—watching her arms, her hands, and then turning his head boldly to watch her face. His attention was unnerving. She glanced sideways at him, hoping he would see how uncomfortable she was with his proximity. Or maybe her discomfort was with his voice, the way he smelled, or his questions. Or maybe she was not uncomfortable, and that was what bothered her.

"I've upset you, Dr. Foster," Devon said, touching her arm with his fingertips. "Let me help you. Tell me what else I can do to help you."

The emotion and bona fide concern in his tone penetrated Audrianna's psychological armor like a high-powered rifle. She shook her head. Why must he say things like that? She would rather he hold a knife to her throat and force her to work under the fear of death. A man's life was at stake after all, and all she could seem to think about was how this boy was making her feel right now. Yes, this boy! And in a cursed whorehouse of all places.

"Cover him with those blankets, and then go fetch me some more hot water," Audrianna ordered with cold, intentional frankness, testing his humility. She stepped back from the bed and watched Devon drape the would-be death shrouds over his motionless friend. He pulled the blankets up to the man's chin with a gentle sincerity that instantly softened Audrianna's will to punish him. She placed her hand on his back and asked, "Look for coffee again. He desperately needs the stimulant of it."

Devon nodded his head. He looked back at her with an obliging "thank you" and then broke for the door without comment. Audrianna followed him with her eyes, unhappy with herself for the way that she had treated him. It was obvious his loyalty and concern for his friend were authentic. Maybe Devon was right about not handing him over to an enemy hospital.

Audrianna realized her anger was more frustration for the feelings he evoked in her. They made no sense, not for her, not for her super-sensible personality. It was part of the reason she had not been married yet. She had never been moved by any one man or by efforts to acquire her affection. It was more than odd, in the midst of such a dissonant mess, someone making no outward attempt to commandeer her interest would gain it all the same.

Audrianna returned her efforts to her previous course of heat therapy, forcing herself back into the reality of the moment. She massaged the dwindling warmth into the muscles of the injured soldier, working through fallen hair and cramping fingers, until twenty more minutes passed and a noticeable sign of life began to reemerge in the pink skin of a once-pale body. The man's color implied concurrent improvement in circulation, prompting her to reassess his breath sounds: improved air movement. She checked his blood pressure one more time. She found a small increase and stood up.

"Here is the coffee. I'm not too late, am I?" Devon said, coming back into the room with two metal pitchers steaming with the flavor of coffee and mocha. He set them down on top of the bedside table.

Audrianna looked over at him. "No," she sighed. "He's a little better, in fact."

"Oh, thank God," Devon breathed. "Thank you." His piercing green stare searched her face as if he were looking for the best place to extract thoughts from her mind. She began to blush and quickly moved to the side to hide that fact from him.

"I know you don't understand why I've done the things I've done—or not done," Devon said, aware of her aversion but unwavering in his intensity. "But I—"

"I don't want to know, Devon," Audrianna interrupted, lying. She wanted to hear everything he had to say, but her heart was aflutter again, and the lump in her throat was an indication she could not handle anything beyond light conversation. She had not slept for more than a few minutes at a time in the past twenty-four hours, and she was beginning to feel it. Her back ached and she felt the weight of her eyelids pressing her eyeballs as far back into her skull as they would go. She had no intention of being his confessor at that moment.

Applauding her own internal resolve, Audrianna removed the now-cold water bottles from beneath the blankets, handing each to Devon. "Will you pour these out the window for me, please?" Devon did so while Audrianna re-tucked the edges of the blankets underneath his friend.

"We need to talk about how we're going to get—what's his name?" Audrianna asked, moving casually around to the bedside table to inspect the contents of the hot pitchers Devon had brought.

"Niklas." Devon drew up next to her with the empty glass bottles and set them down on the table with a clunk. "His name is Niklas."

Audrianna nodded. She poured a tiny amount of hot coffee from the pitcher into one of the bottles and carried it back to the bed. "We need to talk about how we're going to get Niklas to a German-friendly hospital. Here, Niklas. You need to drink this," she said softly, sliding her free hand underneath the soldier's head and lifting him just enough so he could consume the liquid stimulant. Niklas opened his eyes and pursed his lips to accept her offering. He slurped the beverage and then looked at her pleadingly, begging for more in a manner Audrianna was fully practiced in deciphering. "There will be more, Niklas. Just a little at a time, though. You've been badly injured and your friend and I are trying to figure out a way to get you someplace where you will be well taken care of."

"Zurich," Devon said as a kind of postscript to her discourse.

"Zurich! That's where I'm going. I'm conducting some research there!" Audrianna exclaimed, but quickly stopped herself from celebrating the news. "Zurich is a full day away," Audrianna said cautiously. "There must be another, closer option to consider."

Devon shook his head. "Believe me, I, too, wish there was another, quicker way, but the border into Germany is closed and, even if I were able to locate a hospital close by, in his condition, it would be nearly impossible for us to reach it. And I refuse to put your life at such a risk. I can protect you from the people we encounter much more easily than I can protect you from weapons. No. We must make it to Zurich. Niklas' brother is the chief surgeon at one of the hospitals there."

"How are you planning to go?" Audrianna asked.

"By train," Devon replied. He backed up against the wall and slid down until he was sitting on the floor. "There is an 0600 train and a 2200 train every day. The earlier we can get on one, the better off we'll be," he added.

"We should take turns sitting up with him for the rest of the night," Audrianna suggested. She rubbed her eyes with her fists, glanced at her wristwatch, and then joined Devon on the floor. The strange, omnipresent sensuality that existed between them seemed to fade inside their new challenge of getting Niklas to Zurich alive.

"Okay. I'll go first," Devon volunteered without giving her a chance. She did not resist his offer. She scooted off to the side of his legs and laid her head down on the saggy wooden timbers.

"Fill the two empty bottles with the rest of the hot water and put them under the blankets. And try to make him drink a tiny bit of coffee every ten minutes or so, okay?"

"Thank you for helping me, Dr. Foster, for helping Niklas," said Devon. "He would have died without you."

Audrianna opened her eyes and looked at him, braving the eye contact she had been avoiding since the beginning of their acquaintance. "He may still die, Devon. I'm not sure what, if any, damage was done by the gunshot. At this point, it's probably safe to say that blood loss is not the primary factor in his condition, although I just don't know. I have no way of knowing. But you need to understand we are far from being out of the woods, and this trip you're convinced we must take may just undo everything we've accomplished here tonight. He may not make it to Zurich, Devon."

Devon nodded. "Thank you for your honesty." He rose from his position against the wall and started back over to the table to carry out Audrianna's instructions. So she thought. He stopped and squatted down on his haunches so he was very close to her; Audrianna could see him without having to turn her head. The skin of his face was invitingly smooth, perfectly unmarred, absent of whiskers. She felt a compulsion to reach up and inspect it, but suppressed her desire.

"It's time to close your eyes, Dr. Foster," he whispered. "Morpheus is calling to you."

"Morpheus?" she yawned.

"The Greek God of the dream world. His voice is the blaring stillness you hear right as you're nodding off, in that short period of time considered neither awake nor asleep."

"Uh-huh," Audrianna agreed hoarsely, her eyelids dropping over scratchy eyeballs. She tried focusing on his voice, but the monotonous lull only catalyzed her entrance into Morpheus' domain. A buzzing drowned out Devon's voice; a heavy weight pulled on her body like an ethereal magnet, releasing her into a dark tunnel of swirling matter, engulfed in a thick, nebulous fog.

"Stay your fright, Dr. Foster. Nothing here can harm you. The cost of giving fear the power to invade this place is greater than you currently understand."

"What are you talking about?" Audrianna panicked, spinning in circles in search of Devon, recognizing his voice immediately. "Where are you?"

The familiar gleam of two green orbs penetrated the fog, promising safety. She stumbled toward his approach, falling and clinging to his lean figure like a buoy.

"I am here." Devon consoled her. "Everything is all right."

He pushed her gently back and tilted her face up to see his twisted, unusual smile. Annoyed by his amused expression, Audrianna snatched away from him. "Turn me loose," she said. "Your presence here is intrusive." Although she was unsure where "here" was.

"I couldn't be here unless you wanted me to be," Devon replied.

"How dare you!" Audrianna flared. She ran her hand up her neck and kept it there to strangle the successive stutters. "I ... I ... wanted no such thing!" Though she did. She knew she did and that's what made the situation horrendously uncomfortable. In what Audrianna was beginning to discover was Devon's special talent for discerning the indiscernible, he had entered the closet of her subliminal mind and disrobed her of the shameful secret she had been hiding—her interest in him.

Devon looked away shyly and then back with a non-verbal apology. "This is your safe place," he explained. "Nothing, no one, may exist here without your permission. And there is nothing improper about my being here or you giving me sanction to be."

A fire of humiliation spread to Audrianna's cheeks, emblazoning them with a sultry red tinge she attempted to extinguish with her sweaty palms. "What do you mean by my safe place?" she laughed bitterly. "This is just some strange dream arising from the unwise attachment I've formed for you. In that I clearly have no control here, I hardly consider it to be safe."

"You have complete control over everything," Devon replied seriously. "Yes, you are asleep, but what you're experiencing is not exactly a dream, nor does it have anything to do with the way you may or may not feel about me. I am simply here as your guest."

Audrianna shook her head. "I don't understand," she said. "What do you mean, 'not exactly a dream?' What else could it be?"

"Let me show you something," Devon offered, dismissing her immediate questions and beckoning her to accompany him with the wave of his hand. When she did not follow, he came back and took her by the arm, escorting her off through the daunting haze to a single enormous mirror that extended distantly into the sky and to the left and right to the ends of perception. A blazing, blue orb met them in the glass as they approached, banishing the surrounding cloud cover with an incandescent light that disseminated warmth upon their faces. It ebbed up and down, and backward and forward, spinning madly on an invisible axis like a heavenly top that had just been sprung from the fingers of God. Fluorescent pulsations identified fractures in the globe.

"What is that thing?" Audrianna asked, her eyes widening.

"It's you," Devon answered quietly. "It's your soul." He looked into the glass and then at her. "You shed your physical body before you entered this place, and now this is all that remains."

Audrianna raised one eyebrow. "What's it for?"

Devon laughed and said, "Well, it's your eternal body. It's also known as your life force because it supplies the energy necessary for you to live lifetime after lifetime, or for you to return to the God you worship, whichever you choose. It is the library of knowledge that belongs to your being."

"Am I dead?" Audrianna choked.

"No," Devon replied quickly. "What makes you think you're dead?"

"I don't know," Audrianna stammered. "All that stuff about shedding my physical body, I guess."

Devon laughed again. "Oh. I see. No. It's nothing like that. Think of it more along the lines of taking off a pair of muddy boots before entering your house. You certainly wouldn't want to track mud through your house any more than you would want to tarnish your soul with the harmful energies your physical body carries from the outside world."

"What outside world?" Audrianna asked.

"I'm referring to your awakened state," Devon replied. He smirked a little at Audrianna's confused expression and then gestured around. "Right now, you are in the inner sanctum of your soul. You come here each night in your sleep to heal any emotional wounds you've received during the course of the day. You've just never seen it from such an enlightened position before." He drew a breath and then continued. "The conscious mind is completely incapable of understanding the purity of the energy contained here, so it often superimposes inaccurate visual interpretations of the moment across your memory fields. These memories are recalled as dreams, or nightmares, when you wake up." He pointed right and left, then knocked on the glass in front of him. "This wall represents your eyes; it surrounds and protects your soul, and no one, no thing can pass through it without your permission. If you do invite someone or something in here, be mindful of what they bring with them. There are many, many beings out there that would smuggle weapons in here to assault your soul when it is the most vulnerable. Your own weapons represent an even greater threat. Leave them outside with your physical body."

Audrianna squinted and said, "I'm not sure I'm following you, Devon. What kind of weapons are you talking about?"

"Emotion," Devon replied.

"I'm sorry?" Audrianna lifted her eyebrows.

Devon laughed and shook his head. "Emotion, Dr. Foster. Everyone uses emotional weapons when they're out there." He pointed through the glass. "Out there in the awakened world. They're necessary. You couldn't survive without them. Even the most evolved beings must arm themselves when they leave this, their safe place. The big difference between evolved beings and other people is they've learned to carry only defensive armaments like hope, happiness, and forgiveness to dispel their adversaries. They never employ weapons that can hurt others. And because of that, even if they choose to bring such weapons into their inner sanctums, they have very little risk of defiling their souls. Do you understand?"

Audrianna gave her head a little irritated shake. "No, I don't," she said. "Are you implying we have the ability to use our emotions to attack other people, or even ourselves?"

"I'm not implying anything. I'm saying it straight out," Devon replied. "Human beings use emotion just as soldiers use armor, shields, swords, and guns. And in much the same way as with physical conflict, the result can be peace and prosperity, or war and ruination."

Audrianna scoffed. "Okay, Devon. This is getting a little ridiculous." She tugged her fingers through her hair and looked around for an exit. "I'm not sure why my subconscious is suddenly conjuring all of this nonsense, but it's quite enough. How do I get out of here?"

Devon ignored her question. "Your present-life conditioning won't let you accept this information," he said, "yet stored within you is the knowledge of which I speak. If you have the courage to stay and explore yourself, I can show you proof, not only of who you are right now but also who you have the potential to become."

Audrianna's mouth fell open and she sputtered, "You are quite bold, sir."

Devon smirked at her, and then gestured to the orb in the mirror. "Take a look here," he said, "the defects in the integrity of the orb represent various vulnerabilities in your soul. You've acquired them through self-destructive behaviors over the years. The color blue is an expression of your personality and can take on an infinitely different number of hues based upon how you're feeling at the time. For example, I can tell right now by the depth of your color you are using every mental and emotive faculty you have to solve this riddle. You're looking at your surroundings, remembering the stress of recent events and comparing what I've just told you to the theory of life as you've been taught to understand it in this lifetime. And because of those combinations of influences, you are inclined to discount what I'm telling you—yet you can't."

"Is that so?" Audrianna snapped. "Why can't I?"

"Because," Devon chuckled, "whether you know it or not, you've been scanning your library of knowledge since I've been talking in search of some validating guidance from your past lives, and although you weren't expecting to, you have found it."

Audrianna glowered at him. "If you are so well informed about the inner workings of my mind, why don't you just, just," she flipped her hand in the air, "tell me what number I'm thinking of right now?"

"Seven," Devon said calmly.

Audrianna clinched her jaw. "Good guess," she said, and then she took a step forward and met his eyes defiantly. "And now?" she shouted.

"Five hundred million patrillion." Devon narrowed his eyes and tilted his head to the side. "Is patrillion really a number, Dr. Foster? Or was that a trick?"

Audrianna relaxed her stance. "Ha," she said with a pronounced laugh, and lifted her hand to her forehead. She had called Devon's bluff, and he had capitalized on her disbelief. He really *did* know the inner workings of her mind.

"I do not know your mind," Devon said quietly. "I hear thoughts which are forged from emotional energy, and that's entirely different than knowing the depth of someone's mind—if that feat is possible. Even then," he shrugged, "I have to use my own knowledge and experience of emotion to interpret the thoughts correctly. Sometimes I'm wrong."

Audrianna gave him a soft once-over with her eyes and then turned around with her arms crossed. On a whim, she wheeled back around and asked, "Are you an angel?"

"Hardly!" Devon snickered, but then dampened his response upon seeing her vulnerability. "However, I can see why you might think that." He held one of his palms out in front of him in a gesture of accession. "Do you know many angels?"

"No," Audrianna answered gruffly, rolling her eyes. "I don't know what made me ask that."

Their eyes locked in an awkward moment of silence that yearned for release through laughter, but Devon spoke first. "Your curious approach to problem solving is one of the things I find so exceptional about you," he said. "You're all or nothing and that's completely different from who I am. Would you like to rule out demons next?"

Audrianna shook her head and giggled through her nose, then hid her face in her hands. "No! I'm glad you're not ... subhuman. Thank you."

"Come have a look at this," Devon said, changing the subject. He stepped to the edge of the mirror and pressed his forehead into it, beckoning her closer.

Audrianna came forward to look through the glass, squinting past the blinding light of her celestial reflection. "My God. What kind of insanity is this?" she gasped.

"Just as you've said," Devon replied. "Insanity. The thousands of men and women you see out there represent your fellow mankind: children of the omnipotent bloodline—slashing and thrashing at each other with their emotions—doing more harm to themselves with their ignorant offensives than to anyone else." He pulled his face back and ran his hand up and down the glass. "What you're looking at as you sleep is a snapshot of what's going on in the physical world right now from an enlightened point of view. In here, you don't see people as physical beings, rather, psychological beings."

"I can see their souls," Audrianna said.

"No, not their souls," Devon clarified. "The psychological being and the soul are not the same thing. The psychological being is a soldier, armed to the hilt with the emotional weapons of the soldier's choosing. The soul is the innocent child he or she defends." He knocked on the glass. "This fortress protects them both."

Audrianna turned her head and looked at him. "Can they see us in here?" she asked.

"Can they see into your eyes?" Devon replied, laughing. He knocked on the glass again, speaking offhand to himself, "No, they can't see into your eyes—at least not yet. This is very strong, very good, but if you take a closer look here," he pointed at various imperfections in the glass, "you can see blast damages all along the surface. You've been destroying your fortress from the inside for some time now. The damage is irreparable."

"What are you talking about?" Audrianna asked.

Devon pressed his face back into the glass and then beckoned Audrianna to do the same. "Come here. Look. See that crippled man there? Crawling toward the wall?" he asked.

Audrianna peered through the mirror, shielding the glare from her eyes. "What's left of the wall, you mean? The wall is *kaputt*."

Devon laughed, "*Kaputt,* yes, that's right. But if you look past the shards of broken glass, you'll see a pathetic, black lemon of a soul, sucked dry of the vitality required to heal his emotional injuries. His fortress has been shattered and now he is permanently disabled. On the physical side of things, one only has to look into his eyes to see who he has become. When you encounter people like this on the street, they appear in the forms of thieves and murderers, perpetual criminals incapable of being rehabilitated."

Audrianna flattened her hands against the glass and stared at the crippled man without blinking. "What happened to his fortress?" she whispered.

"He destroyed it," Devon replied.

"How?"

"With negativity," Devon answered. "He committed to resolve his everyday battles with as little effort as possible—using negative emotions that require no forethought or finesse to employ." His tone turned stern as he counted out examples on three fingers, "Anger, jealousy, fear. Humans were cast from God's light and cannot carry those dark emotions for any length of time without sustaining some sort of damage from it. Negativity is like a hand grenade: it can destroy other people, for sure—but it is also capable of destroying the person that carries it if it's held for too long," Devon went on.

"The worst of all possible outcomes," he explained, "is when people carry these proverbial hand grenades into the inner sanctum of their own souls." He clapped his hands and Audrianna jumped. "The bombs explode, they shatter the protective fortress from within, and leave the soul vulnerable to pillagers of the life force. In short order, the victim becomes a wickless candle, possessed only of the flicker of energy required to reincarnate into this very same situation again the next lifetime. Energy can never be completely destroyed, only lessened or transferred."

"But if that's true—if they can reincarnate," Audrianna cut in, "that means they must have another chance—to make up for what they've lost here."

Devon shook his head. "There are no more chances after someone has sustained that degree of damage," he said. "Certainly it's possible for a person to have a limitless number of physical bodies and many, many tangible lives. But there is only one soul.

Once the light has been extinguished, there is no way to rekindle it. A person in that situation," he pointed again through the glass, "like that man out there, is doomed to live lifetime after lifetime in the misery of repetitive despair. Without enough life force left to heal his wounds, or to carry him back to his creator, the only hope he has is of running across another dark entity who might find it worthwhile to finish him off altogether."

"Why are you telling me all this?" Audrianna put her hands over her ears and turned away. "I have to get out of this nightmare."

Devon grabbed her forcefully and spun her around to face him. "I've told you this because given enough time, Dr. Foster, that man might very well be you!" He threw up his hands. "You are currently in a troubling situation far outside your realm of comfort. You've employed emotional weapons to soften the blow of the insult. But instead of using any one of the precious, positive resources at your disposal, you've chosen to carry an arsenal of negativity: anger, resentment, self-pity. These are weapons you can't possibly win with—ever! Your fortress is damaged." He pointed to the glass, and then he pointed at her. "Your soul is weakened. Your psychological being is destroying you. Negativity will destroy you!"

Audrianna stared at him.

"Listen to what I'm saying to you and take it to heart," Devon continued, his tone urgent. "When you leave here tonight, leave those weapons behind. If you use them again, or any other of their type, consider the consequences before you do so."

"I can't stay here," Audrianna said numbly. "How do I get out?"

"This isn't a prison," Devon replied, touching her cheek lightly with the tips of his fingers. "Remember, you have complete control over everything while you're in here. And you can leave anytime you want. All you have to do is open your eyes. Open your eyes, Dr. Foster."

———•+•+•———

Audrianna opened her eyes and sat straight up. The room was freezing; she found herself shivering uncontrollably. "Oh my God," she breathed through chattering teeth.

"Yes. It's colder now than it usually is this time of year." Devon appeared from nowhere and dropped down on his knees, cupping her hands and blowing soft, warm air into them. "I'm afraid I have no coat to give you." He took another deep breath and then exhaled a second time into her hands. Prickly needles shot into Audrianna's fingers, but she did not pull away. The pain she felt was inconsequential compared to that which he brought with his touch.

"I feel strange," Audrianna whispered, watching mesmerized as he attended to her.

"You're just cold." Devon rubbed the tips of her fingers together.

Audrianna shook her head. "No, it's more than that," she replied. "I think it's you. I had this strange dream about you while I was asleep and now I ..." she paused, "now, I have to know. Who are you?"

Devon smiled, glancing up and down without making eye contact. "Have you forgotten my name already, Dr. Foster?"

"I think you know what I mean," Audrianna pressed him.

Silence brought a tingle of nervous energy into the atmosphere as Devon's eyes tracked upward from their entwined fingers. "I'm someone you can trust," he finally said. "Someone who will protect you and make sure you remain unharmed until you get back to where you belong." He smiled and brought her hands up to his lips without looking away. "And you will get back. I promise."

"Back to where I belong," Audrianna repeated. She let her eyes fall out of focus and then stifled a bitter laugh. "Right now, I'm not even sure where it *is* I belong, Devon. But that's a whole other story." She cleared her throat, checked her watch, and then changed the subject, asking, "Do you think we have time to make it to the train station?"

"Yes, I do," Devon said in a half whisper. "Do you think it's safe?"

Audrianna turned to face him fully, ensuring herself a good look at his face. "I'm not sure if you're asking me whether it's safe to take a seriously wounded German soldier onto a French train, or something bigger. Perhaps we should just carry on however you see fit. I trust that you'll make the right decision."

While Devon certainly appeared to be relieved by her surrender of control, she could tell he was not as pleased as he would have her believe. The muscles of his cheekbones sank beneath a set of unmistakably sad eyes, his eyebrows arched toward the bridge of his nose.

Audrianna made an inward inquiry of his expression.

"It's nothing," he answered her thoughts.

One of them had to look away. This time it was Devon.

CHAPTER 3

"Let's go," Devon said. "There's a taxi waiting for us downstairs."

Audrianna sat on the edge of the bed with her arm wrapped tightly around Niklas. It had taken them nearly an hour to get him up and dressed in ill-fitting civilian clothing that Devon had stolen earlier that morning. Now they were pressed to make it to the train station on time. Devon took Niklas' arm on the opposite side of Audrianna, and together, with effort, they lifted what seemed to be most of his weight, and headed to the door.

"He's not saying much," Devon huffed as they shuffled out toward the stairs. He grabbed Audrianna's medical bag and slung it over his free shoulder with a heave, struggling as she was, with a man who was well over six feet tall and probably twice their combined weight.

"You'd have very little to say, too, if you were chock full of bullet holes and morphine," Audrianna replied in a snippy tone of voice.

"Bullet hole, singular," Devon corrected her. "Please don't exaggerate. The situation is bad enough as it is."

"It will be bad for that poor man who is going to wake this morning and find his clothes gone, too. Honestly, Devon, you should be ashamed of yourself. I know you had the money to buy those things. Whatever possessed you?"

"Clothing wasn't one of the things available for purchase around here this morning," said Devon. "And Niklas couldn't leave here in that bloody German uniform. Besides, I left that man enough money to buy himself a grand new outfit from Charvet in Paris if he likes."

"Well, that was nice of you!" Audrianna scoffed. "I'm sure Monsieur Charvet won't mind at all that his new patron will be completely naked when he wanders into the store to purchase his new garb. The very least you could've done was to have stolen the right size. I'm not sure this ensemble is any less inconspicuous than that uniform was."

Their squabble stalled with their first inhalations of morning air. The outside was like an icehouse: cold and humid, difficult to breathe in, and impossible to see through. An extraordinary amount of concentration was required to negotiate each step, and it was only after they felt their feet touch the stable dirt of the earth that they even knew they were on the ground. A rickety carriage waited at the bottom of the stairs, attached by bit and bridle to a horse that appeared to have been a last-minute salvage from the local slaughterhouse. A filthy, codger of a man watched from the driver's seat as the three of them stumbled from the fog. He showed no obvious intent to assist them with their load.

"We're in a hurry," Devon said as he unlatched the rusty door. He held Niklas against his hip and, with the other hand, a bill in the air to signal the driver. The man ambled down, practically on top of Audrianna, gagging her with his rancid body odor and the food in his beard.

"*Quel est le probleme avec lui?*" the man asked suspiciously.

"Drunk," Devon replied. "*Ivre. C'est tout.*" He reached into his shirt pocket and handed the man another large bill. Without further delay, the man helped Devon and Audrianna push Niklas up into the carriage, then took his seat and switched the horse to a trot.

After a few lengthy minutes of silence, Audrianna said, "That was quite a bit of money you gave that man." She hoped Devon would catch her questioning undertone.

"I'm sorry, darling," Devon replied. He peered through the crud-covered window at various angles. "I hear the emotional inflection in your voice, but I don't understand your point. Was there a question?"

Audrianna shifted her eyes to the right. He just called her darling. She forgot her question.

"There's the train station," Devon interrupted her thought. He pointed to a hastily constructed lean-to, decorated with an old cowbell and a creaky, petrified sign. The writing was nothing but a shadow, having long since succumbed to the elements of the weather. French troops passed through the crowd of boarding passengers.

"Devon—soldiers!" Audrianna hissed as the taxi slowed to a stop.

"So I see," Devon replied thoughtfully. He examined his pocket watch, then opened the carriage door. "We haven't much time," he said. "We'll make a dash for the train at the last second and hopefully avoid that patrol."

He grabbed Niklas by the arm and pulled him toward the edge of the seat. "Niklas, come on," Devon coached. "You have to help."

Niklas groaned and opened his eyes. He saw Devon and then Audrianna. "Who are you?" he asked her.

"She's a friend, Niklas," Devon told him. "Someone we can trust. That's all you need to know right now." He dragged Niklas roughly from the coach by his shirt, ignoring Niklas' cries of pain and his continued questioning. "Put your feet down," Devon commanded him, "and concentrate on walking as though your life depends upon it. Because it does." Audrianna followed closely with her medical bag, supporting Niklas' balance.

The final whistle of the train burst their bubble of uncoordinated hesitation, forcing them into a clumsy looking three-legged stumble for the platform. The train attendant hung from the outside pole of the locomotive, stretching his hand forward to receive tickets or money from the boarding passengers. Devon pulled out his dwindling but still substantial wad of money and pushed half of it into the attendant's hands. "*Dormeur s'il vous plaît. Rapidemente,*" he said, out of breath.

"*Juste un moment s'il vous plaît,*" a cracked, pubescent voice called loudly from behind them. They spun about and collided with a young French officer and his overweight sergeant, both sharply dressed in the same kind of uniform Audrianna had begun to detest.

"*Excusez-moi, Monsieur,*" the officer said.

"Terribly sorry, but I don't speak French," Devon said quickly in a shaky British accent. He made a move for the train, but the officer stepped around and addressed them in English.

"Just a minute, please," he said with a cloaked French nuance. "The train will wait. Or there will be another."

"Certainly," replied Devon, light and cheery. Audrianna looked away to hide her state of mind. She was not sure what she was doing wrong in aiding these two, but it was probably enough to secure herself a place in a foreign prison indefinitely.

"Papers, please?" the officer asked politely.

Devon willingly gave two sets of documents, read first by the officer, then by his sergeant.

"What is wrong with him?" The officer gestured to Niklas.

Devon snuck a peek at Niklas' downturned face and said, "Oh, a bit of a problem with the bottle, if you know what I mean. You have some fine local wine."

The young officer nodded, satisfied, but still hesitant to let them off. "You've shown me only two sets. What about the lady?" he asked

Devon threw up his hand, exasperated. "So sorry, Lieutenant! The girl has Lodonis Syndrome! Might as well be talking to a bloody monkey."

"She has what?" The officer stepped back with a grimace. Audrianna felt the stinging surge of blood threaten her cheeks and ears. Never having heard of such an illness, she was unsure of how to carry the farce.

"Lodonis Syndrome," Devon lowered his tone. "Type of mutism, Lieutenant. From repeated cycles of inbreeding. Parents also her siblings. Get the point? They traded her to my father for a bottle of whiskey when they found out that local men wouldn't pay to sleep with a retard. My dad took pity, put her to work in the kitchen. Been in our house ever since."

Audrianna stared at the ground realizing if her role were that of a mentally handicapped mute, it would make no sense for her to have an interest in the conversation.

Devon let out a hearty laugh. "She's dumb as a stump, but we just can't live without her shepherd's pie. So she comes on the trips. Papers are in her bag, Lieutenant. I'll get them for you." He adjusted Niklas' weight. "Do you mind just helping out here so we don't fall down?"

The young officer gestured to his larger counterpart to hold Niklas in place while Devon fished through the contents of Audrianna's bag. He fumbled through a collection of neatly folded papers, and then handed one of them to the officer, exclaiming, "Here we are!"

The lieutenant scrutinized the papers closely, and then returned his attention to Devon. "This says her name is Audrianna Foster, citizen of the United States of America."

Devon tapped his foot. "That is her name," he said. "My father is British; my mother is American."

"All aboard!" The announcement was directed at them.

"Anything further, gentlemen?" Devon sighed heavily. "The train is about to be off and I'd like to be on it. My father is an emissary from the British Ballistics Corporation. He is meeting nearby with the war committee for the Army of Alsace, and I'm sure he will be most unhappy when he sees my brother in this condition. His displeasure will be doubled if we miss this train. Do you follow?"

The young French officer lumped all the papers into one big bunch and handed them back to Devon, tipping his hat and voicing his dismissal. "Good day, *Monsieur.*"

"Yes, good day indeed," Devon stuffed the papers into his pocket, pulling both Audrianna and Niklas hurriedly to the stairs of the train. The train attendant counted keys on a large key ring and gave it to Devon in exchange for the large sum of money he had taken earlier.

At the door of their sleeping compartment, Devon worked the key in the lock and fished inside for a light. Audrianna remained in the hallway with Niklas who weighed more heavily on her arm than before. He had not spoken throughout the interrogation, and he did not speak now.

"Niklas, are you okay?" Audrianna whispered. She tried to see his face, but his legs gave way beneath him; he toppled onto the floor. "Niklas!" Audrianna shrieked, dropping to his side and feeling for a pulse.

Devon rushed back out into the hallway. "What happened?" he panted.

"He's fainted," Audrianna said. She gestured for Devon to help. "Hurry. Let's get him inside so I can take a better look at him." They attempted to pick him up, but he was too heavy. Instead, they dragged him by the arms and heaved him up onto the bed.

"Niklas," Audrianna pressed her hand into his chest. A red sap seeped through his second-hand shirt, making her palm sticky. "Oh, no," she muttered, unbuttoning his shirt and pulling it apart to see his chest. The saturated dressing had slipped during their journey. "Jesus Christ!" she cursed. "He's pouring blood again, and I have nothing left to stop it with."

Audrianna turned her sweaty face into the heat of the room and spied a tiny, coal-burning furnace in the other corner of the compartment. "Devon, stir that fire with the poker," she ordered. "Make sure the point is white hot, then bring it over here."

Devon hesitated.

"Now, please," Audrianna barked.

Devon moved to the task. He stirred the listless coals into enthusiasm, and then placed the poker into its guts. After three minutes, he brought it over to her and placed the handle into her hands.

Audrianna held the poker like a branding iron and moved toward Niklas with it, gritting her teeth. "Hold him, and keep him quiet," she said.

"No!" Devon caught her arm. "What are you doing?"

"Don't interfere!" Audrianna snarled. "I have to cauterize the tissue before he bleeds to death. Either help me, or move out of the way."

Devon loosened his grip and edged away, moving to hold Niklas' arms above his head; he put his hand over Niklas' mouth.

Audrianna inserted the hot poker into the wound, searing the flesh into a blackened char. Niklas' eyes stretched open in terror. He easily broke from Devon's hold and grabbed for the poker, wailing, "*Nein! Nein!*"

Devon scrambled to pull him back. He leapt around the side of the bed and sat on top of Niklas, holding his arms down with the weight of his own body while Audrianna reheated the poker. She became filled with confidence in her skill and found a calm in the exercise of torture. This man was alive now because of her, because of her knowledge, her quick-witted improvisations, and her unwillingness to give up on him. She was not about to give up now either.

"Okay, Niklas. Hold on." Audrianna turned back to him. "One more time with this thing and we should get that bleeding under control." She pressed the poker into the wound again, wincing at the sizzle of scorched blood bonding to the iron tip.

She leaned firmly into it until Niklas' bucking sent Devon flying to the floor.

Niklas whimpered with wet eyes as he kneaded the smoldering hole in his chest with his fingers.

"Okay, okay, Niklas," Audrianna soothed him. She dropped the poker on the floor and latched onto his wrists. "Don't touch it. Leave it alone. Devon, come get his hands while I get him something for the pain."

Devon lurched up from the floor to take her place.

Audrianna pulled away and wiped her face on her sleeve, scanning the room for her bag.

"Underneath the bed," Devon croaked out an answer to her unvoiced question.

"Right," Audrianna said as she shot Devon a dubious glance. She snatched her bag from under the bed frame and snapped the neck on the last vial of morphine. She opened Niklas' mouth with her fingers and lifted his tongue, dribbling the liquid underneath. Niklas gagged.

"I guess that's one way to do it," Devon said.

"I'm sorry, are you the doctor?" Audrianna replied indignantly. "Or do you just think you know more than I do?" She rested her hand on Niklas' forehead while he settled.

"Of course I don't," Devon replied. "It was a compliment, Dr. Foster. I think you're an amazing physician. Why are you so set on thinking the worst of me?"

"I'm not!" she hissed, although it was true. She needed to think the worst of him in order to conquer her true feelings.

The locomotive accelerated into a rhythmical jerkiness that seemed to expedite Niklas' fall to sleep, and after Audrianna was certain her voice would not disturb him, she finally vocalized her contrived apology. "Forgive me, Devon," she said, shaking her

Lyovitalis

head. "I'm unaccustomed to compliments from men—especially as they pertain to my medical practice."

"Why is that?" Devon asked.

Audrianna laughed a little. "Medicine is a male-dominated field."

"Life is a male-dominated field," Devon came back. "Do you also shun compliments when they're offered over dinner?"

Audrianna lifted an eyebrow and replied, "I don't go to dinner. I go to work. My work *is* my life." She scratched her forehead, and then looked down, embarrassed by her sour attitude. "I'm sorry for not responding as—I'm sure—most women typically would, Devon. But to be perfectly honest, I haven't much experience with compliments and I've been in trouble for my manners before," she finished with a laugh.

"I happen to find nonconformity to be very attractive," Devon replied softly. He sauntered around the end of bed. "That was also a compliment," he added.

Beads of perspiration popped and trickled down Audrianna's face. Panic percolated within. She jumped past him for the door. "Excuse me. I need to visit the washroom," she said.

"I'll have the porter bring us some breakfast, and then I'll go after you come back," Devon called from behind her.

The thought of food and drink breathed new life into Audrianna, and she found her way to the ladies washroom at the end of the car. After relieving herself, she washed the blood from her hands and face and repinned her hair into place. She considered removing her clothes and scrubbing her entire body down, but decided against it. The lock was broken, and she did not know how someone might react to a naked woman in a public lavatory.

Audrianna retraced her steps back to the sleeper, finding a tray filled with pastries, assorted meats, cheeses, and coffee waiting for her. She crossed paths with Devon halfway across the room; she felt only slightly guilty for having a cup of coffee while he was gone. By the time he returned, she was on her second cup.

"Are you all right?" Devon asked. He drew close to her and dropped his hand down her back, leaving five distinct fingertips in place at the base of her spine.

"Yes," Audrianna's voice cracked. She ran her hand up her neck and cleared her throat. Her skin began to tingle. "Yes. I'm just hungry." She stepped away from him and took a piece of cinnamon bread from the tray, chomping off a larger bite than what might have been considered socially acceptable.

"As I see," Devon said with a grin. He slumped down into one of the two chairs next to the table and followed her lead, dismissing the plates and silverware that had been provided for their convenience, eating out of his hand instead.

"Devon," Audrianna spoke between chews from behind her hand. "I've never heard of Lodonis Syndrome. Is it a European disease?"

Devon swallowed before answering. "Yes, it has European origins." He cocked his head and added, "I conceived it less than an hour ago. How do you like me as an actor? I think your performance was exceptional." He winked.

Audrianna widened her eyes. She threw her hand down laughing and said, "Devon! What if they had realized you were lying? Think of the trouble—"

"I think we were safe enough," Devon cut her off, his eyes twinkling. "After all, I fooled a physician."

———————

"I didn't expect to see you here again," Audrianna said.

"I know," Devon replied. "I really didn't expect to be here."

Audrianna might have interpreted his demeanor as coy, if not for his eyes. Their sparkling glint proclaimed his enthusiasm for her in a manner that seemed almost palpable. She boldly got up and met him where he stood. "So why are you here?" she asked

"I wanted to make sure you were okay," Devon answered too quickly. Audrianna smiled at his precipitous response.

"I don't believe you," she said frankly.

"All right." Devon shrugged with a lopsided smile. "Why do you think I'm here?"

Audrianna brought her fingertips to rest on her windpipe and said, "I think you might be here because you are as interested in me as I am in you."

Devon stepped close to breathe his words on her face. "Our interest in one another is dangerous," he said, seizing the tops of her arms and pulling her forward to whisper a smile in her ear. "If you're wise, you'll walk away from me now, and never let me come in here again."

A deep erotic charge jolted Audrianna. She quickly attempted to pull away from Devon, but he held her in place. "Stop struggling," he said. "Or didn't you want me to keep you from leaving?"

An explosion of anger erupted inside Audrianna. She clenched her jaw and growled, "I think you already know how I feel about having my private thoughts repeated to me, Devon." She flapped her elbows hard to free herself and then jammed a finger in his face. "And I'm not going anywhere until I have some answers to my questions!"

Devon burst into laughter. After a moment he said, "You are quite unpredictable, darling." He started to walk away, but abruptly wheeled back around, capturing Audrianna by the waist and prying an emotive hand grenade from her fingers. "Give me that," he said, and then he made a quick, sharp pivot and chucked the bomb into the air with the momentum of his body. An explosion occurred.

"There. Good," Devon said, nodding. He returned his attention to Audrianna. "Now, where were we? Oh, yes. You have some questions, I believe."

"Wha—"Audrianna's voice got caught in her throat. She pointed to the cloud of smoke in the distance and said, "What was that?"

Devon casually twisted the top part of his body and examined the view, replying, "That? Oh, I believe that was anger." He flipped back around. "Or embarrassment. I'm having a very difficult time differentiating the two in you. Where one is, the other invariably seems to be. Were you teased a great deal as a child, Dr. Foster?"

Audrianna felt her cheeks turn red. A cold metal ball rolled down her sleeve and caught in the palm of her hand. She pulled it up to her face and stared at it.

"Aha!" Devon said, flashing her a smile. "There it is." He seized the grenade in one hand and held out his other hand, saying, "Now the last one, please."

Audrianna patted herself down in a frenzy. "I don't have another one," she cried. "I didn't know I had those two—"

"Dr. Foster," Devon talked over her words. "If you don't give me the other one right now, I shall be forced to strip-search you." A wicked grin spread across his features. "Or is that how you would prefer to be disarmed?"

Audrianna's eyes widened. Her heart began to thud. She felt she should be angry or embarrassed by his threat, but she was not either of those things. She was just panicked. Another grenade rolled down her sleeve and launched off the tips of her fingers before she could grab it. Devon snagged it from the air and lobbed both bombs, one at a time, far into the distance. "No more embarrassment." *Boom.* "And no more panic." *Boom.* He turned back to Audrianna and brushed his hands together. "You may keep your sarcasm with you—so you don't feel completely out of sorts." He snapped his fingers; the scene fell dark.

Audrianna heard the sound of a match being struck, and then she saw Devon's lips speaking over the top of the flame. "Do you like games, Dr. Foster?" he asked.

"Look, Devon," Audrianna snapped. "The formality is quite out of place right now. You don't hear me calling you 'Mister Devon', do you?" She rubbed her forehead absently and laughed at herself. Normally, such a mindless response would have embarrassed Audrianna, but instead, she felt smug. The flame petered out and she allowed herself a moment alone with the feeling.

Devon struck another match, this time at the level of his eyes. "Do you like games, Audrianna?" He teased her with the sound of her name.

Audrianna shuddered. She took a deep breath through her nose and slowly let it go, replying, "Games? I haven't played games since childhood. Why do you ask?"

"I was wondering if you would like to play one with me," Devon replied. He blinked softly, "Of course, you could just ask me your questions and I may or may not answer them. But I don't commit to anything unless there is a contest involved."

"What game?" Audrianna raised a sly eyebrow.

"Your choice," Devon replied. The light went out again.

"Under what terms?" Audrianna croaked in the darkness.

"You may ask me questions the entire time the game is in progress, and I will answer consistently true, or consistently false," Devon talked lowly. "If you win the game, I shall reveal the nature of my responses."

"And if I lose?" Audrianna whispered.

"You will answer a single question of mine," Devon finished.

There was a lengthy pause in the black abyss while Audrianna thought through the rules. She felt certain she could discern the nature of Devon's responses without having to be told, and she had absolutely nothing to hide. The choice seemed clear. "Chess," she snorted. Chess was a tedious game. She would probably run out of questions before the match was complete.

"Chess," Devon repeated. His tone was equally confident. He struck another match and cupped the flame with his palm, flashing his eyes at Audrianna and whispering, "Let's play." He tossed the match into the air and the entire area became illuminated with soft white light.

A theatre decorated in blue crush velvet came into view. A crowd of fifty people filled upper and lower sections with private boxes on the sides. An overused gaming table with two rub-marked chairs dominated the floor. An ornate silver chess set topped the table; the players were grotesque beasts with emerald and onyx eyes.

"Good evening." Devon moved to address the crowd. "Thank you for coming. Please do have a pleasant time." He projected his voice across the heads of the people and then made a majestic bow. Applause erupted.

"Are you serious, Devon?" Audrianna asked, perturbed.

Devon stood tall and glanced sideways at her. "I'm not sure I understand your question, darling," he replied. "Would you mind asking it another way?"

Audrianna rolled her eyes. "I mean, are we really going to play in front of all these people?" The applause died and silence consumed the space.

Devon's eyes darted toward the crowd. He laughed once and said, "I might ask *you* that question."

"Why me?" Audrianna hissed through her teeth.

Devon cupped his mouth to hide his reply from the audience. "Because these are your guests, Audrianna. I have no power to invite people into your safe place." He gestured to the chess set. "My only contribution is this board. Everything else has been conjured by you." He snagged Audrianna's elbow and sat her down in one of the chairs. "I had not seen you as an exhibitionist, darling." Devon touched his lips to her ear and said, "But I am most intrigued." He took the opposite chair without waiting for her to answer and ceremoniously announced, "You may make your first move, and ask your first question."

Audrianna stared at him. She shook her head, vexed, and then after a moment said, "Fine, how old are you?" She picked up the queen's knight and moved it up two spaces, and over one.

Devon moved his king's pawn ahead one space and replied, "Twenty-six."

"Ha!" Audrianna laughed out loud. "I'm sure. Twenty-six and no hair on your face, right?" The audience burst out laughing, and Audrianna encouraged their involvement with an oscillating hand gesture. She laughed for a few seconds longer, and then moved one of her end pawns forward on the board. The audience quieted.

"Where do you live?" She asked her next question, grinning because she already felt she had the advantage.

"Various places," Devon shrugged. He moved his king's bishop diagonally until it rested in front of her queen's bishop.

"I spend as much time as I can at my home in Bavaria. I have apartments in Paris and Berlin, but I am only in those places when I have to be. I try to get to Zurich at least once a month to see Dirk? When I'm there, I stay with him."

"Dirk?" Audrianna asked. Curiosity sharpened her gaze. She picked up the same pawn and moved it ahead another space.

Devon cut his lustrous eyes across the board at her and replied, "Niklas' brother, Dr. Dirk von Traugott."

Audrianna made a lazy upward nod of her head and chuckled out her next question. "What makes your eyes glow like that?"

"They glow when I am filled with energy," Devon replied. He moved his queen diagonally three squares, and then continued. "The color of my eyes match my level of existence. Green is life, black is death. Anything in between is, well, anything in between."

Audrianna laughed and said, "That's convenient! The rest of the world has to depend upon the advice of doctors for that sort of insight." The audience erupted into a flurry of chuckles, and Audrianna threw out her palms at them, saying, "Isn't that right?" The crowd clapped their hands and vocalized their agreements. Devon smirked, but he made no reply.

After the noise died down, Audrianna moved her queen's rook forward two spaces. She bit down on her bottom lip and slowly turned her eyes up. "What causes the color to change?" she asked, playing along.

"Emotion," Devon replied. His tone was even-keeled and without guile.

An empty feeling swept through the pit of Audrianna's stomach as she recalled details of her previous dream. She cleared her throat and said, "Emotion? What do you mean?"

Devon tilted his queen to and fro with a single finger and tracked the movement with his eyes. "Emotion drains life from me," he said. "Fear, sadness, happiness, anger. All have the same effect. If I do not replace the energy required to fuel these feelings, then I will die." He moved his queen to capture one of Audrianna's pawns.

"What about love?" Audrianna whispered.

Devon looked up and said, "Love is a dagger that would prick so many holes in my heart that I could never acquire enough energy to equal the amount I've lost. To love, for me, is suicide." He flicked his forefinger and Audrianna's king fell over. "Checkmate, darling."

Gasps arose from the crowd as Audrianna stared at her slain king. She ran the fingers of both hands through her hair and let her eyes go blank. "That was quick," she said disbelievingly. "I only got to ask four questions."

"That's three more than I'll get to ask, and I won the game," Devon replied, smirking. He rose slowly from his chair and swaggered over to Audrianna, pulling her up by the elbows and drawing her eyes up with an unspoken command. "Now for my prize," he said.

Audrianna licked her lips. "Fine," she whispered, "what do you want to know?" The audience stood row by row to get a better view of their exchange. Whispers permeated the air.

Devon waited for them to hush, and then he asked, "May I kiss you?"

Audrianna swallowed hard. She diverted her gaze. That was the last question she had expected! Or was it? Who was she trying to fool? She had been thinking about this moment, shamefully thinking about it, fantasizing even, for some time now. Her secret desires had obviously precipitated this dream, but what was she supposed to do now? Let him kiss her here in front of all these people?

A solid metal projectile dropped from the ceiling and zipped toward their heads at a high rate of speed. Devon intercepted the grenade with his bare hand, and shook it gently in her face. "Don't do that!" he said, irritated. "You don't need your weapons here! What's gotten you so bothered again? The crowd of onlookers that *you* invited?" He flung the grenade to the back of the theatre and blew a hole through the wall. Wooden joists popped and snapped; the infrastructure of the building shifted. "There," he pointed at the suddenly stampeding crowd, "they're leaving now."

Audrianna cupped her hands over her mouth and watched as the audience escaped the building amidst an orchestra of shouts and screams. She stifled a laugh. "Oh my God, Devon. I can't believe you just did that," she said, certain she should be angry or panicked herself, but she wasn't. She was amused.

"You believe very little about me," Devon said with a hint of annoyance. He drew Audrianna closer and swept her hands from her face. "Presently, that is of little concern. I'd like an answer to my question, please."

Audrianna took a quick shallow breath and then started into a stutter, "I … I …"

"Stop." Devon captured her quivering chin with his fingers. "May I kiss you?" he said. "Yes or no?"

A lump popped in Audrianna's throat. She decided she should deny him—not because she meant to deny him, but so she would remember to chastise herself later for allowing it.

"Yes," she whispered.

Devon pulled her forward by the chin until their lips touched. After a moment, he pressed further into the kiss, taking his time at tasting her without attacking her with his tongue, without drowning her in saliva, or overwhelming her with clumsy roughness. Audrianna breathed in his potion as he conjured arousal from the deepest, darkest part of her, a part she had intended only for her future husband. When he caressed her buttocks, she began to tremble. Her nipples hardened and chill bumps wrapped themselves around her body.

In response to her excitement, Devon's reservation dissipated. He knocked the chess set onto the floor with one broad sweep of his arm, and picked Audrianna up with legs straddling him. He laid her down on the table and cycled his pelvic bone slowly between her legs, shifting his lips to suckle the wet skin of her neck. "Devon," Audrianna panted. She pulled the back of her hand to her forehead and closed her eyes. "We shouldn't be doing this."

"Of course we should, darling," Devon whispered. He closed his eyes and brought his lips to murmur on hers. "We have wanted each other like this from the moment we met, and we are safe to enjoy that pleasure here. You've believed nothing else I've told you; please believe that."

Easily persuaded, Audrianna waved him onward with a reciprocal sentiment. "I do believe," she mumbled.

The words had no sooner left her mouth than Devon pulled away from her, looking back over his shoulder at something Audrianna could not see. His eyes fixed on the distance and he listened to something she could not hear.

"What is it?" Audrianna breathed, still laboring in eroticism.

"There's something wrong," Devon said without looking at her. "I have to go back."

"What? Wait!" Audrianna reached for him, but it was no use. Within seconds, Devon was gone.

Audrianna opened her eyes, seized heartlessly from sleep by the sudden, short stop of the train. She raised her head just enough to see Devon peering out through the curtains of the window, dodging the spattering rays of sunlight as they infiltrated the room. "What's the matter?" she asked.

Devon turned his head at the sound of her voice, but then rapidly returned to his study of the outside. "French soldiers are boarding the train," he said.

Audrianna yawned. She sat up and rubbed the sleep from her eyes. "How long have I been sleeping?" she asked, rising from the floor to look out the window over Devon's shoulder.

"Four hours," Devon replied. She could tell he was worried. Audrianna recognized this change in his countenance immediately.

"What are they doing?" she asked, watching as the soldiers paraded up the stairs.

"They are looking for Niklas," Devon answered. He did not make a move from the window, and Audrianna was forced to vie for his attention.

"Why, Devon?" She grabbed his arm and turned him toward her. "How do they know he is on this train, and why do they care? Who is he?"

"We're almost to the border," Devon said without emotion. "Someone must have recognized him and alerted the officials. They most likely want to exert their authority while they still have the opportunity to do so." He released the curtain and backed into the darkness of the room.

Audrianna caught him by the shoulders and drew her face to his. "Devon, how do you expect me to help you if you won't tell me who you are and what is really going on here? How would anyone be able to recognize a German officer not in uniform?

And more importantly, why would they care? Why would the French government commit so many soldiers to finding one man? It just doesn't make sense!"

A loud knock sounded a couple doors down, followed by voices, slamming doors, and the heavy shuffle of clunky boots. Audrianna held her breath as she strained to decipher the muffled commentary. "Can you hear what they're saying?" she asked Devon.

"They're questioning the passengers in the other sections," he replied calmly. "I have to turn myself in before they get to this car."

"Turn yourself in for what, Devon?" Audrianna cried. "What have you done?"

"Dr. Foster, please. We've been through this," Devon said, stalling. "It's not that I don't trust you. I think I trust you more than I should, or could imagine I ever would. But I will not involve you in anything that could risk your way of life."

Audrianna shook her head and said, "Devon, I am already involved. You cannot ask me to go blindly into this. I am more harm than good to you if I don't know what to expect. Now, tell me what the hell is going on!"

Devon rubbed his hands over his face and shrugged. "Very well, Dr. Foster. You win. We are carrying war plans from the headquarters of General Paul Pau, the commander of the French Army of Alsace. These documents outline major offensive tactics that will be used against the German armies. If we fail to deliver them, a great many lives will have been lost for nothing. And a great many more will be at risk."

Audrianna stared at him blankly. She heard what he said, but what did he mean? They were carrying war plans, so what? There was a war on, after all. Did the soldiers simply want their war plans back? Perhaps if Devon just handed them over, nothing more would come of this.

"It's not that simple. They were stolen, Dr. Foster," Devon chided her impatiently. "Niklas and I stole them. We are spies for the German government."

Audrianna felt her throat tighten. "Dear God," she choked out, placing one of her hands over her mouth to suppress more astonished outcries. "You can't be serious!"

Devon grabbed her roughly. "Listen to me," he said. "I am going to walk out that door and turn myself in. I may be able to convince them that Niklas is dead. They already know he has been shot. They just don't know if he was mortally wounded or not."

"No, Devon," Audrianna pleaded. "What makes you think they will believe you? They'll shoot you, too, and search anyway. There must be another way."

"There is no other way," Devon countered.

A heavy fist pounded on their door, forcing them to lower their voices. "You're not going to do this!" Audrianna exclaimed. "Let me answer the door. I'll try to get rid of them. It's our only chance!"

"No! You don't even speak French."

"All the better!" Audrianna hissed.

"No. They'll arrest you and you'll spend the next ten years of your life rotting away in some French slum, prostituting yourself for bread and water to survive," said Devon. The banging on the door became louder and more insistent, magnifying the tension inside the compartment and dissolving Devon's typically composed demeanor. "Dr. Foster! We are through arguing about this! I want you to climb out the window and

run around to the main car until after they've taken me away.
Do you understand?"

Audrianna snorted and said, "Oh, no. I don't think so."
She broke away from him, opened the door and stepped into
the hallway before he could stop her.

"*Bonjour, mademoiselle.*" A tall gentleman with dark hair
and mustache greeted her. He wore the same kind of uniform
as the young man who had detained them at the train station
earlier, only with more adornments: ribbons and bars. His pistol
was a standard, older looking service revolver, holstered over the
top of his gray tunic with a wide black belt. A small group of
soldiers accompanied him, all sporting slung rifles with bayonets
jutting from the barrels. "*Bonjour, mademoiselle,*" he repeated,
leaning forward for emphasis.

Audrianna's heart began to thump so vigorously she could
feel it in her throat. Perhaps she had not really thought this
through. But Devon's idea was no better. In fact, it was worse.
Did he really think giving himself up would prevent Niklas from
being discovered? What a laugh, almost as funny as the thought
of her crawling out the window.

"Hello, sir. Do you speak English?" she asked sweetly, trying
a play off her femininity again, despite her past failures.

"Yes," he replied. "Are you British?"

"No, sir. I'm American."

"Ah, I see. May I speak with your husband or father, please?"
he asked politely, looking past her toward the compartment door.

"I have no husband, and my father is deceased," Audrianna
answered.

"With whom do you travel, *mademoiselle?*" he frowned
and asked.

"I am traveling to the Medical University of Zurich with two critically ill patients who are to be treated there," Audrianna explained, ignoring his misogynistic implications. "I am their physician."

The French official scoffed at her. "I do not believe you are a doctor," he said. "May I see your credentials, please?"

Audrianna nodded her head without openly replying. She turned to unlatch the cabin door and stopped when the officer made an attempt to follow her in. "If you'll wait here, please," she brushed him back with a slight turn of her shoulder. "I'll bring the information to you."

"If you do not mind, I must follow," he smirked. "I will need to talk to your, ah, patients also." His disrespectful manner was a slap in the face, belittling not only of her sex but of her professional position as well.

"Why, of course you may come in, sir," Audrianna said, infuriated but emboldened by his arrogance. She swung the door open wide in a gesture of compliance, and stretched her arm across the empty doorframe, protecting the indwellers with the worthless barricade of her body. "However," she cautioned, "you really shouldn't come in here if you have anyone at home who depends upon you."

The officer pulled up short of his charge into the room and stared at her. "Pardon?" he said.

"Do you have anyone at home who depends upon you?" Audrianna repeated. "A wife? Children, perhaps?"

"I do not understand the relevance of the question," the man stammered.

Audrianna pulled the door to and lowered her voice. "The two patients in my care suffer from a highly contagious, rare disease that affects men only. It's called Lodonis Syndrome. Contact carries the risk of death."

The officer took a step backward. "Death?" he said.

"Yes," Audrianna replied. "Lodonis Syndrome is caused by a rampant infestation of flesh-eating microbes. Fortunately for me, the bugs are only attracted to men, specifically to the male genitalia. But don't worry. The microbes won't kill you instantly. It will take a few days for them to metamorphose. When they do finally hatch, they emerge with fangs so long they can be seen with the naked eye, and a thirst for blood that is only superseded by their desire to procreate more of their kind. A pestilence like that is capable of masticating both the testicles, and the penis, in under two hours." She sniffed the air. "Smell that? The stench of rotting meat is so difficult to cover up. These poor men will be lucky to have any lower extremities left at all by the time we reach Zurich."

The Frenchman inhaled deeply through his nostrils, taking the bait she laid out for him. He looked around at the small band of men who encircled him, all standing, watching their interaction.

Audrianna scratched the top of her head, imitating puzzlement. "Surely you must have heard of it? It seems to have hit France particularly hard. Probably brought here by those horrible Germans." She held her stance as the officer carefully considered the scenario she had depicted for him. He studied her, too, searching for the slightest inkling of inconsistency or fear in her appearance. She did not give it to him. Rather, she jumped upon his hesitation, saying, "Let me fetch my medical certification for you."

"Yes, let me look at it," the officer replied quickly, quelling the unrest Audrianna was trying to incite. "As well as the traveling papers for both you and your patients. I need all three sets."

Without giving him a second's opportunity to change his mind, Audrianna entered the room and closed the door behind her. "Give me all the papers," she whispered to Devon, rebuffing his objections with the wave of her hand. "And not your real papers, for God's sake," she added. "The fake ones. The ones you two have been using to get by on."

Devon reached into his pants pocket and removed all three sets of folded papers and handed them to her. "Dr. Foster, you just lied to a French officer. Do you understand the seriousness of that offense?"

"It's only serious if you get caught," Audrianna replied flatly.

Devon grabbed her by the arms and pulled her into him with an aggression she had not seen in him before. "Godammit! You are not playing a game. I cannot protect you if you are out of my sight. If they arrest you, I—"

"Devon, let me go," Audrianna interrupted hotly, pulling away from him. She made her way over to her bag and extracted her medical certification. "I appreciate your chivalry, but you are not invincible, either. Now, if I don't return in a matter of seconds, that man is going to come in here and collect me. He'll haul all three of us off to prison where Niklas will most certainly perish. We stand a much better chance if I continue with the deception. Okay?" She did not wait for an answer but carried out the door with the momentum of her resolve.

"Here you are, sir," Audrianna said, handing over the documents. The once-stoic-looking gentleman, now appearing unsettled and indecisive, took the papers from her and studied them for several minutes. He shifted his weight back and forth restlessly, demonstrating an uneasiness that Audrianna found contagious.

"*Mademoiselle* Foster, have you seen this man while you have been aboard this train?" He pulled a small worn picture from a pocket on his belt and handed it to her. Audrianna took it from him and looked at it. She recognized Niklas' image instantly but was careful not to let anything show on her face.

"He may be traveling with a German woman," continued the officer. "They are both fugitives, wanted for high treason against France. Anybody caught helping them will also be treated as such."

Audrianna shook her head. "No, sir. I'm afraid not," she lied, meeting his eyes fearlessly. "Because of the infectious nature of the disease I'm dealing with, I am not allowed to mingle with the other passengers."

The officer did not budge. He loomed above her, teasing her with the distribution of his justice as he continued his examination of the papers. A sickening feeling of fright crept back into Audrianna's heart, overpowering the effects of free-floating adrenalin in her system. She leaned backward into the door, her extremities weakened from the sheer terror of the lies she had just told and from the imagined punishment for such. What would they do to her? Would she be condemned to a lifetime of prison prostitution? Or would they execute her outright? Governments had little tolerance during wars, especially where espionage was concerned.

"Very well," the French official said, breaking into her panicky self-flagellation. He handed her the stack of documents. Audrianna tempered the tremble of her hand, forcing a smile that depicted the honesty he needed to see in order to let her go. They both made brief, gratuitous eye contact with one another in an acknowledgement of time spent together, and then the officer and his men continued down the narrow hallway to the next car.

Audrianna waited for their disappearance before returning to the room. Inside, she latched the bolt and slid with her back against the door to the floor.

"Dr. Foster!" Devon dropped down next to her. "Are you hurt? Did he hurt you?"

"No, Devon," she replied. "I'm a little weak, that's all. The important thing is that you and Niklas are safe, at least for now."

"Thanks to you, Dr. Foster," Devon whispered.

Audrianna half-laughed with her eyes turned down, chattering through her teeth. "Must you always address me so formally?" she asked, glancing back up.

Devon's gaze wandered over her face. "I speak to you that way because you've worked hard to earn that respect," he said. He reached up to her face and gently detached stray strands of hair that had fallen and become trapped in her eyelashes. "Audrianna," he whispered sweetly.

Audrianna felt the warmth of his breath on her face. His scent filled her nostrils, sparking a recall of her dream from earlier. She shook her head and quickly changed the subject.

"Devon?"

"Hmm?"

"That officer was looking for a woman, too," Audrianna said. "Do you know who she is?"

"Yes," Devon replied. "I know who she is."

Audrianna narrowed her eyes and asked, "Is she dead?"

Devon shook his head "No, she's not dead. Though I sometimes wish she were."

CHAPTER 4

"Come with me. I want to show you something," Devon said. He took Audrianna by the hand and led her to a silver door suspended in midair. It opened as they approached.

"Where are we going?" she asked.

"I'm taking you somewhere you've never been before," Devon replied. He was excited, giddy even. Intrigued, Audrianna followed him eagerly through the floating doorway. The two emerged headlong into a breeze on the other side, one that froze their exhalations and tickled their faces with flurries of snow.

"My God!" Audrianna gasped, sucking her breath in sharply, anticipating the searing coldness. But there was no cold. Shockingly, it was warm, and it evoked in her the sensation of a rain shower on a sunny summer's day.

A lush blanket of vegetation covered the ground, popping with leagues of multicolored wildflowers. Snow clouds billowed down from stiff mountain peaks, smothering the vision with an opaque fog. Audrianna became oddly overtaken with a feeling of playfulness and took off laughing and running through the snow-swept field of green. Devon caught up with her about halfway down and raced her to the edge of the meadow where they drew up together, gasping for air, and watching their breath materialize into frosty condensation.

"Would you look at that!?" Audrianna exclaimed, standing in the driveway to a gray slate manor house. Imposing and ominous, its baroque architecture taunted her with a history that belittled even the oldest structures in New England. "What is this place? This snow," she marveled, holding her arms up to the sky, "it's like magic dust falling from heaven. Look at how it sparkles in the sunlight."

Devon beamed. "This is a section of the Bavarian Alps that my family has owned since the reign of the first Hapsburgs over seven-hundred years ago. The inconsistent weather is a façade I created. It's usually quite chilly this time of year, but I warmed it up for you so that you could enjoy the site without shivering to death."

Audrianna shook her head at her own subconscious, giggling as she thought out the magnificence of her dream. Why shouldn't the boy she liked also be a prince? And why shouldn't that prince, if he chose to do so, be able to change the weather at his whim?

"This is the most beautiful sight in the world," she shouted, and then laughed at the echo.

Devon chuckled, "Well, almost," he said.

"What do you mean almost?" She tilted her face to the sky, celebrating the falling snowflakes as they melted on her skin.

Devon put his arm around her and pulled her close to his side, saying, "Every year since I can remember, I've come back here to watch the first snow of the season. It doesn't matter where I am, or what I'm doing. I stop. I stop, and I return home to witness the same spectacle. I tilt my head up, just as you're doing now, and rejoice in the awe of Mother Nature's grace. Until now, it's all I've known of God. Until I met you."

Audrianna stared at him, dumbfounded. He had not really said that. Had he? She never quite understood the concept of blasphemy, but surely his comparing her to God qualified. Yet he was relaxed and unapologetic, staring up into the heavens irreverently, fearless of celestial reproach or condemnation.

Devon lowered his face to her level and moved his hand to her cheek. "This vision you see before you is a mental reconstruction of my home in Germany, Audrianna. I built it from the sediment being discarded from your soul."

"What does that mean?" Audrianna asked.

"It means that you have so much expendable life force that you are unable to store it all within the confines of your soul. You've been spilling the excess into the world, and I have collected some of it to use in this creation. Let me show you," Devon said, placing his fingers over the tops of her shoulders and dragging them slowly downward toward her hands.

A sparkling cloud of blue glitter rose from Audrianna's arms, dislodged into the surrounding air by the friction from Devon's fingers. He reached up and gathered it with his hands, molding the dust like putty into a swirling sphere of color that was neither completely solid nor completely permeable. The wind picked up and blew against them as he tossed it between his palms, accelerating in turn with the momentum of the rotations he applied. Surging puffs of darkness swept in and commuted the beautiful snowfall into a torrential blizzard that startled Audrianna.

"What's happening?" Audrianna cried.

"Audrianna, please don't panic." Devon flashed her a stern look. He steadied himself against the strength of the wind without breaking concentration with the orb and said, "I'm using the gravity of your essence to pull forth a storm."

"Why?" Audrianna screamed.

"So you may understand that any impossibility you can imagine is yours to create here," Devon replied. "Any feat you care to conquer, any wonder you care to experience. Call your desires into existence with your mind, and they will materialize just as you've commanded. Watch this!"

Devon reached up into the air with one hand and then followed the trajectory with his eyes. The clouds parted to the right, then to the left, exposing a large, sunflower-colored sun. He drew back with his other arm and threw the oscillating ball of energy into the sky, right into the dead center of the sun. It bore down through the middle, slowly dissolving into the mass. The sun began to pulsate with a frequency that Audrianna could hear. It swelled until a massive explosion seemed imminent.

Audrianna ducked her head and covered her eyes with her hands, but Devon pulled them away just as quickly as she placed them there. "There is nothing here that can hurt you, Audrianna," he assured her. "This is a manifestation of your own power—it is you! I'm bringing it to life, but you could easily surmount anything I am doing with a single bat of your eye. Remember, all I have to work with is the excess energy you've shed. You have your entire soul. Just figure what you could create with such a store, if you had a mind to do it. Give it a try!

It's just like painting, only a thousand times better. Think of something you'd like to add to the picture."

Audrianna squinted her eyes in thought. She tried to ignore the blustery wind, the spattering chips of frozen rain, and the ominous, pre-exploding sun. Storms frightened her, even if they were only figments of her imagination. The only good thing about storms was that when they were over, you could sometimes catch a glimpse of a rainbow—a rainbow!

Streaks of multicolored prisms shot to the ground from the heavens, all around them, surrounding them in columns of kaleidoscopic light. Audrianna's eyes widened in amazement as she watched her thoughts coalesce into the background. She spun around and around, afraid to miss any part of the theatrical light show she had conceived. Gradually, her uneasiness transformed into a sense of emancipation as she threw off the chains of reality and revoked the sun's control over the sky, forcing it back into normal size with the flip of her fingers. The snow stopped pouring on their heads, replaced by … popcorn—thousands of toasted corn kernels spilling over the tops of the clouds.

Devon began to laugh. Not his normal reserved laugh, but rather the laughter of someone who was truly having a great time. "I love popcorn!" he shouted, snatching it out of the sky with his mouth and then giggling to himself when he caught one. Audrianna began to chuckle, then stopped. Her smile transmuted into a cock-eyed half grin as she contemplated Devon's playful change of countenance. His whimsical spirit, one he never apologized for or attempted to hide, was endearing. It was a sneaky little offset to an otherwise exquisitely profound personality and also a perfect complement to her own sense of humor.

Tingling warmth emerged in her chest as she tried once more to talk herself out of wanting him, out of falling in love with him. His lessons, his insoluble demonstrations, had granted her the privilege to behave as she pleased, but the influence of conventional thought continued to drive her judgment. She could not help it!

Right on cue, Devon targeted her thoughts with insightful precision. "It's really very easy," he said gently. "There is nothing to be afraid of, no risks, no consequences. This is your world, and here you can have anything you want." He snapped his fingers, and the sun shot from the sky like a falling star, vaporizing the remaining backdrop as it fell. He caught it in his hands, and it instantly reverted to the same glowing globe he had thrown minutes earlier. The electric warmth of blue light illuminated their faces as they drew close to one another, their eyes locked in an inseparable stare.

"Is there anything else that you want, Audrianna?" Devon asked.

Audrianna felt her inhibitions drain from her body through her feet, whisked away by the ghosts of prior hesitations. The sound of their breathing heightened the delay of her response, but not enough to sway her course. She stayed in the moment, built upon the tension, and matched his intensity with a fire of her own.

"I want you to take me somewhere we both long to go," she said, caught up in the candor of his intimated suggestions. It did not take a linguist to decipher his code of suppressed desire, especially when it was the same as her own.

"Are you certain?" Devon asked.

"Quite."

Devon's pupils dilated. His facial muscles twitched around the outer corners of his lips, as though he were attempting to conceal an impetuous excitement he was not sure he should express. "I know of such a place," he said, testing her confidence.

Audrianna blushed, but she did not look away. She lifted her chin and goaded him through the final seconds of their banter with a whisper. "Take me there."

Darkness folded the light into its depths, and when it returned, it returned as firelight on their faces. They sank into a plush, feather mattress molded from corner-to-corner and end-to-end into the frame of an ancient four-poster bed ringed by sheer silk curtains, drawn back but not tied. The room was warm, the air was still, and the silence was soft and tranquil.

"Where are we now?" Audrianna asked.

"My bedroom," Devon replied. "My bed."

He slowly began to unbutton her blouse, skipping his fingers from one button to the next without diverting his eyes from hers. Audrianna felt her nipples sharpen into sensitive, swollen tips at the first touch of open air, responding to Devon as he unlaced her corset and pulled it from her body.

He brought his lips to her bare breasts, not kissing, not nuzzling, not moving at all, merely breathing through his mouth and nose as though he had discovered an exotic flower to savor before plucking. "I wonder how much of your skin I can absorb just like this," he whispered. He lingered in that position for a few seconds before drawing one aching nipple into his mouth. He fondled it with his tongue.

"Oh!" Audrianna gasped. She folded her hands over her face and turned her head to the side, unaccustomed to the sensation of being suckled.

Devon stopped and looked up at her. "You're trembling," he said. "Have I hurt you?"

Audrianna shook her head. "No, Devon, you haven't hurt me," she whispered back. "It's just, I've never done this before, and I guess I didn't realize how lovely it would feel. I'm sorry." She inwardly forbade the welling tears from falling, but without success. A single, renegade tear escaped from the corner of her eye, slipping down her cheekbone. She wiped at its liquid trail in frustration, and then exhaled deeply.

"There is nothing to be sorry for, darling," Devon soothed her. "Do you want me to stop?"

"No." She answered quickly, scared that the patron saint of morality would appear and drag her kicking and screaming back to the world of appropriate behavior if she gave the matter any more thought. And she did not want that. She wanted him to make love to her. She just needed to get past her own discomfiture.

Devon sat up on his haunches and looked at her. He ran the warm, palmar surface of his hand down her sternum to her navel, dragging the tips of his fingers back up again in a seductive tickle. His passive sexuality stirred Audrianna into the kind of restless squirm that comes with carnal expectation. Although he could see her growing impatience, he did nothing to hasten his flow. "I hadn't expected a woman so well versed in birth control methods to be quite so shy," he chuckled.

Audrianna's nostrils flared. "That's my work, Devon, not my life!" She started to sit up, but Devon put her back on the bed by her neck and gently held her there.

"I thought your work *was* your life, doctor," he said. He reached underneath her skirt with the opposite hand to caress a stocking-clad thigh—deliberately, slowly, his movements choreographed and controlled, a ballet of arousal.

"That's different." Audrianna struggled weakly.

"Why?"

"Because this isn't medicine!" she snapped. "It's lust!" Sweat began to saturate the sheets beneath her, as she wriggled. She wanted to disappear and hide just as much as she wanted to stay and experience what he was doing to her.

Devon turned loose of her neck and slid his hands inside to remove her stockings; they clung to her thighs in a mix of sweat and silky lubricant. "Is there something wrong with lust?" he asked, parting the folds of her skin with his fingers, releasing the pent-up heat, allowing her only minimal relief from the ache.

"When carried to extremes," Audrianna panted. Her legs shook, she threw her hands over her open mouth and arched backward on the bed, closing her eyes, bracing herself for—for what? She had no idea what was coming.

His balmy breath fell first upon her thighs. "No, we mustn't carry things to extremes. I agree," he said, and then he brought his tongue to her, electrifying her with its precision as it moved across her clitoris and nothing else. *Oh my God! This couldn't be it!* This could not be all she could tolerate! Only it was. The intensity of the sensation was too strong, and she knew something inside of her would explode if she did not pull away.

"No, Audrianna." He seized her above both knees and forced her to stay with him. "We have both wanted this. Move with me, not against me." A challenge! Audrianna spread her legs wider for him. She was not a coward. Tenderness gave way to tension, an eroticism of a different flavor, and it made her feel powerful, liberated, and brazen enough to watch him as he slid his fingers into her.

They locked eyes as Devon stroked her, speeding or slowing his tempo to match Audrianna's movements. He slid his thumb beneath her clitoris and applied firm pressure, trapping a river of blood inside so it flooded the nerve endings. She gasped at the surge, and rocked herself more forcefully against his hand. A cool, indescribable wetness doused her from somewhere inside, providing an initial burst of satisfaction that quickly turned into something else. Her legs began to tingle. Her momentum slowed to a crawl. She felt feeble and incapacitated.

"What's happening to me?" she cried, propping herself up on her elbows and letting her head dangle back.

Devon placed one of her legs over his shoulder and brought his mouth back into her core. He continued his gentle finger thrusts as he darted his tongue up and down, working her over until she could not hang on to her sense of control anymore. Audrianna screamed. She felt muscles from deep within her pelvis contract more than a half-dozen times, delivering a kind of blissful release that she never even knew existed.

"*Leute die nach Zurich fahren muessen hier absteigen!*"

A brash voice cut into Audrianna's climax. Devon stopped; they both looked around. She sat up and covered herself shyly with her dismantled clothing.

"It's the train attendant," Devon replied. "We have to go." He rose from the bed and started to walk away, but she seized an iron-trap grasp on his arm.

"Go where?" Audrianna cried.

A familiar fog began to choke the room with the haze that represents every end of every dream. It muddied her vision and crippled her sense of hearing with its buzzing white noise, but Audrianna did not turn him loose. "Tell me!" she insisted. But he did not say another word, and Audrianna, immobilized by the heaviness that belongs to the earthly plane, gave in to its call and woke up.

─────◆─────

"*Leute die nach Zurich fahren muessen hier absteigen!*"

Audrianna opened her eyes. Devon lifted his head from her lap and looked around. His skin was flushed with a crimson hue that extended all the way from his ears down to his neck. He sat up and rubbed his face in what appeared to be an attempt to stimulate alertness, although it did not seem to help much.

"We're in Zurich," he said. "We have to get off this train before it sets off again." His voice was hoarse and cracked, words slurred like he was intoxicated on whiskey. He stood and reached for Audrianna's hand, pulling her from the floor so they stood face-to-face and eye-to-eye.

Audrianna gasped, surprised by his appearance. His once-sparkling emerald eyes were now a drab olive, more yellow than green. "Your eyes are—"

"Yes, I know." He cut her off, turning from her view. He stooped to collect her bag and handed it to her without looking up. Audrianna took it, but did not move to leave. It was obvious something was wrong.

"Devon, what happened?" she asked him. "You look like a different person! Please tell me what is wrong."

He glanced at her sideways with a half-hearted smile. "I assure you, Audrianna, there is nothing wrong that can't be corrected with a day or two of rest."

"All right," Audrianna said, though she knew he was lying. She had seen tired before and that certainly was not his principle affliction. But he clearly had no intention of confiding in her, and she refused to beg him for his divulgence. She had to protect her own fragile state of emotion after all, one that he had so recently riled up whether he knew it or not.

"Niklas. We're home," Devon said. He moved past Audrianna and shook Niklas, gently at first, and then more aggressively when he did not respond.

Niklas' face was colorless. His lips were dry, cracked, and cemented with mucosal secretions that had hardened into a white, textured paste around his mouth. His much-too-small shirt was drenched with sweat. Audrianna rushed to examine him, placing one hand on Niklas' forehead and the other on his chest to make sure he was still alive.

"Lorna?" Niklas opened his eyes and looked at Audrianna.

"Niklas. We're home," Devon repeated, stepping in front of Audrianna in a hurry. "I'm taking you to Dirk. Help me get him up, Audrianna." He presented her with one of Niklas' limp arms and took the other himself. Together, the two of them pulled Niklas up to the side of the bed.

Audrianna pried one of his eyelids open to assess his level of consciousness. "He's still very sedated," she said. "I don't know if he'll be able to—"

"He has no choice," Devon cut in with a short, sharp retort. He pulled gruffly on Niklas' arm, forcing him into a clumsy wobble the injured man could not sustain for more than a few seconds. He fell backward onto the bed and Devon yanked on him more forcefully.

"Devon, stop it!" Audrianna grabbed him. "You'll pull his arms out of their sockets."

Devon bowed his head and lowered his eyes. He seemed weak and defeated. His fortitude had been shaken. Audrianna was not sure how, or why now—now at what seemed to be the end of their journey. But she could not waste any more time thinking about it.

She rested her hand on his shoulder and softened her tone. "Don't you understand?" she asked. "He's got a bullet in his chest, a collapsed lung, and I've given him enough drugs to tranquilize a horse. What in the world has gotten into you?" She snatched her bag off the floor and plopped it onto the bed, digging around inside.

"I do understand," Devon muttered. "I just don't know how we'll get him out of here and we only have a few minutes left before the train leaves again."

"We're going to get him out of here like this," Audrianna replied. She ruptured an ammonia capsule and stuffed it into Niklas' nose. He shot straight up on the bed, and when he did that, Audrianna stomped her foot and screamed at the top of her lungs, "On your feet, soldier!"

Niklas stood up.

"Why did you scream like that?" Devon asked as he took hold of one of Devon's arms.

"Adrenaline," Audrianna replied, taking the other. "He needed a jolt of adrenaline."

They flung his long, well-muscled arms around their shoulders, inching forward with tiny, painful steps. The weight of his body dragged on them like an anchor as they trudged out the door, unbearably slowly. Eventually they arrived at the exit. The sun set against the oncoming starlight with an orange flaming glow. The potency of the light illuminated the entire station, making it easier to see the steps, the railing, and the platform. It alleviated some of the effort required to clear them.

"I can't feel my body," Niklas croaked as they shuffled across the threshold. His sweaty limbs slipped down, forcing Audrianna and Devon to drag him across their backs like a sack of rocks.

"It's okay, Niklas," Audrianna encouraged him, although she was not at all encouraged. "Concentrate on your feet. Bring your arms back up and put your weight on us. Use us like crutches. Understand?"

"Yes. Thank you," Niklas replied, seemingly grateful for her lack of admonishment and her simple, calm instructions. He moved his arms back up onto their shoulders and swung his body forward, conquering one stair at a time until there were no more to conquer. Using the propulsion of the descent, the three of them lumbered ahead another few steps to safety, collapsing to their knees just as the train began to pull away from the platform.

"How much farther must we go?" Audrianna asked Devon, unable to hide the strain in her voice. "I'm afraid we're about to lose him." Niklas' head bobbled loosely around on his neck, splattering her face with salty driblets of perspiration. His dark, hollow eyes rolled back into his head as he floated to and from the edge of consciousness.

Devon looked around quickly. "There's Jakob now. Jakob!" he screamed, throwing his free arm up into the air and signaling for someone in the crowd to come to his aid.

A gangly young man turned in the direction of Devon's call, searching through the droves of passengers. He wore a driver's uniform of gray wool pants and jacket, black accents at the lapel and sleeves, a matching hat, and black leather boots up to the knee. He picked out Devon's waving hand through the swarm and made his way toward them. "*Warum bist duo?*" he asked Devon in bewilderment.

Devon held up his hand, silencing the young man's questions without a word. He gestured with his head, first to Niklas and then into the air, issuing silent orders to a person who seemed to understand his dictates. The young man maneuvered himself into Audrianna's position, and she took a stance behind them. She pulled up on Niklas' belt loops so his feet would not drag the ground, and together they moved him down the gangway through the multitudes of onlookers in the train station.

By the time they reached the outside, night had drawn its curtain completely across the sky, and street lamps provided the light to see. Devon pointed toward a long row of motorcars lining the cobblestone. "Is the car there?" he asked Jakob.

Breathing heavily, Jakob replied, "Yes, over there." He spoke in perfect English, much to Audrianna's surprise. She was no authority on foreign literacy, but found it most odd that a hired driver would be able to speak anything other than his native language.

"Dr. Foster. Get the door, please," Devon broke into her thoughts.

Audrianna jumped to open the back door of the car, but drew up short of actually doing so, shocked. The car was a Rolls Royce. Not any Rolls Royce, but a Silver Ghost. Her father had been a motorcar aficionado, and Audrianna had grown up reading magazine articles on luxury vehicles. She came away from her childhood with a knowledge of cars, not the relationship with her father she had sought.

"Dr. Foster!" Devon groaned, "the door!" Audrianna opened the door and moved out of the way.

"All right, Niklas, in you go," Devon huffed as he and Jakob heaved Niklas' body into the back seat. Audrianna started to climb in behind him, but Devon stopped her with a hand on her arm. "Wait," he said. "You've more than fulfilled your favor to us. I'll have a taxi take you to a hotel and have your luggage delivered within the hour."

"I'm not leaving you—" Audrianna caught herself. "I mean—
I'm not leaving Niklas until we reach the hospital. As we agreed."

They locked eyes. She could tell Devon wanted to insist, but
was no more ready to say goodbye than she was. He nodded his
concession. "Let's go," he said, patting Jakob affectionately on
the back, then gesturing to Audrianna. "This is Dr. Audrianna
Foster. She is here visiting us from the United States. Dr. Foster,
this is Jakob Schultz, the von Traugott family chauffeur."

"How do you do?" Jakob asked Audrianna.

"I am well, thank you," Audrianna replied with a smile.
Aside to Devon she said, "His English is beautiful."

"Jakob's parents were lifelong employees of the von Traugott
family," Devon explained. He encouraged her into the backseat
of the car, and then climbed in on the other side to help support Niklas. Jakob swung around to the driver's side to crank
the engine before sliding behind the wheel and steering the car
onto the road. "They died when he was only three years," Devon
continued. "Afterwards, he was made a ward of the family.
Thus, he has been educated in the highest tradition of the von
Traugotts, a family considered to be one of the oldest known
lineages of Frankish royalty in the world. He speaks English
fluently, along with French and, of course, German."

Audrianna stared at Devon. Everything was beginning to
make sense: the manner in which Devon conducted himself, the
money he carried, the sense of urgency, and the outrageous lengths
he had gone to get Niklas home. He was accountable to this family, the von Traugotts, in some fashion, and it definitely seemed
more than just a professional courtesy. He knew things, details
and histories that a common acquaintance would be unlikely
to know. In addition to the obvious familiarity he displayed
toward Niklas, he was also warm and protective—qualities that

would be nearly impossible for anyone, despite their impressive lineage, to purchase. Devon must be, she decided, a ward of this family, too.

Devon flipped his eyes out the window. There was a continued sadness in him that Audrianna felt she finally understood. He was embarrassed by his station in life—his change in mood, an anticipatory reaction of how he thought Audrianna would feel about him once she found out the truth. Only he was wrong, terribly wrong. She was completely smitten with him, and it did not matter if he were absent a family, if he had no title and no money. The fact was he had captured her heart with nothing more than his own distinctive manner. And now, even his age seemed an irrelevant deterrent for her affection. She was in love with him, and felt it was finally time he should know it, if he did not already.

As the car rolled down the streets of the city, Audrianna found herself thinking of her father. She had all but hated him for beseeching her on this long, tough road to Zurich, but now she was excited to be here. How strange, she thought, that fulfillment was the same thing as sharing the air with a young man whom she would have otherwise never known.

———

All was quiet, save the hum of the Silver Ghost as it left the town center. House lights dotted the mountains around the outskirts of Zurich, shining like stars against a winter night's sky. Minutes passed; Audrianna lost track of time. The swift arrest of the engine reoriented her succinctly as the car ground to a stop in front of a solemn looking stone building.

"We're here," Devon announced. He tapped Jakob on the shoulder. "Go and get Dirk," he said. "Quickly!" He slid back into his seat beside Audrianna and said, "Let's try and get him inside as discreetly as possible. We won't be able to avoid everyone, but there is no need to alarm the entire staff." He opened the door and got out of the car, scanning the area right to left and front to back before popping his head into the backseat again. "Come this way," he said, as he motioned for Audrianna to slide toward him.

Audrianna skimmed her body laterally along the pearl-colored leather until she was able to free her legs from the cage of the car. She planted her feet on the stone driveway next to Devon; he reached in and took hold of Niklas' shirt.

"Come on, Niklas," he said, giving a hefty yank on the fabric to pull him closer. "Dr. Foster, are you able to grab his hand?"

Audrianna took Niklas' palm into her own and helped tug him from the car while Devon maneuvered the bulk of Niklas' body.

"*Was zum Teufel wird geschehen?*" a voice exploded from behind them and Audrianna snapped her head about to see who it was. A tall man of perhaps thirty, with dark hair pulled back into a ponytail, shot from the doorway as though he had been launched from a cannon. He stopped uncomfortably close and stared at Devon in a fury. "*Was zum Teufel wird geschehen?*" He repeated his question, lowering the volume of his voice without lightening the level of his rage.

Audrianna felt her heartbeat kick into overdrive, frightened for Devon, who stood speechless under the scrutiny of the man's glare. The man did not wait long for a response. He brushed them aside and scooped Niklas up in his arms as though he were an oversized rag doll. Devon and Audrianna followed closely behind him into the hospital. They passed by Jakob, who stepped back quickly from their rush through the doorway, calling, "I'll wait for you here, Dr. von Traugott." But the man did not respond. He charged past several open rows of hospital beds and gawking nurses in long white dresses, to a private surgical suite away from the main ward. He placed Niklas on a stretcher and examined him from head to toe with various medical instruments from the drawers around him. He inserted a single finger into the wound in the man's chest to assess its depth and diameter, provoking a howl from Niklas that made Audrianna wince. He wiped the blood from his hands on a nearby towel and turned to Devon.

"What have you done?" he flared.

Devon narrowed his eyes and flattened his lips. "Dirk, he's been shot," he said icily. "I brought him home to you. I thought—"

"You couldn't just leave well enough alone, could you?" Dirk shook his head. He turned back to Niklas and tore into the hem of his shirt, exposing his entire chest. "It wasn't good enough for him to be an artillery officer, was it? You had to fill his thoughts with visions of heroism and glory. A spy! And for what?" He removed a basin and a bottle of antiseptic solution from underneath the stretcher, dropping a small heap of gauze in it, then poured the liquid over the top.

"I'll tell you for what!" Dirk continued as he began to clean Niklas' wound. He threw the dirty wads of gauze on the floor as he used them with force so strong they left red smudges on the concrete where they slid. "For a cause that doesn't even exist! A game! I wonder sometimes how you're any different from the rest of them." He turned around and wagged his finger once in Devon's face. "He's your mirror! You've all but gotten him killed!"

Devon lowered his voice and gritted his teeth. "Fine," he said. "If it makes you feel better to say so—but I'm hardly alone in my culpability. If you had—"

"That's enough," Dirk stopped him sternly, but the anger had faded from his intonation. "I have work to do. Please wait for me in my office, and we'll talk about it then."

Devon scowled at him, then turned a sharp about-face. He glanced at Audrianna with soft, apologetic eyes before starting out the door. She turned to follow, but did not make one full step before Dirk's voice instructed her to halt. "Not you, Dr. Foster," he said. "I need to talk to you."

Audrianna stopped, but did not turn around. He was addressing her by name, yet they had not been introduced. Devon must have wired him a message about her somehow—but when? And why would Devon just leave her there by herself to defend her actions to a skilled surgeon?

"What is your assessment of Niklas' condition?" Dirk asked her.

Audrianna pivoted slowly on the balls of her feet to face him, nervous, but deciding an interjection of politeness might be in order. "We haven't met," she began lightly. "My name is Audrianna Fos—"

"I know who you are," Dirk cut in. "Is Niklas any better? Is he any worse? Is there anything important I need to know? Has he had a fever?"

"Fever, no," Audrianna replied quietly, even more intimidated by him now. "His level of consciousness has been diminished since my first encounter with him, and I believe that he was in a state of cardiogenic shock in the beginning." She licked her lips before continuing. "He had a collapsed lung, you see, so I treated him as well as I knew how to, under the circumstances."

Dirk moved in closer to her. "How was that?" he asked.

Audrianna tilted her head back to look up at him. Like Niklas, he was over six feet tall, but aside from that, the two men looked nothing alike. Dirk's glossy-gray crystalline eyes could not have been more different from Niklas', and they might well have been the oddest color she had ever seen.

"Well, I, um," she stuttered, "I created a one-way valve with a ... condom, and then I used hot water bottles and coffee to restore and maintain body heat. He started bleeding again when we were moving him to the train, and I had no choice but to cauterize the tissue with a hot-fire poker in order to stop it. I used morphine to ease the cardiac load and employed his own natural adrenalin when necessary."

"How did you do that?" Dirk asked, disbelievingly.

Audrianna tilted her head back down and cleared her throat. She took a few steps backward and replied, "I scared him."

"You scared him?" Dirk repeated with a bemused laugh. "Did he respond to that?"

"Yes," she said. "I've found fright can be a powerful stimulant—at least in labor it can be, Doctor." She pointed over at Niklas. "He's been like this for at least twelve hours now. It's not great, but it's better than he was."

Dirk took several slow paces toward Audrianna, who had inadvertently trapped herself against the wall. "I'm sorry you were involved in this, Dr. Foster," he apologized. "Forgive me if I've frightened you. It certainly wasn't my intention. I'm in awe of your resourcefulness. I don't know that I would've thought of any of the measures you employed to save my brother's life. Thank you."

"How do you know my name?" she asked with trembling lips. Dirk smiled weakly at her, but Audrianna did not reciprocate. She found his mannerisms unsettling and wanted nothing more at that moment than to escape from him and return to Devon.

"You're safe here," Dirk said. He closed his eyelids tightly, as if concentrating, then inhaled deeply. As he exhaled, he placed the fingertips of one of his hands on Audrianna's shoulder. "Be easy," he whispered.

Audrianna began to melt under the warmth of his hand. She could feel each individual finger distributing heat into her muscles, first into her shoulder, then her arm, and throughout the rest of her body. She became sedate. Her heart rate slowed, trembling stopped, and her breathing became long and easy. It was nearly the same feeling she had when first meeting Devon. Only this was not as debilitating. This time, she could still feel her arms and legs, could still speak if she wanted to.

Dirk retracted his hand and turned back to Niklas. "Have you ever seen Locke's solution used intravenously, Dr. Foster?" he asked.

Audrianna put her hand up to her forehead to steady herself. There was a ringing fullness in her ears that she tried to clear by yawning. She felt muddled. Suddenly, she could not remember the details of the past few hours. "I'm sorry. What did you say?" she asked him.

Dirk turned around and looked at her. "Locke's solution," he repeated. "Belgian military surgeons have used it quite a bit. It's helpful for restoring electrolyte imbalances like acidosis."

Audrianna struggled to focus. Locke's solution? Acidosis? She scanned the room for Devon, but did not find him. He had left. Audrianna could not remember why she had not gone with him.

"Dr. Foster?" Dirk repeated.

Audrianna shook her head, trying to clear the fog that accumulated. "Um, no. I don't think so," she finally managed.

"Come here, and I'll show you," Dirk offered, seemingly unaware of her state of confusion. "I doubt you'll find as much need for it in your field of medicine, but it never hurts to have more knowledge."

Audrianna scratched her head. Had she told him her field of practice? She must have. Why was she having such a hard time remembering things right now?

"This solution is a mixture of sodium chloride, potassium, calcium, glucose, and sodium bicarbonate," he said, perforating the rubber stopper of the bottle with a cannulated needle and then attaching a length of tunneled tubing to it. "Dr. Foster, would you mind holding his arm down for me while I do this?" Dirk placed a tourniquet around Niklas' arm.

Audrianna stepped to the stretcher and applied pressure to Niklas' hand and forearm while Dirk inserted a large, bored needle under the skin into his vein. Intravenous therapy, while having been practiced for hundreds of years, was just now beginning to be implemented in common medical regimens, although its use was still mostly limited to trauma, surgery, and battlefield medicine. This was the first time she had seen an actual demonstration of the technique.

"Good," Dirk said, as he watched blood begin to dribble from the hub of the needle. "Now if you'll hand me the end of that tube, please."

Audrianna handed him the tubing that was attached to the bottle of Locke's solution. He slid it over the hub of the needle and released the clamp that had dammed the fluid in the line, dispensing nutrients into Niklas' body.

"How do you know how much to give?" Audrianna asked him.

"Well, you don't, really," Dirk replied with a soft chuckle. "It's kind of a wait-and-see approach." He removed a clean gauze roll from a drawer and wrapped it up and around Niklas' arm. "Let's give him 250 milliliters at a time, in several doses, to start. He'll need surgery to remove the bullet, of course, but not now.

Maybe sometime tomorrow if he is much improved." He went to one of the cupboards and pulled out several blankets and covered Niklas with them. "I need to leave for a few minutes to get some tetanus toxin and morphine," he said. "Could I trouble you to remain here for a little longer and clamp that tube once he has received the first 250 milliliters?"

"Yes, of course," Audrianna replied.

Dirk bowed his head in appreciation, then he hesitated. He looked at Niklas and then at her. "Thank you," he said. "You've done more to help him than any other reasonable human being would have. May I ask why?"

Audrianna chuckled. "If you'd have asked me that two days ago, I would have told you I had momentarily lost my mind."

"But not now," Dirk finished her thought.

Audrianna shook her head. "No. Not now. Now I'm prepared to believe that some of life's most poignant lessons come with the oddest tutorials and from the most unlikely teachers. This whole experience has been one such example."

She opened her mouth to speak again, but caught herself, deciding instead to rehearse her thought in her head before saying it out loud. "You know, Dr. von Traugott," she continued, "it was Devon's determination that really saved Niklas. I don't know how he convinced me to get off that train, but his courage, strength, and sense of devotion are what motivated me. It would be disingenuous of me not to tell you that I've done what I have as much for him as I have for Niklas. Devon is a very special young man."

"Devon. Right." Dirk acknowledged her praise, although his tone was biting. "Excuse me, Dr. Foster. I'll be back as quickly as I can, and then we'll get you situated. Where in town are you staying? I'll have Jakob contact them to prepare for your arrival."

"I have reserved a room in a ladies boarding house near the university," Audrianna replied. "Although, I'm quite certain they aren't equipped with a telephone, so perhaps you would just allow him to drive me there."

Dirk smiled softly and said, "I'll have him keep the car warm. That is the very least I can do. Also, I believe I may have your luggage at my house."

"Oh! My luggage!" Audrianna said, realizing now how Dirk had known her name. "I'd forgotten all about it! Thank you so much for taking care of it."

"It was my pleasure," Dirk replied. "I'll have Jakob deliver it to you in the morning, if that is amenable?"

Audrianna nodded. "Yes, the morning would be fine."

"Very good. Excuse me, Dr. Foster," Dirk said, and then he left the room.

Audrianna monitored the infusion of Locke's solution closely. When 250 milliliters had emptied into Niklas's arm, she clamped the line. More than twenty minutes had passed, and Dirk had not yet returned, so she stuck her head out into the hallway in the hopes of flagging a nurse to come and sit with Niklas. Her swollen bladder had called to her hours ago, but now, the urgency had become unbearable, and she was desperately in need of the ladies room.

With no one in sight, Audrianna forged her way deeper into the corridor, following a faint light at the end of the hallway. The walls were cold bare concrete, marked with indistinct doorways and windowless doors. She opened several of them looking for a washroom to no avail; she then decided to return to the entrance of the building. Just then, Audrianna heard two voices in quiet conversation. In curiosity, she quietly traversed the remaining length of the hallway to the light spilling from underneath a door; she peeked through the crack of the door.

"She is not to be touched," Dirk said. He paced, carrying a decanter of scotch in one hand and a highball glass in the other, which he would periodically fill and down in single gulps. Devon leaned against a large wooden desk, arms folded toward Dirk.

"Do you really think I would do that?" Devon said, shaking his head. "After all she's done for us?"

Dirk rolled his eyes and laughed. "Who are you trying to fool? I can see where you've been already. The color of your eyes gives you away!" He downed another glass and slammed the decanter on the desk next to Devon. "She's not one of your little whores! Have you no decency?"

Devon's eyes protruded. "I haven't treated her like a whore!" he screamed. "She wasn't harmed." He poked himself in the chest. "I'm the one who bore all the loss!"

"Your loss is temporary and you know it," Dirk rebutted. "You'll have rectified it by the time the sun rises, no doubt. I'm sure you have a reserve of women in every city you visit for just such a crisis."

Devon sprang from his perch and slapped Dirk across the face with an open palm. "Fuck you, Dirk," he spat. "None of this would've happened if you had been focused on the game!" He pointed at Dirk's eyes. "What word would you use to describe that color of gray, anyway? Inept? No wonder Niklas got shot!"

Dirk trapped Devon's arms behind his back, clamping his wrists using just one of his own hands. He pushed Devon back into the edge of the desk with his much larger body, bending him backward over the top of it in the process. Devon fought feverishly at first but eventually fatigued.

"What will she say when she finds out?" Dirk asked with a malevolent laugh. He slid his free hand down Devon's pants, and Devon's gasps turned into involuntary moans. "Or didn't you think of that when you were doing this to her?"

Audrianna looked away, mortified. Her own breathing became short and pronounced; she placed a hand over her mouth to contain the noise. The sound of tearing fabric drew her eyes back to the fight.

"Amazing she didn't see through the ruse," Dirk scoffed as he ripped the seams of Devon's shirt. The garment fell in swathes around Devon's waist, revealing a cloth bound tightly around a soft, white chest. Panting, Dirk removed a switchblade from his pocket and sliced the fabric with surgical expertise.

"You son of a bitch!" Devon yelled in a renewed burst of energy, breaking free of Dirk's hold, attacking him with closed fists. Dirk tossed away the switchblade and blocked the punches with his forearms, catching Devon's wrists over his head. Without his arms to hold the fabric place, the cloth around Devon slipped down. And with its loss, two small, naked breasts with jutting nipples appeared.

Audrianna gasped. She collapsed sideways into the wall in a sudden state of shock, quickly recovering when she realized the commotion she had made. Whispers overtook shouts; feet shuffled inside and then fell close to the door. Audrianna shot to her feet and fled back down the hallway as the door to Dirk's office swung open, flooding the passageway with tangerine light.

"Audrianna! Wait! Come back!" Devon pleaded after her.

Tears blinded her escape as she rounded the corner and made her way to the entry. She ran out the front door and flung herself into the backseat of the car. Jakob was already there.

"I'm ready to leave!" she cried. "Let's go."

Without hesitation, Jakob steered away from the hospital. Audrianna sobbed without dignity or grace, burying her face in her hands as betrayal bit hungrily at her heels. Rain drummed the windshield as the car sped back into Zurich.

CHAPTER 5

"Are you hungry, dear?"

Audrianna squinted through sleepy eyelashes at the sound of the voice. She propped herself up in the bed and brushed her hair out of her face. A short, robust woman of middle age leaned over and patted her lightly on the head. "It's Mrs. Brindle, dear, from last night. Remember?" she said.

Audrianna continued to squint but did not answer, and the woman simply set about opening curtains throughout the room. Thousands of long-dormant dust particles danced in the daylight. Audrianna coughed.

"Sorry about that, Miss Foster," Mrs. Brindle said. "Me and my husband came from England six months back—been least that long since the room was used." She grabbed a dust broom and swung it through the air fruitlessly, agitating more of the flying crud. "If I'd known you was coming last night, I would've had it ready for you."

Audrianna rubbed her nose. "Don't worry, Mrs. Brindle," she said. "I didn't know when I would arrive."

"Of course you didn't, dear!" Mrs. Brindle tut-tutted. She sat next to Audrianna on the bed. "And my, what a journey you must have had! You was soaked through last night, and so terribly upset! What happened to you dear? Why, I could barely get you to tell me your name last night."

Audrianna shook her head to clear unpleasant memories. She rose from the bed, noticing aching muscles, and steadied her wobble against the bureau. She turned to face her benefactress.

"Yes, it's been quite a journey," Audrianna answered offhandedly. "And now I'm hungry—and filthy. Might I have a bath?"

Easily distracted, Mrs. Brindle replied, "Well, it's certainly the place for that! The previous owners had hot and cold installed in each suite last year. That was my mother's brother's wife's family, you know?" She looked down and away, trying to remember something. "They died on that boat, the *Titanic*, the big one that sank. Remember that, Miss Foster? They was in second class, so …"

Audrianna feigned interest. She heard Mrs. Brindle patter on, but wasn't listening. Every once in a while she interjected a well-placed "yes," or "that's interesting" for the sake of being polite.

"They wasn't as rich as that lady that came by to see you this morning, but they made their way decent—"

"Lady?" Audrianna snapped to attention.

"Yes, the lady with the big green eyes. The one who brought your bags." Mrs. Brindle pointed to the luggage in the corner of the room. "She asked to see you, but I told her you was still asleep. She tried to insist, but I told her you wasn't in any condition to receive visitors, regardless of who they was. She was a tad miffed with me, I think, but finally that fancy motorcar took her away. You know her well, dear?"

Audrianna shook her head. "Not well at all." She turned away, lest her facial expression give her away.

"Didn't think so," Mrs. Brindle said. "Aristocrat, she was. Ladies and gentlemen of the upper crust tend not to mingle with the likes of you and me. Your luggage must've gotten caught up with some of her things. Wonder why she didn't send one of her servants with the chauffeur instead?"

Audrianna took a deep calming breath through her nostrils, and then whispered, "What makes you think that she was upper-crust?"

Mrs. Brindle chuckled. "Oh, you can tell them apart, all right—that's the way they want it, too." She winked and headed into the adjoining room. "I'll start the water for your bath, then fix you up something to eat."

"Aristocrat. Ha!" Audrianna muttered, barely noticing Mrs. Brindle's departure. She did not believe it. Surely no one with that kind of pedigree would ever risk the scandal of parading around like a member of the opposite sex. Or maybe she had not planned it that way, Audrianna suddenly considered. Maybe she had no choice but to alter her identity once Niklas had been shot. Audrianna shook her head at her own ignorance. Niklas had been calling for a woman named Lorna. The officer on the train also mentioned Niklas traveling with a woman.

Audrianna shuddered. All the clues! His delicate features, his skin, his scent. It had all been right there in front of her eyes! But she had not seen it. She had not seen it because the senselessness of falling in love with a younger man had been at the forefront of her mind. And as bad as that was, the reality of this situation was so much worse.

"It's nearly afternoon now," Mrs. Brindle announced, reappearing in the doorway. "How does sandwiches and tea suit your fancy?"

"Nearly afternoon!" Audrianna lamented out loud. "Yes, that would be fine, Mrs. Brindle. Thank you." She glanced at her wristwatch to confirm the time. How embarrassing to have slept so late. She should get dressed and take a stroll over to the university to find out what had happened to Dr. Adler. In the months leading up to her journey to Europe, she had written to Dr. Adler repeatedly about her father's work. In a way, Dr. Adler was the very reason she had made the trip to Zurich. She knew Dr. Adler was a close colleague of her father's and would thus be a great place to start in regard to her own research. However, since he had never replied to any of her correspondence, Audrianna could only surmise that Dr. Adler had either passed away, or no longer worked at the university. Unfortunate as that was, the school would have at least retained the research notes on lyovitalis.

Audrianna walked over to her luggage to forage for a change of clothes. She took a semi-fitted, dressy suit of wool serge into the bathroom. Hot water cascaded from the copper faucet, filling the room with a steamy mist. Audrianna shed the clothes she had worn for three days, twisted the faucet closed, and slipped into the ceramic tub, one foot at a time. Eventually submerged up to her chest with a bar of oatmeal soap, she washed away the grime first from her skin, then from her hair. Her scalp massage turned to clawing at her wet head to drive Devon's image from her psyche. She felt dirty; her mind was still sullied with fantasies of him—dreams that should be too humiliating to admit they even existed. Only they did exist.

Audrianna slapped the water. "Stop!" she growled at herself, and then she rubbed her dripping hands over her face. "Stop thinking about it!" she quietly added. She got out of the tub.

After she dried off and dressed, Audrianna applied makeup and sat down for roast beef and tomato sandwiches in the parlor. She picked up the newspaper left for her and read the headline: *Local Nurse's Death Ruled A Suicide, Third Case This Year.*

"Dreadful thing." Mrs. Brindle crept up behind her and poured water into her glass. "All them poor girls from that *cursed* refugee hospital. If you ask me, they all died from broken hearts."

Audrianna choked on her sandwich. "I'm sorry?" she coughed.

Mrs. Brindle sat down across from her and made casual conversation despite Audrianna's sputtering. "Of course, I'm not one to spread gossip, Miss Foster, but every young nurse that goes up there to work at that hospital goes in the hopes of catching that doctor."

Audrianna guzzled her water, and then wiped her mouth with her napkin, keeping it there while Mrs. Brindle chattered on. "Dr. Dirk von Traugott," she laughed. "A bachelor, a baron, and as rich as Croesus—so charming, it's said—he need only look at a girl and she becomes hopelessly infatuated with him." She lowered her voice to a loud whisper. "Locals call him a predator. They say he seduces the young girls, preys on their love, and sucks their souls dry—"

"That's ridiculous, Mrs. Brindle." Audrianna put her napkin down, feeling the need to defend Dirk, if only on a professional level. She stood up and gathered her belongings, continuing, "Medicine is a demanding profession. Many are unsuited for the work, especially in a time of war. If Dr. von Traugott has lost some of his staff to suicide, it merely indicates the atrocities they must all be enduring as a result of this conflict. The community should have more compassion for him, not less."

"Of course, I've never met the man myself," Mrs. Brindle said, unfazed by Audrianna's defense. "I'm just telling what I've heard said around the town, you know? Where are you off to in such a hurry, dear?"

"I've got some errands to run." Audrianna left it at that. She slung her messenger's bag across her body and headed toward the university, an easy half-hour stroll down the old brick streets of Gloriastrasse and Ramistrasse. From the directory, Audrianna located the section of buildings housing the school of medicine, and then proceeded to the information desk. *"Guten Tag,"* she greeted the attendant and continued to speak in German. "Whom might I speak with about disease research conducted here by Dr. Gustav Adler?"

"I suggest you speak with Dr. Adler," the attendant replied flatly. After a moment he added, "Will there be anything else, Fräulein?"

Audrianna shook the blank stare off her face and said, "Yes, I'm sorry. Do you know where I might find him?"

"Upstairs; second floor; Room 213."

Audrianna lifted her brows. "Do you mean he still works for the university," she asked.

"That is what I mean, Fräulein," the attendant replied. He looked around Audrianna and waved the next person in line forward.

Audrianna stepped to the side and scratched her head. If Dr. Adler still worked here, why had he not responded to her letters? She dropped her hand and started up the staircase. He must not have received any of them, she decided. The letters must have been misdirected.

Audrianna located Dr. Adler's office on the second floor and rapped lightly on the door. No answer at first. Another rap, and a tiny old woman with salt-and-pepper hair opened the door with a smile.

Having established Audrianna's identity and the purpose of her visit, the woman shuffled off into the second of the two rooms; Audrianna took note of the mess in the outer office area. Open boxes were stacked around the room. Half-empty shelves lined the walls; books cluttered the floor. The space felt transitional.

"Fräulein Foster?" A stately looking gentleman appeared and extended Audrianna a handshake.

"Yes, sir." Audrianna accepted his hand.

"I am Dr. Gustav Adler," the man said. He gestured to the inner office. "Would you like to come in?"

"Yes, thank you." Audrianna followed him inside. He pulled out a chair for her, and then seated himself behind his desk, beginning the conversation without preamble.

"I am afraid that I am no longer in a position to be of any assistance to you," Dr. Adler said. He pulled his reading glasses from their perch on top of his nose and twirled them between his fingers.

Audrianna fell against the backrest of her chair and stared at him. Finally she said, "What do you mean you are not in a position to help me?"

"The university has suspended my research grant, and I have no plans to appeal," Dr. Adler explained. "I have submitted my final report to the board of directors to which I attest that I have been unable to find any evidence to support lyovitalis as a legitimate disease process."

"What do you mean no evidence?" Audrianna demanded. "There are sufferers, individual cases," she softened her tone and then shook her head. "What about my mother?"

Dr. Adler let out a deep sigh. "I'm sorry about your mother, child, but as I said, there is no evidence to link any of the so-called cases to one another. The university is satisfied, and so am I."

Audrianna was momentarily dumbfounded. Her father had devoted the final years of his life to this study. She had traveled halfway across the world, at his dying wish! How could his research partner stand in such a sharp contrast to his beliefs?

"I would like to have my father's medical journal, please," she said indignantly.

Dr. Adler made a tent with his hands and stared at her over the top. He cleared his throat and said, "You know about the journal?"

Audrianna stared at him. "My father always kept a medical journal," she replied. "It was not at home, so I am assuming he left it with his work—with you."

Dr. Adler cupped his hands over his lower face, hiding his mouth while formulating a cautious, unnaturally spaced response. "Yes, I have the journal," he admitted. He took his hands away from his face. "It is rightfully yours and, therefore, I will release it to you. However, I must tell you it saddens me to see a bright young lady such as yourself caught up in this farce."

Audrianna snapped. "Dr. Adler, I don't understand. You've been my father's research partner for years. What could cause you to change your mind so suddenly?"

Dr. Adler relaxed against the back of his chair. He reached into his pocket and pulled out a single golden key, unlocked his top desk drawer, extracted a leather-bound notebook, and slid it over to Audrianna. "Fräulein Foster," he began, "I have wasted a good deal of my life chasing an illness that has parameters so vague and so elusive it doesn't even warrant medical merit. It was a hard truth, but I accepted it. Your father's grief fueled his research with vengeance. It would be unfortunate for you to contract his obsession."

Audrianna took the journal and put it in her bag. Something was wrong, she thought. His entire interaction with her seemed uneasy, staged. Not being particularly blessed with the ability to disguise her feelings, Audrianna decided to leave before her temper got the better of her. She pushed her chair back to go, but stopped short. "Dr. Adler," she said.

"Yes?" he replied.

"I see you've been packing. Are you relocating?"

Dr. Adler stood and walked around the desk to where Audrianna was. He placed his hand on her back, applying steady pressure—a nonverbal cue to continue her exit. "As a matter of fact, I am," he said. "I have come into a bit of money and have decided to retire. Next month will be my last with this university."

Audrianna wondered if the change in his domestic situation had prompted his reversal, or vice versa. She was not sure what was going on, but knew she needed to think about things, read the journal, and consider all her options before engaging the doctor again.

Deanna Rhamsden: Female
Age: 19
Race: Caucasian
Place of Birth: Zurich
Occupation: Laundress
Class: Lower

Meeting with patient's mother—only living relative. Similar aberrations to other lyovitalis cases. No inherent physical defects or susceptibility to illness. Before affliction, patient presented with blonde hair, blue eyes, sturdy build, and extremely attractive features—similar to other cases.

Patient reported as well fed, well clothed, and well chaste through most of young life. Mother reports exception beginning two months prior to death. Deanna reported as keeping bizarre social hours, including complete absences from home for days at a time.

Differentials: lyovitalis; pathogen capable of paralyzing and destroying nervous system severely, aggressive or mutated form of Gonorrhea or Syphilis.

Impossible to rule out …

Audrianna turned to the next page. Blank. She flipped through the rest of the journal. All blank. She was six days into her time in Zurich and had spent the entire time reading her father's written account of his research. The journal was in complete disarray. Many pages were torn from the binding and much of the writing was deliberately inked out. The decipherable cases were eerily akin—not only to one another, but also to Audrianna's mother's behavior prior to her death. Audrianna's parents had taken a world tour in 1909, ending in Berlin where her mother contracted and died from lyovitalis. She disappeared one night from her hotel room and turned up three days later at *Charité Hospital* in the full throes of the disease. Audrianna was notified by post, two full weeks after her death.

A tap came on the door and Audrianna heard Mrs. Brindle's voice on the other side. "Dr. Foster," she said, "that lady is here to see you again. Shall I have her wait downstairs or would you prefer to see her up here?"

Audrianna felt the pinch of pin pricks run across her cheeks and her forehead. "Tell her I'm not receiving visitors today," she replied with a cracking voice.

Mrs. Brindle laughed nervously and said, "Dr. Foster, I told her that yesterday, and the day before that. This is not the type of lady to be put off in such a manner."

"If that's true, Mrs. Brindle, it won't be long before she stops calling," Audrianna replied. She got up and took a peek at the Rolls Royce parked outside; Mrs. Brindle plodded back downstairs. The front door opened and a decadently dressed woman emerged from the house; she turned her face immediately to the window where Audrianna stood looking down.

"Damn." Audrianna ducked behind the drapes. She popped her hand over her mouth and remained hidden for a few more moments until she heard the car drive off. After that, she tiptoed back to her writing desk and gingerly sat down.

"Dr. Foster." Another knock sounded at the door, and Audrianna jumped right back up. She clasped her hands over her heart and squeaked out, "Yes?"

A small cream envelope appeared under the door. "She left that for you," Mrs. Brindle said, her tone annoyed.

"Thank you, Mrs. Brindle," Audrianna quietly replied. She picked the envelope up off the floor and tore the elegantly embossed card from inside: *Countess Lorna Mehlinger.* Audrianna flipped the card and read the hand written note: *My darling, I cannot mend what is broken if you refuse to see me.*

Audrianna closed her eyes and ran the card under her nose, keeping it there for a few additional seconds while she breathed. She put the card down when she realized what she was doing, ashamed of herself. Why was this high-ranking woman so intent on making contact with her? In all reality, she should be trying to avoid her. It served no purpose for her to continue their ill-conceived relationship. Why was she making such an effort?

Audrianna looked down at the card and ran her thumb over the imprinted name. She looked over at her father's journal and an unrelated idea dawned on her. She rifled through the desk drawers for a pencil, then opened the book to the first empty page and grazed the edge of the pencil back and forth in large fine sweeps across the paper. She blew the excess dust away from the page.

GAVRILEK

The massive letters were set alone on the page, written in a childlike scribble.

Audrianna turned one page back and read the last sentence on the paper. "Impossible to rule out," she flipped quickly to the rubbing, "Gavrilek." She wrinkled her nose and whispered to herself, "What the hell is Gavrilek?"

"Come in, come in!" Dr. Adler greeted Audrianna at the door with an overly delighted handshake. She was wary of this sudden enthusiasm.

"Thank you for meeting with me, Dr. Adler," Audrianna said. "I understand you are a very busy man; I appreciate your time."

Dr. Adler offered her a chair in front of his desk and then sat himself. He folded his hands over his elbows, looking her squarely in the eye. "You must be missing America by now, Fräulein. Best get back there before the food rations begin," he laughed.

Audrianna ignored him. She pulled her father's journal from her bag, opened it, and pushed it forward on his desk. "I was hoping you could help me understand why these contact addresses have been scratched out—why complete pages have been ripped out."

Dr. Adler looked through the journal slowly. Audrianna scrutinized his facial expressions, mentally recording them to compare with the coming explanation. He stood and moved to a nearby bookshelf, plucking the two remaining volumes and tossing them in a box on the floor. "In three weeks I'm off to the Mediterranean to wait out this war in peace and comfort." He gestured to a hefty metal safe behind his desk. "The contents of that thing are about all I have left of value to move."

"Dr. Adler, please," Audrianna redirected. "Tell me why my father's medical journal is in such a mess. He didn't do this to his own journal, I'm sure of it. Was it out of your possession at any point?"

Dr. Adler brushed his hands together and placed a lid over the top of the box. The silence persisted.

"Surely you have no reason to withhold answers from me?" Audrianna pressed him.

Dr. Adler retook his seat and was contemplative. Finally, he said, "I could tell when we met you were not going to be put off easily. It was wrong of me to act that way. I should have told you everything straight off instead of trying to protect you from the ugly reality."

Audrianna shrugged her shoulders and said, "Protect me from what? What 'ugly reality' do you believe I need protection from?"

Dr. Adler leaned on his elbows, clutching his hands as if in prayer. "Your father, Fräulein Foster, was my friend. It pains me to say I believe he was suffering from dementia praecox, what my colleague, Dr. Eugene Bleuler, now calls schizophrenia. Have you studied this disease in school?"

Audrianna's eyes bulged. Her father had been a lot of things in his life, but he was not crazy. She would bet her life on it. "I was at his bedside on the day of his death, talking with him. He exhibited no symptoms of such a condition," she cried.

Dr. Adler shook his head. "Fräulein Foster, there are times of clarity, where no signs or symptoms can be detected. As you know, the absence of notable indication does not preclude its presence."

Audrianna got up, unnerved. It was not possible. What proof did he have?

"Take a look at this," Dr. Adler said, pointing to the open page in the journal. "He sabotaged his own work! He tore out these pages and then confronted me the next day asking who had tampered with them. I couldn't help him. There is no treatment, no cure. At the point of complete paranoia, I had to disband our partnership and send him home."

Audrianna ran her hands through her hair, bristling against the possible accuracy of the story. When was the last time she had a meaningful conversation with him? Had she ever?

Dr. Adler continued, "I was forced to step back and analyze the validity of 'lyovitalis'. Your father brought the information to me, and I signed off on it. I kept no notes myself. When I took a good look at this journal, I decided I had been subject to a fool's errand. Fräulein Foster, no sane man would send his daughter halfway around the world into a war zone based on this!" He slammed the journal down on top of the desk.

Audrianna took a deep breath, staving off her anger. She did not want to believe him. She was not prepared to disbelieve him either. His story made some sense, but she needed time to consider the information he had given her before accepting his revelation as the truth.

"Thank you, Dr. Adler," she whispered, needing to withdraw for deeper consideration. "Everything makes perfect sense now."

Dr. Adler closed the journal and handed it back to her. "I'm sorry to have been the bearer of such bad tidings, Fräulein Foster," he said. "But I couldn't, in good conscience, leave you here in this situation without telling you the whole truth. I should think returning to America would be your safest course of action now."

"Thank you. My father was blessed to have a friend like you," Audrianna replied without looking at him. She took the journal out of his hands and turned around to leave—but then she remembered something. "Dr. Adler, have you ever heard the word Gavrilek before?"

"I don't think so," he said without pause. "Why?"

"It was one of the words obliterated from the journal," Audrianna replied. "I was wondering if it were a new microbe or virus being researched."

"Nothing I've heard of," said Dr. Adler. "Honestly, Fräulein Foster, it's probably just another product of the poor man's mental illness. Pay it no mind." He moved to open the door for her. As Audrianna brushed by him, she felt the draw of his eyes and turned back around to face him. "Fräulein Foster?" he said as he took a deep breath. "I wonder if you would be interested in attending the commencement ceremonial ball for the university tonight? I would be pleased to escort you as my guest."

Audrianna hesitated.

Dr. Adler continued, "I owe your father that much. It would give you the opportunity to meet with many world-renowned physicians. It never hurts to cultivate professional relationships in this field."

Audrianna nodded. "Yes, sir, I'm sure you are right. I would consider it an honor," she said.

"Very well, then," Dr. Adler answered with a surprised expression. "I'll send the car around for you at 5:50. We'll have dinner and then attend the ball. Where are you staying?"

"Ausleiden Boarding House on Gloriastrasse."

Dr. Adler nodded and said, "Until tonight then, Fräulein."

———•◦•———

"I met your mother once, in Berlin, before she got sick," Dr. Adler told Audrianna as they departed the restaurant. "You are every bit as lovely as she was," he continued. "Only you have your father's eyes."

Audrianna blushed. She spent the better portion of her life in the shadow of her mother's stature, reaping the rewards of her likeness but never really feeling like she deserved to do so. Her mother had been stunningly beautiful and graceful, a true lady. Audrianna could never see herself this way.

Dr. Adler offered her his arm as she stepped from the cab; Audrianna took it obligingly. He led her up the carpet-lined staircase into the foyer where a doorman took their coats. Audrianna fiddled nervously with the short choker of pearls around her neck, spinning the clasp until she finally let it rest at the base of her hairline. She did not like formal balls, being forced to mingle with vacuous poseurs who spent their days gossiping in self-righteous circles of wealth.

"Here we are, my dear," said Dr. Adler, encouraging her forward with a sweep of his hand. "There is a ladies' lounge just down the hallway there if you have need of it," he whispered, leaning close to her and pointing to a corridor off to the right.

"Yes, thank you. I would like to freshen up a bit," Audrianna replied. As usual, she had been mildly perspiring all evening and was not at all sure it could not be noticed through her silk charmeuse gown. If she were going to meet Dr. Adler's "world-renowned physicians," she should look her best.

She left Dr. Adler's company, following a typical crowd: elegantly dressed young ladies clustered into tightly formed groups, led by one or two matriarchs at the head. Their processions were very exclusive, and Audrianna felt uncomfortable as a single person in their wake. She accelerated her few beauty rituals in the ladies' room: blotting her face, securing her hair, and retracing her lips. She ignored the gleam of prying eyes until one set spoke to her in the mirror.

"I saw you come in with Dr. Adler," an older, heavyset woman said to Audrianna's reflection. "Are you a relative?" Her tone was easy and non-intrusive, perfectly honed for passing as a friendly acquaintance while procuring unknown, possibly scandalous gossip.

"No," Audrianna answered coolly, turning to face her. "I'm a physician from the United States. Dr. Adler was my father's research partner, and I am here tonight as his guest."

"Oh my," the inquirer frowned. "What a waste of an attractive young lady on a gentleman's career."

Audrianna laughed at the absurdity. "Well, thank you," she replied, "but I see it quite the opposite. Have a good evening." She turned on her heels and exited without another word. Her parry hid the tears that began to well as she searched the crowd for Dr. Adler. It had been a mistake to accept his invitation. She did not belong here with these people. She would leave.

"There you are, Fräulein Foster," Dr. Adler's voice called. "I was beginning to wonder if you had gotten lost."

Audrianna spun, and gasped. Standing with Dr. Adler, handsomely dressed in a black tuxedo with tails, was Dr. Dirk von Traugott. They locked eyes as Dr. Adler proceeded with the introductions, clearly unaware of her horror. "Fräulein Foster, Dr. von Traugott is an associate professor of medicine at the university, and he is also Chief Surgeon at the International Refugee Hospital of Zurich. He has been—"

A fuzzy, static noise surged inside Audrianna's head and overtook the sound of Dr. Adler's voice. The dizzying force left her waving like a leaf dangling in the wind. She placed her hand against her forehead to steady herself, but it did not help. She broke into a cold sweat. Her heart accelerated, and a cloak of heavy blackness weighed on her.

"Are you ill?" Dirk asked, taking a step forward with his hands outstretched. Audrianna managed a nod.

Dr. Adler wrapped his arm around her for support. "Fräulein Foster!" he exclaimed. "You look positively pale! Are you faint?"

"I'm afraid I might be," Audrianna whispered. "Would you take me outside, please?"

"Of course, of course," Dr. Adler replied. "Dirk, be a good man and get the coats, will you?"

Dr. Adler guided Audrianna through the swarms of people to the far side of the verandah outside the grand ballroom. Crisp night air smacked her in the face, bringing her back into a fully functional state of consciousness, penalizing her with the harshest degree of humiliation imaginable.

"I'm terribly sorry, Dr. Adler," Audrianna apologized as she looked around for an alternate means of escape. "It's been a tiring trip. I should leave." She had to get out of there before Dirk

returned, coat or not. She could not see him again. She knew
he must be laughing at her, laughing at her reaction, laughing
at her weakness. Oh God! Why had she done that in front of
him? Of all people!

"Don't be silly." Dr. Adler refused her attempts at elope-
ment. "You'll feel better once you've gotten some fresh air into
your lungs. It's a good thing you didn't go into surgery, Fräulein
Foster. It gets awfully hot in those operating rooms, you know?"

Audrianna made a brief attempt to concur, but was cut short
as Dr. Adler waved to someone behind her. "Here comes Dirk,"
he announced, "and look at whom he has with him, Countess
Mehlinger! Good evening, Lorna! I haven't seen you in ages! I
hope the Kaiser doesn't intend to keep all of the nobility hidden
away in their villas through the remainder of this mess."

Countess Lorna Mehlinger had been an exceptionally
attractive young man, but now, standing there draped in her
swanky black silk, strands upon strands of diamonds and the
most expensive fur coat money could buy, Audrianna decided
that she was also the most beautiful woman she had ever seen.

"Not at all, Gustav," Lorna replied—Devon's voice. "I've been
away on business." She kissed his cheek and stepped around to face
Audrianna with a transfixed smile, linking her arm underneath
Dirk's. Dirk, too, watched Audrianna intently, although his look
was more one of concern. Audrianna continued to divert her
gaze from the two of them. How could she have been so stupid?

"Hello, Dr. Foster," Lorna purred, staring mercilessly through
now-shining green eyes. Audrianna felt a sickening wave-like
motion creep from her stomach, to her chest, to her throat. She
nodded, but did not reciprocate the statement, and she certainly
did not make eye contact.

"What's this?" Dr. Adler exclaimed. "Have you ladies met?"

Audrianna opened her mouth to offer a justification, but Dirk stepped in, sparing her the need to. "Gustav, Lorna and I already have the pleasure of having recently met Dr. Foster," he said. "She was of some service to my family recently."

Dr. Adler eyed the three of them dubiously. "Is that right?" he asked. "How so?"

"My brother sustained an injury while he was vacationing in France," Dirk explained. "He had the good fortune to meet Dr. Foster on the train home, where she treated him with most unexpected skill."

"Well, good for you, young lady." Dr. Adler patted Audrianna on the back. "Now if you ask me, clinical practice is a much better use of your time than pointless research. I'll bet Dr. von Traugott would be more than grateful for your services in his hospital. You don't have a dedicated physician for women and children's medicine, do you Dirk?"

"No, we don't," Dirk replied.

"See there," Dr. Adler continued, "think of the indigents who might benefit from your expertise. Trust me, Fräulein Foster, lyovitalis is a dead project. There is no sense in prolonging the end, not when there is so much need elsewhere."

His statement captured Lorna's attention, and for the very first time since her arrival, she turned her eyes from Audrianna to him. "What are you talking about, Gustav?"

"Didn't you know?" Dr. Adler said. "Fräulein Foster has come to Zurich to continue her father's research into lyovitalis."

Dirk scoffed. "There is no such disease. You are wasting your time."

All at once, after the long set of time she had just spent coddling her nerves, Audrianna exploded, completely enraged by his patronization. "Thank you for your self-important opinion, doctor," she flared, "but it will take quite a bit more than that to convince me that I am 'wasting my time' as you put it."

"It's not opinion, Dr. Foster," Dirk replied calmly, "but a scientific fact. Lyovitalis is nothing more than a severe presentation of Landry's paralysis."

Audrianna lifted her chin. He ought not challenge her on this front: she had read and memorized every comparison of lyovitalis made since it was considered its own disease. "Is that so? How then, sir, do you explain the inconsistencies between the two? Landry's paralysis is most commonly diagnosed in young men ages twenty to thirty, and the mortality rate in known cases has been less than fifty percent. Lyovitalis has a 100 percent mortality rate and its population is overwhelmingly female."

Dirk held out his palms and chuckled a little. "Dr. Foster, as you know, medicine is not an exact science. There are many diseases where parameters are still being established. The worst thing we can do as healthcare providers is to make up new illnesses every time a discrepancy exists. We cannot overlook the likenesses between Landry's paralysis and lyovitalis, and therefore, should work to link them through discipline and eliminate the weaker position."

Audrianna shook her head. "I guess it is fortunate for me that we aren't having this discussion in a country where women's oppression is celebrated as a sport. For now, I will settle for my own assessment, until I find a reason not to." She made a halfhearted bow to her escort. "Dr. Adler, I had a lovely evening. Thank you very much for inviting me, but I do need to go."

"I'm sorry if I've upset you, Dr. Foster," Dirk said in the same, infuriatingly condescending manner. He stepped forward to help her into her coat, then stepped back into place next to Lorna.

"On the contrary, Dr. von Traugott," replied Audrianna. "Our conversation has been quite helpful in reaffirming my objectives here. Thank you very much."

Lorna reached out and touched her forearm. "Let me drive you," she said.

Audrianna felt a shiver from Lorna's touch but was determined not to let it affect her. "That's not necessary, *Countess,*" she said sharply. "I only have a few blocks to go and I could use the time alone for a quiet walk. Good night." She quickly turned and exited back through the grand ballroom and then off down the road.

The frozen, fall night transformed her breath into steam as she trudged in formal party regalia. Audrianna dissected and chastised herself for her brazen remarks. Dirk was allowed an opinion: it was one shared by Dr. Adler and, apparently, the entire medical community there. She had been overly defensive: a compensatory mechanism for feeling such a fool already. She thought of her mother, at how disappointed she would have been in her daughter's conduct. "Anxiety should never influence the manner of your address," she would have said. A lady should never reveal the true inner workings of her mind. Oh! When was she ever going to learn to just keep her mouth shut?

"Audrianna."

"Oh my God!" Audrianna jumped and shrieked. She was caught up in her thoughts and completely missed walking past that magnificent Rolls Royce from last night, and right past Lorna, who was standing just outside the car. She cinched her coat tightly around her and slowly backed away. "Why are you following me?" she panted. "What do you want?"

"Why are you running away from me?" Lorna replied. "I just want to talk to you, to explain."

"Explain? Ha!" Audrianna locked her footing and mocked her. "Explain what? Why you didn't tell me that you were really a Countess, not a common laborer?" She laughed. "Although I do have to tell you that you weren't very believable in that role. I think your noble heritage must've kept you from adopting that mentality entirely." Audrianna lifted her eyebrows continuing, "Or perhaps you'd like to explain why you let me believe you were a man the entire time we were together? Or why you played with my heart? Did you think me incapable of helping you without such a seduction?"

Lorna took a step forward and said, "Audrianna, be fair. I never at any time—"

"You did! You did!" Audrianna broke down. She buried her face in her hands and began to weep. "You came into my mind. You made love to me in my dreams! I don't know how you did it, but how *could* you? All along, knowing that nothing could come of it? Is human emotion worth so little to you?"

Lorna grabbed both of Audrianna's arms and pulled her into her body aggressively. She touched her lips to the side of Audrianna's face and whispered in her ear, "I could make you understand, but I won't. You're such a naïve little girl, Audrianna. It's impossible for you to know how I feel about you, or why I can never feel that for you. You want to know who I am, but you are scared of what you might find out. Well, you should be!" Lorna released her and Audrianna stumbled backward on frail legs. "No, Dr. Foster, I am far from being out of touch when it comes to human emotion. Believe me, if it weren't for the way I've come to feel about you, I would make you know why."

"Why must everything be a puzzle?" Audrianna wept. "Why can't you just tell me what it is you're trying so hard not to say?"

"Because you would never be free," Lorna replied in a much softer tone of voice. She reached out and stroked Audrianna's cheek tenderly. "And neither would I."

Audrianna closed her eyelids over a spring of tears, slowing their flow to a trickle. She tried to memorize Lorna's touch, prolong it. She knew she should not want her. But she could not help it. A passion re-emerged inside her tortured heart, flooding her with images: Lorna's breasts pressed against her in an embrace, Lorna's lips on hers in a kiss.

"I'll be leaving tomorrow for Bavaria," Lorna announced abruptly, withdrawing her hand. She opened the back door of the Silver Ghost and started to get in, but Audrianna stopped her.

"You're going to see the first snow of the season, aren't you?" she sniffed. "You always go home at this time, ever since you can remember."

Lorna looked back at her. "I wish you hadn't remembered that," she whispered.

This time, Audrianna did not shy away from her stare. "Why?" she cried.

"Because I don't need another reminder of what I've done to you," Lorna replied coarsely. She slid into the backseat of the car and then closed the door behind her. Exhaust from the engine billowed from the pipes of the Rolls Royce as it lurched forward into a roll, and for half a second, Audrianna thought Lorna might lower her window and say something else to her. But she did not. She drove away, leaving Audrianna to cry like she had never cried before.

CHAPTER 6

"Dr. Foster?" Mrs. Brindle knocked. "There's a gentleman here to see you, says it's about your research."

"Thank you, Mrs. Brindle," Audrianna replied through the closed door. "Ask him in, please. I'll see him in the parlor."

Her visitor was undoubtedly Dr. Adler. She had been expecting his call, preparing herself for the questions she knew he would ask. She had not quite figured out how to account for last night's unpleasant behavior just yet, but having been in similar predicaments in the past, was quite certain she would be able to convey a convincing apology nonetheless. She got up from the writing desk in her room, straightened her Bulgarian-style afternoon dress, and then went down the stairs to meet her guest.

"Good afternoon, Dr. Foster. I hope you're feeling better."

A chill shot through her body at the sound of the voice. Dirk von Traugott stood up from one of the armchairs to greet her.

Audrianna's subconscious secreted a subliminal glue to cement her feet to the floor.

"What are you doing here?" she asked him with as much composure as she could muster. She felt exposed, deceived.

"I'm sorry to have disturbed you without first calling," Dirk started. "To be frank, I wasn't sure you'd see me if I had."

Audrianna rolled her eyes and said, "Likely not. But here you are. What is it you want, and what has it to do with my research?"

"I'll be brief," Dirk replied. "First of all, I would like to apologize for my conduct at the ball. Coming so quickly on the heels of what you learned the other night at the hospital, I can fully comprehend why you would have no interest in meeting with me. I'm afraid all you've ever seen of me is the worst man I can possibly be."

Audrianna blushed. He was being quite delicate in his allusion to the interaction she had witnessed. She had to admire his courage for bringing it up, nevertheless. Most people would have swept the affair under the proverbial rug.

"I was caught off guard by your presence," Dirk continued, "as I'm sure you were with mine. And with Lorna's." He looked down and scoffed. "I'm afraid I'm not very good at on-the-spot recoveries."

Audrianna relaxed somewhat. She hated to admit it, but she identified with him, not being particularly adept at on-the-spot recoveries herself. "Nor am I," she confessed. Dirk seemed grateful for her disclosure.

"I am very sorry for everything that you've been through," he continued. "I was hoping we could start over."

Audrianna sighed. She did not have a good reason to dislike him. He was not responsible for what had happened between her and Lorna—that was all Lorna's doing. "All right," she agreed. "Although I'm not quite sure of what we'd need to start over."

Dirk smiled, although it seemed like a momentary slip of the mind rather than a concentrated effort. "I was hoping you might consider visiting the hospital again," he said.

Audrianna scoffed. "Doesn't your work keep you too busy for social calls?"

Dirk smiled again, but this time it was genuine. "This is something closer to a professional call. Niklas would like to see you. He's well enough now to receive visitors, and I believe that seeing you may hasten his recovery."

"Really?" Audrianna replied flatly. "Our mishap acquaintance can't be a pleasant memory for him."

Dirk shook his head and said, "On the contrary. He feels deeply indebted to you and wishes to extend his gratitude personally. In fact, he has spoken of nothing else."

Audrianna looked around the room, buying time to respond. She had made too many wrong decisions recently, and did not want to add another. Dirk recognized the delay and offered her an outlet for her indecision. "I understand your hesitation," he said. "Maybe you had hoped to put this all behind you."

"Yes, I had." Audrianna glanced at her watch and then rubbed absently at her forearms. "Although Niklas is not the reason why. Nor is he the reason I hesitate."

"Then why?" Dirk asked.

Audrianna looked at him. He was easy to look at, even in the eyes. He had an affable manner about him that she had not noticed until that very moment. This heightened her state of caution. She decided to be forthright. "I'm not sure I trust you," she said. "You tricked me into coming down to meet you, and, by your own admission, there is something more you want. Perhaps you should tell me what it is now."

Dirk paused, and then said, "I will tell you, if you insist. But I'd rather show you. Will you take a chance?"

No. She had taken enough chances this trip. It was not like her. The whirlwind she rode the last week was a complete contradiction to the regimented life she lived up until now. But maybe that was why she found his proposition so irresistible. Maybe it was the possibility of seeing Lorna again. Either way, the sorcery of risk won out and Audrianna consented to go with him.

"We see mostly orphans here," Dirk said, gesturing to a group of children on the pediatrics ward. "Serbians, some Hungarians. Switzerland has long been known as a safe haven for those who need sanctuary from just about anything. These little ones were all rescued from workhouses. Their task masters stopped feeding them because they had become too sick to work."

Audrianna watched a dozen or more children of all ages playing inaudibly amongst themselves. Any one of them could have been an illustration of starvation in one of her medical books. All of them were an unfortunate reality of the state of the world.

"It must be very difficult for the Swiss people to bear the burden of such atrocity," Audrianna remarked.

"I wouldn't know," Dirk replied, "I'm not Swiss."

Audrianna gave him a dazed look.

Dirk laughed and said, "I'm Austrian. My father, the late Baron von Traugott, was the Emperor's second cousin."

Audrianna nodded. It made sense that he and Lorna were cut from the same royal cloth. Obviously they were lovers. "I see," she said. "Then your connection with this war should be one of a personal nature. Why are you here taking care of people who assassinated a member of your family? People you should hate?"

Dirk stepped in front of her, towering like a cathedral. "I can't afford to hate anyone, Dr. Foster," he replied with a tinge of melancholy, "and I'm not especially proud of my heritage." He turned his back to her and delivered a soliloquy. "What happened in Sarajevo was a tragedy, but Bosnia bent over backwards to make amends for it. The Ottoman Empire wouldn't relent. Now we have another war and the common folk—who fight and suffer most—don't know what the fighting is about." He turned back around. "I live here in Switzerland because I don't believe in war. I work here because I want to help those who've had no choice in the matter."

Audrianna felt goose bumps cover her body. How could she not be moved by the passion of his statements? He was a baron. He could be visiting the opera, entertaining dignitaries, and sipping brandy at the family estate. But he was running a hospital for refugees and talking politics with a woman well below his station. How unusual. How fascinating.

"Perhaps I should see Niklas now," Audrianna said, cognizant of her thoughts and their implications. She hardly needed to complicate her already bizarre relationship with these people.

"I'm sorry if I've offended you, Dr. Foster," Dirk responded to her abrupt change of subject. "My convictions carry me away and sometimes I forget my manners. Forgive me."

Audrianna looked at him in earnest, replying softly and steadily. "On the contrary, I'm flattered you respect me enough to discuss the matter with me." She smiled and laughed a little, mostly at herself. "However, you've caught me at a disadvantage. I'm afraid I just don't know enough about the war to be able to speak intelligently on it. I didn't want you to think me brainless."

Dirk began to laugh too, relieved. "I don't generally judge people based upon their knowledge of foreign politics, Dr. Foster," he said, shaking his head, "My, what a miserable impression I've made on you."

"No, not really," Audrianna replied. "I only know what I have lived, and I have lived only knowing men whose agendas for me included cooking, cleaning, and childbearing."

"Well, then, perhaps you've entered a new phase in your life," Dirk said. Their laughter gradually petered out, and the two of them were left with a comfortable silence. Dirk then continued, "I think you're incredibly gifted."

"I'm not gifted, Dr. von Traugott," Audrianna scoffed. She ran her hand through her hair and looked around the room. "I'm bipolar. Naturally, I've undergone various medicinal therapies, but I've found medical practice to be my best stabilizing agent. I've never spoken of it to anyone, so I would appreciate it if you kept it to yourself. I'm not sure why I even told you."

"Audrianna." Dirk caught her shoulders and held her until she looked at him. "You *are* gifted," he said, ignoring her compromising disclosure. "And, what I have in mind for you is something much more fulfilling than cooking and cleaning. My apologies, but I can't speak to childbearing."

Audrianna smiled. Handsome, gentle, charming. Dirk's reputation was incredibly well-deserved. He escorted her out of the hospital bay, down one of the side hallways, and into the entrance of a private room. "Niklas is here. When you're through with your visit, I wonder if you might stop by my office? I have something very particular that I'd like to show you."

Audrianna twisted the knob on the door, but did not quite open it, considering how to respond to Dirk's proposition.

"Think about it," Dirk said. "If I don't see you again, I'll know you've decided not to come, and I'll understand. Don't give it another thought." He backed out of the doorway and walked away.

"I'll come," the words accidentally slipped off Audrianna's tongue. "I'll be there."

Dirk turned around and grinned, then carried on. Audrianna was left contemplating the choice she, perhaps, should have made.

"I should let you rest. I'm surprised your brother hasn't come to chase me out of here yet," Audrianna told Niklas.

Niklas laughed. "He's not like that really. A little overprotective, but I don't mind."

"We all need someone to watch over us," Audrianna remarked.

Niklas smiled. He looked at her thoughtfully. "Who watches over you, Dr. Foster?"

Audrianna exhaled and said, "I don't know. Just me, I guess. If there's another watcher out there, I have no idea who."

"Then it shall be me," Niklas pledged, placing his hand over his heart. "From now on, I will be your protector."

"Your future wife might resent that a bit, don't you think?" Audrianna chuckled.

"Not if she's you."

Audrianna stopped laughing. "I'm sorry? What?" she said.

Niklas leaned in toward her with caricaturist eyes. "What a great thought!" He clapped his hands together. "We should get married!"

Audrianna snorted and quickly shook her head. "Niklas, that's certainly not what I was suggest—"

"But you're right!" he interrupted her. "I should propose. I'll get a ring, and we'll go on a honeymoon."

Audrianna allowed him to prattle on. His boyish charm lightened her spirits. He was uncomplicated to be around, and she savored the change of mood.

"We'll have to get married before I return to the war, though," Niklas finished nonchalantly.

Audrianna's smile faded. "The war? Oh, Niklas, you're not thinking of going back? Not after what happened!"

He dropped his eyes below the level of hers, retaining his grin, but curbing his enthusiasm. "Yes, but not as a spy," he confessed. "I wasn't a very good spy. Probably because I'm not a believable liar."

Lies. Audrianna felt a piercing pain shoot through her heart. She thought of Lorna and all her very convincing lies. How good *she* was at it. Audrianna tried to reconstruct the details of last night's encounter but became caught up in a much more abysmal memory: the memory of Lorna's touch, the memory of wanting to hold her, wanting to kiss her. The thoughts pummeled her with a series of psychological blows that she could not dodge.

"That is certainly nothing to be ashamed of, Niklas," Audrianna managed.

He looked up at her and said, "I know. That's why I decided to transfer to artillery."

Audrianna nodded, but said nothing more, choosing instead to stage her exit then before being drawn into another topic of conversation. Her peacefulness had become unseated by a tizzy of nervous energy. "I'm leaving," she announced, getting out of her chair and moving to the door.

"I'm sorry that Lorna made you think she was a boy," Niklas called out as she walked away. "If I had been well enough to tell you otherwise, I would have."

"I'd rather not discuss it," Audrianna replied. She turned around and met his eyes, "Other than to say that what I do in your regard has nothing to do with her. Okay?"

"Okay," he agreed. "Will you come back to see me again?"

"Shh! I promise." Audrianna put her finger up to her lips, and then motioned for him to lie back in his bed. "Go to sleep," she said, and she slipped out the door.

Audrianna lost her sense of direction in the corridor. She walked the opposite way Dirk brought her, and made a couple more wrong turns in the adjoining passages. She wandered aimlessly through the enormous hospital, eventually losing the sound of other peoples' voices. When that happened, Audrianna became nervous. She began knocking on and opening doors in search of someone. The last door she knocked on opened on its own, then someone found her.

A beefy, hulking man, with shiny green eyes like Lorna's reached out and grabbed Audrianna by the arm and pulled her into the room. "Who are you?" he asked her. "Von Traugott, who is this?" he added, bobbing his pocket pistol at Audrianna.

"Audrianna! How did you get back here?" Dirk cried. He stood in the middle of the empty room, restrained by two medium-sized men, one on either side of him. Both wore holstered pistols over heavy coats.

Audrianna froze in wide-eyed terror. Her legs began to shake.

"Von Traugott," the big man said with a huff, "this is really getting very tiresome for me, year after year, coming down here to deal with you." He looked right and left, then rolled his eyes around the room. "I don't like Switzerland. I don't like sick houses." He jiggled Audrianna's arm and added, "I don't like all the crazies roaming the halls around here! Won't you play the game just like all the rest of us?"

"Not in this lifetime, Oskar—you filthy hawk," Dirk spat out with a forced kind of calm. "These games are nothing less than jealousy enacted upon those who have the life we want. Earth is not our playground. The people aren't our puppets."

Oskar kicked Dirk in the stomach, and Audrianna screamed as he crumpled to the floor. "That's an interesting theory, *Doctor*, but hardly the case," Oskar said. "If you weren't so crippled, you'd have a more accurate idea of what we're playing for." He poked himself in the chest. "*I* want to go home. The master has promised me," he waved his hand in the air, "an emerald castle in the sky."

"You're an idiot. The master will give you nothing. *Nothing!*" Dirk shouted. "He's in it for his own interests! He doesn't care about the group—"

Oskar kicked him in the jaw; blood splattered on the wall.

The two smaller men lifted Dirk's body and forced him to stand. Oskar took a handkerchief from his pocket and wiped the sweat from his brow before continuing on with his tirade. "You're a disgrace to the order, von Traugott. You always have been. You're the worst blocker we have. The only reason the master hasn't sent you to the line already is because of Lorna—but she's not here to save your ass this time." He laughed and then pointed his gun at Dirk's head. "Let's pick this conversation up again in about fifteen years. Maybe you'll have changed your mind about playing by then." He cocked the hammer. "But I doubt it."

Audrianna lunged for the gun. "Stop! You can't do this!" she yelled. The two men who held Dirk turned him loose. They drew their pistols and aimed them at Audrianna with well-rehearsed proficiency.

"Audrianna!" Dirk shouted. He groped for both the brandished weapons in an ineffective attempt at distraction. "She has nothing to do with this," he told the men. "Just let her leave."

Audrianna ducked her head and surrendered with her hands; Oskar quickly devised an alternate plan. "How sweet!" he mockingly said to Dirk. He placed the barrel of his revolver against Audrianna's temple and nodded at his partners. "I guess we don't have to kill him after all! This may be a more effective consequence for disobedience. What do you think, boys?"

"Let the lady go, Oskar. She's mine." Lorna's voice sliced through Oskar's intimidations with razor-sharp authority. Audrianna felt Oskar's grip relax on her arm. She tugged loose and slammed against the wall, covering her gaping mouth with her hands.

"Lorna!" Oskar flared. "Fuck!" He wheeled around at Lorna's unhurried entrance into the room, glancing from her to Dirk and back. "He called you here, didn't he?" She did not respond. "You pussy motherfucker, von Traugott! Well, this time I won't have it! I'm here on the master's business and—"

"I told the master I would handle this," Lorna broke into Oskar's raving with a soft, calm voice. A smile played on the corners of her lips, like she was entertained by his explosive mannerisms, although Audrianna could not understand why. She found them terrifying.

"You've been telling him that for the last hundred years, Lorna!" Oskar shouted. "This time you almost got caught! This time you almost lost the play! And it's all because of him!"

"But I didn't lose the play, did I, Oskar?" Lorna patronized. "The plans were stolen and delivered to the master as ordered." She took three drawn-out steps to confront him head-on. "You've delivered your message," she said. "Now leave. Before I send *you* to the line."

"You don't have the authority to do that!" Oskar scoffed.

"Don't I?" Lorna taunted him. "The only command that trumps mine is the master's. You know it, and I know it." She started to laugh. "You're a hawk, and I'm the best player he's got. Which of us, do you think, is more expendable? I could have these gentlemen haul you off right now, and the master would never even notice you were gone until he needed you to brutalize someone else. And you can be replaced. I know a number of ambitious hawks who would love to fill your shoes."

Oskar flared his nostrils and said, "I'm not scared of you, Lorna. If you think you can manipulate me like you do that asshole over there, think again. I won't be a hawk forever. I'll be a better player than you, and you'll be sorry for this."

"You'll never be a player, Oskar," Lorna cooed. "You're ill-bred, ill-mannered, and have no sense of control whatsoever." She pointed at a mirror hanging on the wall. "Take a look at yourself. You're wiped out from five minutes of this insignificant bit of parley. What makes you think you could ever survive the kind of intricate maneuvers I'm involved in?"

Oskar twisted to look in the mirror, and Audrianna saw his reflection. His eyes had transmogrified into polished copper disks, his skin was ashen and dripping with sweat. "Dammit!" he cursed, reaching into his pocket for his handkerchief and then re-wiping his face with it. He pointed his gun at Lorna but she did not flinch.

"This isn't finished, you bitch," he barked. "You can't protect Dirk forever. The master won't tolerate one lost play in this conflict, and when that happens—I'll be back to settle this."

"Get out," Lorna said, but her humor was gone. She stepped again toward Oskar, and he disengaged. "Let's go." He motioned to his minions, and they left.

"Lorna, I'm sorry," Dirk said once they had gone. She looked at him, but did not communicate an acceptance or rejection of his apology. Her prolonged state of hush perpetuated the tension in the room, making the witness of their interaction even more uncomfortable for Audrianna to watch. She could sense that whatever was happening was something she was not supposed to be part of, but she had know idea what it was.

"What were you thinking, Dirk?" Lorna crossed her arms and spoke at last. "Involving her in this? What if I hadn't arrived in time?"

"I hadn't planned to involve her," Dirk replied. "I didn't know they were coming."

Lorna rolled her eyes and said, "How could you not know? His thoughts were fixated on you; he was making no effort to contain them at all."

Dirk nodded and looked away. "I should've known. You're right. It was a careless mistake."

"It's one of many careless mistakes, Dirk," Lorna replied. She threw one of her hands down and continued, "France? Their searchers were tracking me. They were locked on my every move because your screen didn't protect my thoughts. The players are better this time. I can't do it by myself."

"Please, Lorna. Let's not get into this right now," Dirk said, peering at Audrianna. "Dr. Foster is frightened enough."

Lorna gave way. She held her face between her hands for a second in what appeared to be a self-quieting gesture, and then stepped toward Audrianna.

"Are you all right, darling?" Lorna asked her, pulling Audrianna off the wall and into her arms. She held her there. Audrianna nodded but did not say anything. Honestly, she was more confused and curious now than frightened—and that was secondary to an even more substantial realization: Lorna had said, *She's mine!* And she was now holding her in her arms. Her scent, that same intoxicating scent, infiltrated Audrianna's nasal passages and lit her senses on fire, bringing with it a tingle that Audrianna knew she should be ashamed to feel.

Lorna moved to engage Audrianna's gaze. "What would ever possess you to place yourself in such a dangerous situation?" she asked with a gentle shake. "Have you lost your mind?"

"I. I—" Audrianna stuttered. She could not think straight. It was too much for her to bear, being that close to her, looking into her eyes, tortured by the memories, by what she still wanted, what she knew could never be.

"Never mind, it's all right now," Lorna said, pulling Audrianna back into her arms and rocking her. "Senseless, impetuous creature. One of these days your instinct to help people is going to get you hurt." Lorna held her for another few seconds and then released her.

"I'm going home now," she told Dirk. "I'll be in Berlin by the end of the week to get the details of the next play. I'll be gone for several weeks. Please prepare yourself or we'll both be facing the master's wrath."

"Lorna." Audrianna called out, trying to keep her there. It was the first time she had said the woman's real name out loud, and it generated another erotic charge that Audrianna felt everywhere she wished she would not.

"Yes, Audrianna?" Lorna's eyes twinkled as though she had tapped into the same sensations.

"What's happening here? That man, his eyes—your eyes."

Lorna stepped closer and said, "Do you really want to know?"

"Yes."

"Lorna, don't!" Dirk pleaded. But Lorna walked over to Audrianna, cupped her chin in her hand and drew Audrianna's face to her own.

"Come with me," she whispered. Lorna kissed her on the lips and everything went dark.

———•◦•———

An outdoor scene gradually materialized. Twenty women clad in rich medieval attire danced around a violent bonfire. Musicians played. A feast of food and ale was laid out and attended by servants. Green-eyed children cowered in their nursemaids' arms. Audrianna drew a quick, sharp breath; she began to panic.

"Stop," Lorna commanded. She gently captured Audrianna's throat from behind. "Be still," she whispered in her ear. "I will not show you this if you are not prepared to see it."

Audrianna overlaid her hand on Lorna's and swallowed hard. "What is this?" she croaked.

"It's a party, of sorts," Lorna replied. She nuzzled Audrianna's cheek and added, "They're about to slaughter my father." Audrianna gasped, and Lorna tightened her grip. "Are you prepared to see it?" Lorna asked.

"No, I don't want to see it," Audrianna replied. She twisted her head to the side and closed her eyes.

"Then you don't really want to know," Lorna said. She withdrew her hand and darkness fell again.

———❖———

"Dr. Foster."

Audrianna felt a tepid dribble of wetness on her forehead. She flitted in and out of focus, fighting the spindle of gravity that wrenched her eyelids shut. She was on the floor. Her upper back, arms, and buttocks were frozen. She forced her eyes open and sat all the way up.

"Take it easy," said Dirk. "Are you okay?" He wiped her face with a damp cloth, and then helped her up from the floor.

"What happened?" Audrianna asked.

"You tell me," Dirk quietly responded. He ran his hand over the back of her scalp. "Did you hit your head?"

"No," she replied. "I think I must've slipped." Even though she knew she had not. She remembered everything. She remembered Lorna's apothegm; she remembered her kiss. She remembered the darkness that crept in with that terrible dream which had not answered any of her questions as Lorna had promised. "Where is—" Audrianna stopped. She pinched the bridge of her nose and squeezed her eyes shut.

"She's gone," replied Dirk.

Audrianna nodded. Dirk had to have seen her reaction to Lorna's presence, and she was certain he had watched them kiss. He had to know she had not fallen accidentally. Audrianna opened her eyes and said, "I should go, too." She felt uncomfortable there, embarrassed.

Dirk sighed heavily. "I understand, and I am more sorry than words can express. May I show you this before you leave?" He reached into the pocket of his lab coat and pulled out a square of yellow, grainy paper. "This came earlier today," he said, handing it to Audrianna.

"A telegram?"

"Yes, read it," said Dirk.

PERSONAL ATTENTION DR. D. VON TRAUGOTT, CARE TIRHZ, ZURICH

RE RECIPROCITY CLINICAL EDUCATION REQUIREMENTS FOR DR. AUDRIANNA FOSTER STOP CONDITIONALLY GRANTED PENDING BOARD APPROVAL STOP CONTRACT AND TERMS VIA POST STOP PLEASE COMMENCE IMMEDIATELY

DR. CLARA MARSHALL, DEAN, WMCP

Audrianna touched her bottom lip. "What is this?" she asked.

"May I speak plainly?"

"Please," Audrianna replied. She blinked hard and then gave her head a little shake. "I would prefer that, for a change." It was a backhanded stab at Lorna's historically covert method of communication, one which seemed to be lost on Dirk, but still felt good to say.

"Dr. Foster," Dirk began. "I know why you've come to Zurich, and I know that you've taken time out of your residency to be here. I'd like to offer you a way to keep up with your requirements whilst pursuing that endeavor."

"Why?" Audrianna responded with a suspicious glance.

Dirk chuckled. "Call it atonement. I want to make amends for the difficulty you've had—with Niklas, Lorna, me, everything. Call it curiosity; I've never met someone like you, Dr. Foster."

Audrianna hesitated. "Like me?" she asked.

"I mean to say you're instinctual; you don't wait, you act."

"You mean I *react*," Audrianna chuckled.

Dirk looked down and shrugged, replying, "Whichever perspective you prefer."

Audrianna cleared her throat. "What would I have to do?" she finally asked.

Dirk looked up. "Nothing more than if you were still enrolled in your traditional program: see and treat patients." He leaned against the doorway and talked with his hands. "To be honest, my surgical load occupies the majority of my time here. I do have a few interim physicians who attend to the women and children when I am unable, but all-in-all, they are largely neglected. I could use the extra help, and it would help you out, too. What do you think?"

Audrianna hedged. "You are very kind, Dr. von Traugott, and your offer is a most generous one. But, I'm not sure after what happened today that I feel safe here."

"You have every right to expect to feel safe," Dirk replied. "In the future, I plan to be more attuned to outside threats. I promise."

Outside threats? Audrianna ran her hand over her face and laughed once. She looked at the telegram again, and said, "I think I would be more inclined to believe that if I knew more about this 'game' everyone keeps referring to."

Dirk pressed his lips together while he considered his choice of words. Finally, he said, "What if I could never explain it in a way you might understand?"

"You're patronizing me," Audrianna responded. "You cannot know what I'm capable of understanding until you try."

Dirk paused. A quick smile played across his face. He motioned her into a chair, saying, "Then sit, please, I shall try."

Audrianna pulled a chair closer and gazed up at him expectantly.

Dirk began to pace. After a few moments he asked, "Do you believe in God?"

"Yes," Audrianna answered automatically. "I mean—" she looked inward. "I was taught to believe in God. My parents took me to Mass every Sunday morning and forced me to sing psalms." She looked at Dirk and softly shook her head. "What does that have to do with anything?"

"Do you believe in the teachings?" Dirk pressed.

Audrianna thought for a moment. "I suppose so," she said. "I've never given it much thought. Are you telling me all this trouble is over religion?"

Dirk cocked his head sideways and replied, "In a manner of speaking."

"What kind of manner?"

Dirk forced a laugh. He put his hands in his pockets and rocked from heel to toe. "A very perverse manner," he eventually said.

Audrianna ran her fingers through her hair and asked, "Are you saying you don't believe in God?" She had heard of religious extremists before, sects of fascists inflicting horrors on detractors. Was that what was going on here?

"No, I believe in God," said Dirk. He shrugged. "It is God who does not recognize me."

They held unblinking eye contact until Audrianna dropped her face forward into her hands, chuckling. The irony of another complicated situation was amusing. Dirk von Traugott was the provost of a large hospital, an associate professor of medicine at the university, and Dr. Adler's associate. He had influence. He made it clear he did not support the research of lyovitalis, but if she offered him her services, she might persuade him otherwise. If she refused him, doors would close in her face; she would never have a chance to unravel the mystery of her mother's killer. She thought of Lorna. This might be the only way to see her again.

Dirk continued, "God is—"

"Okay—" Audrianna held up her hands and turned her face to the side. "That's fine, Dr. von Traugott," she said quickly. "I really don't want to know. Just give me your reassurance that people don't routinely come here and threaten you. If you can give me that, then all I really need to know is when to report."

Dirk laughed. "In the morning." He seemed relieved that she did not want him to continue his explanation. "There is an Austrian woman here on the verge of delivering, and I've got a full day of surgery scheduled."

"How clever of you," Audrianna remarked with a smirk.

"Yes, it was, rather, wasn't it?" Dirk reciprocated her jocularity, clearly content to let their discussion end. He held his hand out to her as a gesture for ratifying the professional agreement.

Audrianna took it and said, "I hope tomorrow brings less excitement than today has."

CHAPTER 7

"I give up," Audrianna said. She folded her arms on the book and laid her head atop them. Three weeks since arriving in Zurich, and she was no closer to formulating a hypothesis about lyovitalis. The journal reference to Gavrilek had forced her to broaden her theories, consider more possibilities, and search through more unknowns. As of yet, she had not found one single mention of the word.

"I'm worried about you, Dr. Foster."

The gentle lilt of Dirk's words moderated Audrianna's self-pity. She sat up and looked at him as he entered the room, surprised to see him there at such an early hour. The two of them routinely ate lunch together to exchange patient information, but she rarely saw him before noon.

He sat down next to her on the petrified workman's bench, straddling it so he faced her. His cologne carved the air around her nose into sharp, clean edges.

"Every morning and evening, I see you in this library poring over these books like a monk in a monastery. Now, you're alone and talking to yourself? Should I have a bed on the psychiatric ward prepared you?"

"Ah, yes. Thank you, Dr. von Traugott," Audrianna teased back. "Please handle that for me. And then, if you would, please provide my boss with a list of my patients so he can take over my rounds."

Dirk chuckled. "I know your boss. I don't think he'll agree to that."

"I guess we'll have to forgo the psychiatric therapy for now," Audrianna said.

"Perhaps you would have breakfast with me instead?" Dirk suggested. "I know the chef personally and I am told he has a great deal of experience in the preparation of … ahem … grits."

Audrianna chomped down on the insides of her mouth to hide her amusement. After a moment, she said, "That's very funny, Doctor, but your ridicule of American cuisine is a bit off. That dish is served in the southern states, and I've never tasted it in my life."

Dirk smiled and offered her his hand. "That's a shame. How about some eggs and extra salty sausage?"

Audrianna laughed. She placed her hand in his and allowed him to help her up from the bench. "I can't go with you, Dirk," she said. "I'm eating breakfast with Niklas this morning. How do you think he'd feel if I stood him up for his older brother? Would you like to join us?"

"No. That's all right," said Dirk, seemingly disappointed. Audrianna found herself a little disappointed, too. The truth was, the more she had gotten to know him, the more she wanted to know him, the more she wanted to see him, and the more she wanted to be in his company. She really liked him, admired him. He had a temper, but he also had an indescribable sweetness about him that was magnetizing.

"You're not sleeping well," Dirk said. It was a statement, not a question.

Audrianna felt a stinging warmth creep up the front of her neck into her face. What was he talking about? How could he know that?

Dirk stared at her with his mesmerizing gray eyes. "Are you here every morning at this time because you'd rather not be sleeping?" he continued. "Is Lorna still meddling with your dreams?"

Audrianna turned her face away. "I'm not sure what you mean," she replied. She pulled at the collar of her blouse and reflected on Lorna's nightly presence in her dreams.

"Is Lorna still tormenting you, Audrianna?" Dirk half-whispered.

Audrianna scoffed softly. Their garishly sexual romps left Audrianna writhing in sodden sheets when she awoke every morning—so real they were that the memory of Lorna's taste would emerge in her mouth throughout the day. Or the sensation of her fingers inside her would return. But how did Dirk know that?

"Good morning, you two," Niklas said, cutting in like an adolescent schoolboy. He slapped Dirk on the back and extended his hand to solicit a handshake. "You're here early. What's the occasion?"

Dirk shook Niklas' hand, standing, changing mental gears without batting an eyelash. "I have a bit of paperwork to catch up on," he said. "I should see to it. Excuse me, Dr. Foster."

Audrianna flipped her head around. "Dr. von Traugott? How did you know?"

Niklas glanced at Audrianna and then at Dirk, gathering that he had interrupted a rather intense moment. Audrianna rescinded her question. "Never mind," she said. "Dreams are nothing more than the purging of the subconscious, right?"

"Right," said Dirk without conviction. After a step away, he turned. "Dr. Foster, if you are still having those dreams, I suggest that you banish the monsters, lock your doors. Unless—secretly you *want* the monsters there."

"What in the world are you two talking about?" Niklas interjected. "Dreams and monsters! What have I missed?"

Audrianna tucked her arm underneath his to divert his scrutiny. "You haven't missed a thing, Niklas," she said. "Your brother and I were just arguing the various theories presented by Dr. Sigmund Freud."

"*The Interpretation of Dreams*," Dirk added, winking.

"Precisely. *The Interpretation of Dreams*." She patted Niklas' hand and removed her arm from his.

"Doctors and their theories," Niklas scoffed. "Shall I come back later?"

"No, no," Dirk insisted. "You two go ahead. We can finish our musings later, Dr. Foster?"

Audrianna squinted at him. He knew about the dreams, but how? Was he calling Lorna a monster?

"Dr. Foster?" Dirk repeated.

"Yes, we can finish later," she said distractedly. "That's fine."

"Very good. Enjoy your breakfast." Dirk slapped his hand on the doorframe, dismissing himself.

Audrianna closed the open books she had been using. Niklas joined in. "We should take a ride this afternoon," he suggested. "It is very fine out today, and I have a convertible car—nothing at all like that stuffy car of Dirk's."

"That's kind of you, Niklas," Audrianna replied absently. She replaced the books on the shelves and then turned around. "I've been wanting to go to the university library and Dirk has extended his privileges to me," she continued. "Maybe you'd take me there?"

"Okay," Niklas replied brightly. "Afterwards, I'll take you to dinner."

Audrianna shrugged. She had to eat, but she did not know if accepting Niklas' dinner invitation was practical. She was exhausted already and had an entire day ahead. "I'll think about it, Niklas," she said. Audrianna gathered her belongings and then started out the door, softening her indifference with a touch on his shoulder. "Let's get through one meal at a time, okay?"

"Okay," Niklas replied.

———•◦•———

"Yes. Here it is, Dr. Foster," the librarian said, reaching into a weathered wooden box with creaky hinges. She took out a piece of paper no thicker than a postcard, and handed it to her.

"Library passes are generally restricted to staff and students, but for Dr. von Traugott, I'll make an exception—a rather impressive gentleman, wouldn't you agree? How long have you been working for him at the refugee hospital?"

"About a month," Audrianna replied. She looked at the card and then added, "Do I keep this? Or do I give it back to you when I leave?"

"You keep it with you." The librarian smiled and said, "Is there something specific you're looking for?"

"Yes, as a matter of fact." Audrianna reached into her bag and pulled out a scratch sheet of paper with the word "Gavrilek." She handed it to the librarian.

"Oh," the woman lifted her eyebrows. "I assumed you were doing only medical research." She returned the paper to Audrianna and pointed to the left. "This will be in the Arts and Literature wing in the Mythology section."

Audrianna stared at her for several seconds without speaking. *Mythology?* What kind of wild goose chase was she on?

"Are you all right, Dr. Foster?" the librarian asked.

"Yes—I'm sorry," Audrianna stammered. "Did you say 'mythology'?"

The librarian adjusted her thick-lensed glasses so she could peer over the rims. "That's right. Gavrilek in mythology," she said. "Is something wrong?"

Audrianna placed her fingertips against her forehead. Her lips parted to speak, but she forgot what she was going to say. Eventually she managed, "It's just that I had assumed a medical connection, or a virus, or—"

"Come with me," the librarian said. She slithered around her podium and motioned for Audrianna to follow her. "I'll direct you. You don't look as though you quite understand."

Thoughts of people high on ergot, executing forty thousand women as witches, came to Audrianna's mind. Common hallucinations of the 1600s were blamed on witches, warlocks, and the devil while poisonous food, common in the diet of the age, was the true culprit. The fact that her recent acquaintances seemed to dabble on the same boundary of fantasy and insanity did not quell her sharpening apprehension. Perhaps her father had proposed such a connection, and Dr. Adler had pulled the plug on his financial support and branded him a similar village idiot. Or perhaps her father had hidden the possible connection from Dr. Adler for fear of ridicule.

"Here we are," the librarian said. She felt her way down the spines of the books, stopping at the only vacant position on the shelf. "*The Children of Gavrilek* should be right here; it appears the book has been checked out. Come to the desk and we can find out when it's due to be returned."

Back at the desk, the librarian looked up the card in another file box. "You're in luck," she announced. "The book was checked out by someone from the School of Medicine, Dr. Britton Foster." The woman looked up, surprised. "Is that a relative of yours?"

Audrianna nodded. "My father."

The librarian smiled over her the tops of her glasses and said, "You'll know where to get it from, then." She turned the card over and read. "Oh, wait! I'm sorry, Dr. Foster. I've made a mistake. Your father wasn't the last one to have the book. It was Dr. Gustav Adler. Gracious! He's had it for over a year." She flipped her eyes back up. "Do you know Dr. Adler? I think he's retiring very soon."

Audrianna felt her blood drain from her face. He lied. He deliberately lied to her about his knowledge of Gavrilek. Worse than that, he tried to make her believe that her father had fabricated the idea under the influence of mental illness. That bastard! What else was he lying about?

"Oh, yes," Audrianna whispered, "I know Dr. Adler."

The librarian seemed not to notice Audrianna's change of tone. "Excellent," she said. "If you happen upon him, would you remind him that the time limit for checked books is two weeks? In view of his imminent departure, we could perhaps waive the overdue fee if he just brings it back right away."

"You've scarcely spoken a single word since we've arrived, Audrianna. Are you all right?" Niklas asked her.

Audrianna gritted her teeth. She was not in the mood to answer questions about her current state of mind, or offer excuses for her silence. After leaving the library, she descended upon Dr. Adler's office in a fury, only to find the space completely unoccupied. Despite her continued refusals, Niklas was persistent in his invitation to dine out. Audrianna begrudgingly agreed to a late tea at the majestic *Dolder Grand*. Still in her work clothes, she was underdressed and out of fashion compared to the rest of the women there. Their stares intensified her irritability.

"I wish you'd advised me on the correct attire, Niklas," Audrianna grumbled under her breath. "I don't enjoy the scrutiny." She took up her napkin and placed it in her lap. Niklas did the same.

He glanced around the room in dismay and replied, "I'm sorry, Audrianna. I should have given the dress code more thought, but the truth is, I hadn't even noticed your outfit past your lovely face. If you're uncomfortable here, we'll leave." The sincerity of his sentiment melted Audrianna's frigid demeanor. She blushed, and then looked down to hide it.

"I am uncomfortable," Audrianna quietly acknowledged. She fiddled with her hands for a moment while a waiter situated a three-tiered dish of pastries and sandwiches on the table. Realizing it would be even more conspicuous to abandon the meal, Audrianna decided to endure the scrutiny. After the waiter left, she looked up and said, "I'm not sure fleeing the restaurant is necessary. Thank you, Niklas."

Niklas beamed. He relaxed his posture and waited for Audrianna to have first choice of edibles before helping himself to a hot buttered scone. "Did you get much accomplished at the library today?" he asked.

"In a way," Audrianna replied without expounding. She nibbled her cucumber and foie gras sandwich, then continued, "I stopped in to see Dr. Adler afterwards only to find his office completely vacant—I mean except for that enormous safe. Do you know Dr. Adler very well, Niklas?"

Niklas shook his head and replied, "Not very well, no. He's dined at the manor on a few occasions since he's been here, but to be honest, I don't know if we've had two words between us."

"Since he's been here?" Audrianna asked, confused. She lifted her teacup to her lips and took a tiny sip. "I don't understand. Hasn't he always lived in the area?"

Niklas shook his head whilst chewing, and then spoke after he swallowed. "Two years or so, I think." He looked inward for a moment, reconsidering, and then nodded to himself. "Yes, two years, that's about right."

Audrianna put her cup down and stared at him. "Two years? Niklas, you must be mistaken," she said. "My father spent the last *four* years in Zurich. He had a research partner the entire time he was here. I'm certain of it. I had letters from him stating as much."

"I don't know," Niklas shrugged. "Maybe their partnership was via correspondence—"

"No," Audrianna interrupted him.

"Or maybe he had another research partner prior to Dr. Adler," Niklas offered. He took another bite of his scone, adding,

"You should ask Dirk. He would know. Dr. Adler comes to the refugee hospital regularly."

"Ask Dirk what?" a familiar voice declared from over the top of Audrianna's head. Audrianna whirled around and nearly choked on her own heart. It was Dirk and Lorna. They stood together arms linked: Dirk in white tie and Lorna draped in burgundy chiffon. They were magnificently overdressed for afternoon tea. She stared at them in stunned silence as Niklas jumped up and shook hands with Dirk.

"I wasn't sure if you'd gotten my message," Niklas said. "Audrianna wasn't feeling up to dinner so I thought this might be suitable…"

Internal panic muted the remainder of his words. Niklas had planned an elegant evening together with Dirk and Lorna, intended it as a surprise for some reason. No wonder he had been so insistent.

"God," Audrianna whispered, turning back around and pressing her dewy palm against her cheek. She glanced down at her dowdy brown skirt and reflected that she did not need this added stress, not now when she was so overwrought with emotion already.

A chilly set of fingertips grazed the side of Audrianna's neck, sending a shiver down her spine. "Good evening, my darling," Lorna whispered in her ear, leaving her scent behind when she rose. Audrianna licked her lips and watched with rapt attention as Dirk escorted Lorna by the elbow to a chair across the way.

A popular socialite, Lorna drew a buzz from the crowd. She toyed with their fascination by scanning the room for acquaintances and then nodding to no one. Afterwards, she fixed herself elegantly in her chair and donned her usual expression of superiority and sex. She found Audrianna's eyes and teased her with an impish smirk.

"Good evening, Audrianna." Audrianna jumped at the sound of Dirk's voice. He sat down next to her, and then took her hand and kissed it. Audrianna fluttered her eyelashes down and away, embarrassed to be seated beside him clothed as she was.

"Good evening, Dr. von Traugott," she replied, instituting a formality that matched his level of refinement.

"Dirk, be a darling and get us a bottle of champagne, won't you?" Lorna entered the conversation. She pulled an ornately decorated cigarette case from her clutch and lit one up, taking a drag, and then laughing it out. "Fine," she rolled her eyes at him. "I'll do it, then." She raised her arm in the air and a waiter rushed to her call.

"Yes, Madame. How may I help?" he asked with a respectful bow of the head.

Dirk quietly objected, but his appeal was ignored. "Kindly arrange a bottle of Chateau Latour for the table," Lorna told the waiter. "If pretenses must be observed, you may serve it in a teapot. We're celebrating."

As far as Audrianna knew, she was there for a short meal and a long walk home. What were they supposed to be celebrating?

The waiter hesitated.

"Have I spoken in a language you don't understand?" Lorna asked him. "*Englisch? Französisch? Spanisch?*" She showcased her intelligence with effortless multilingualism, finishing the exposition in German. "*Welche Sprache sol lich sprechen?*" Which language should I speak?

The waiter quickly got the point. He nodded once and backed away from the table, mumbling, "Very good, Madame." His expression was equal parts shock and trepidation.

"That was unnecessary," Dirk mentioned under his breath. "You've garnered the scrutiny of the entire room. You know she's shy of attention."

"She's anything but shy," Lorna laughed, taking another leisurely drag. "Trust me."

Audrianna narrowed her eyes. She suspected she was the source of their banter but decided against argument despite her annoyance.

Dirk precipitously changed the subject. "So, what were you going to ask me, Audrianna?" he said.

Audrianna looked up at the waiter and said, "Thank you," when he poured champagne into her cup. She had never indulged in alcohol before, but was not about to betray that innocence now. "Um, I was going to ask you about Dr. Adler," Audrianna said, taking a tentative sip. The liquid fizzled sweet and dry in her mouth, sparking courage to her tongue. She took another *generous* taste.

"Dr. Adler?" Dirk asked with a laugh. He reached for his cup, but he did not drink. "Yes, we can talk about Dr. Adler," he said, shifting his seat. "What would you like to know?"

"Do you know why he's resigned so hastily from the university?" Audrianna asked, jumping to the heart of the matter. "Do you where he's gone—"

"My, my, Sherlock Holmes," Lorna cut in, stealth as a fox. She took another puff off her cigarette and chuckled out the smoke. "Trying to unravel the *Mystery of the Missing Professor,* are you?" she asked.

Audrianna felt her heart begin to thump. She clinched her jaw and consciously tempered her respirations, determined not to let Lorna's intimidation get to her. She drained the remainder of her champagne and replied, "Yes, *Countess*. I am. Dr. Adler is purposely withholding—"

"Does it please you very much to call me that?" Lorna's voice speared itself into Audrianna's brain. She housed her cigarette in an ashtray and leaned forward on her forearms. Her lips did not move. *"Would you prefer the distinction of rank preserved in bed, as well?"*

Audrianna fumbled her cup on the saucer, quickly righting it with both hands. Fire exploded into her cheeks like a surge of dynamite. She glanced at Dirk and Niklas with horrified eyes, gauging their reactions, but neither of them appeared to be affected—not until they saw Audrianna's face.

"What's the matter," Dirk asked her. Niklas inched his hand over and touched her on the wrist, echoing the question in his stare.

Audrianna stammered, "I'm fine, I'm fine." She pulled away from Niklas and placed both palms against her cheeks, staring across the table at Lorna who buttered a piece of toast, seemingly disinterested. "I think I must be very tired." Audrianna dropped her hands and fanned herself for a moment, playing off the hallucination with an uncomfortable laugh.

"Perhaps you should take her home, Niklas," Lorna said as she bit into her toast; Dirk agreed.

Audrianna shook her head. "No, thank you. I'm okay." She glanced at Niklas with a reassuring smile, and then she pointed at the teapot. "May I have a little more of that, please," she asked, suddenly very thirsty, but unsure why. Niklas poured it for her and she drank half of it despite the burgeoning tingle in her lips. Afterwards, she said, "I'm sorry, what were we talking about?"

Lorna laughed. She blew out the smoke from her final puff, and stamped the cigarette dead. "I believe we were celebrating something, right, Niklas?" She looked at him casually and attempted a half-hearted smile.

"Yes, right," Niklas slowly responded, blushing. He turned to Audrianna and started, "Audrianna—"

"No." Audrianna cut him off with a touch on the arm. She allowed her hand to linger there while she continued. "I'm sorry, Niklas, but just a minute. That wasn't what we were talking about." She shot Lorna a fierce look and then glanced over at Dirk. "We were talking about Dr. Adler," she finished.

Lorna laughed again, and this time it made Audrianna angry. "What, Lorna?" she shouted. A hush fell over the room and Audrianna registered her volume. She squeezed her eyelids shut, and that's when the room began to spin.

"I first met Dr. Adler when I was studying medicine in Berlin." Dirk's gentle voice soothed the tone of the conversation. "He was the head of medicine at *Charité Hospital* and also the most influential physician in Berlin. He was hired to ensure my graduation when success seemed unlikely."

Audrianna struggled to focus on his words. "You nearly flunked out of medical school?" she eventually managed. She reached for her cup again, but Dirk snapped his fingers and Audrianna found the cup too heavy to lift. She leaned forward and turned the saucer counterclockwise, attempting to lift the cup again without success. Dirk continued to speak as if nothing were amiss.

"Yes, I didn't care to sit in class all day," he explained. "I already knew more than they were teaching me, and I preferred to be out in nature."

"What are you doing, Dirk?" Lorna eyed him with icy curiosity. Her smile tightened; her pulse slowly pounded the side of her neck.

"It's too much for her, Lorna. She's unfamiliar," Dirk growled.

Lorna snapped her fingers with twice the gumption Dirk had used and the cup instantly lightened. Audrianna picked it up and looked at it, baffled. "Are you her keeper now, too?" Lorna asked Dirk in a venomous tone of voice.

The comment infiltrated Audrianna's haze. She jolted back into the moment, leaving inhibition behind. "Are you talking about me?" she asked, loudly. "Are you two really talking about me like I'm not even here?"

"This was a poorly executed impromptu." Niklas wiped his mouth and signaled for the check. "I'll take you home, Audrianna. We can do this another time."

Audrianna shook her head. "Wait a minute, I'm not going anywhere. Do *what* another time?" she asked. "You all clearly have some sort of secret agenda that I'm unaware of. Would someone like to tell *me* what's going on?" She tilted the cup to her lips to drink, but overfilled her mouth. She tried to catch the spillage with her fingers, but it ultimately dribbled down the front of her chin and saturated her blouse. Embarrassed, she fought the instinctual urge to hide under the tablecloth. Instead, she gingerly replaced the cup on its saucer, then turned and spoke to Niklas with as much grace as she could muster. "May I have your coat, please? I need to be excused."

Niklas and Dirk both hopped up as Audrianna rocked her unsteady self out of her chair. Niklas placed his coat on Audrianna's shoulders and held her until she found her balance. "Thank you, Niklas." She patted him sloppily on the hand, and she stumbled out of the dining room amongst a flurry of suppressed giggles. Eventually, Audrianna wound up in a vacant ladies lounge, not remembering exactly how she got there. She sat down in one of the chairs and propped her elbows on the table, burying her face in her hands. Her head was spinning; silence thumped against her eardrums. She should have been more careful with the alcohol, but she had no clue two teacups of champagne could have this kind of effect.

The door squeaked open and Audrianna recognized Lorna's distinctive footsteps falling across the floor. She closed her eyes as Lorna gently captured her face from behind and tilted her back by her forehead. She cuddled Audrianna's skull against her taut body and stroked her falling hair. "Poor darling," she said with a little sympathetic laugh. "You didn't quite think that one through, did you?"

Another torrent of anger swept through Audrianna's countenance, but quickly lost its vigor, undermined by Lorna's touch. She wound her sweaty face between Lorna's cold hands, replying with a raspy whisper, "Do you enjoy punishing me, Lorna? Is that why you followed me in here?"

"I'm not punishing you, Audrianna," Lorna softly answered. She petted Audrianna's head a couple more times, and then she pivoted around to face her. She pulled her up by her elbows and tracked her down with her eyes. "Darling, I adore your impulsiveness, but sometimes it *does* get you into trouble. Now, let's see about your ... ahem ... blunder. And then I'll have Niklas take you home." She led Audrianna into the toilet room by the hand and sat her down in there, pulling the curtain closed behind them.

"Take your blouse off," Lorna commanded. She stripped Niklas' coat from Audrianna's shoulders, then turned around and hung it on a rack. By the time she turned back around, Audrianna had managed only one of twenty buttons. Lorna seized her fumbling fingers whispering, "Allow me." Audrianna let go of her shirt.

"You look amazing," Audrianna slurred her words. Her hands drifted to Lorna's hips. She looked up into Lorna's face, unconcerned with impropriety.

Lorna made brief eye contact whilst working her way through the buttons. "Are you flirting with me, Dr. Foster?" she teased.

"I guess I am," Audrianna replied, acknowledging her own state of mind. She pressed her forehead into Lorna's abdomen and breathed deeply through her nose. It had been many weeks since Audrianna had seen Lorna, but not so long that she had forgotten her smell, her indefatigable combination of sensuality and safety. "How long have you been in town?" she mumbled.

Lorna cleared her throat. She skipped a button but then quickly came back to it. "I've only just arrived," she said. "I'm here in support of Niklas. He wants to get married."

"Married," Audrianna repeated. She talked to buy her time with Lorna's scent, not because she cared about Niklas' wife-to-be. "I didn't know he was that involved with someone. Was it arranged?"

Lorna chuckled. "Yes. It's been carefully arranged," she said. "Whether or not it comes to fruition is yet to be determined." She picked up Audrianna's chin and looked into her eyes. After a moment she whispered, "Audrianna, why are you still here? I told you to go home."

Audrianna felt a sting in her soul. She pulled her face back and let go of Lorna's hips. "You know why I'm here, Lorna," she said, anger brewing again. "Is that what you hoped for? That I'd be gone?"

"Yes."

"Why?" Audrianna demanded. "Because the idea of wanting a woman sickens you!? The idea of wanting me sickens you!?"

She patted herself on the chest. "You did this to me, Lorna. I didn't bring it on myself!"

A little smile appeared on Lorna's face as she continued to work through Audrianna's buttons in silence. Her expression invoked a malicious personality that lay dormant in Audrianna until alcohol liberated it. She shouted, "You know what, Lorna? The idea of wanting you sickens me, too! I hate you!"

Lorna tilted her face upwards in a maniacal laugh. "My, my, my little girl," she said shaking her head down. "Who let you play with the knife box?" She pushed the last button through the loop and snatched the shirt down Audrianna's back, trapping her arms behind her. She twisted the fabric in her fists so it tightened like a straight jacket, and then she pulled Audrianna to her feet. The shirt fabric began to warm.

"Now you listen to me," Lorna slit her eyes and jiggled Audrianna's body. "I've been attracted to dozens of women, and I've fucked a good many more than that. Do not flatter yourself otherwise."

"You're disgusting," Audrianna shouted at her. "Disgusting!" She was not disgusted. She was jealous. She bucked her open bosom against Lorna a couple times. The temperature of her shirt fabric continued to climb, searing her skin.

"Yes, you've said that to me before. Although," Lorna laughed, "we were in quite a different position than we are now, and I'm certain it was *you* who asked me not to stop."

Audrianna squirmed from the discomfort of the burning cloth. "Lorna, please!" she gasped.

"What's the matter, Dr. Foster? Does this *hurt*?" Lorna pulled her close to whisper in her ear. "Welcome to *my* world."

Audrianna cried out and was turned loose. Her blouse instantly cooled. She doubled over with her mouth hanging open, mortified as much by Lorna's banter as by the magic she seemed to employ. Lorna took advantage of her vulnerability. She drew Audrianna's skirt up to her knees and twisted her around to straddle the toilet seat backward. She clamped both hands firmly around Audrianna's neck and forced her to sit down.

"As for the idea of wanting you," Lorna said, rocking her back and forth a little. "Well, that's *my* blunder."

"Go to hell," Audrianna bit back, grabbing at Lorna's hands.

Lorna tightened her grip. "Yes, I'm in need of a holiday," she said. "And, I hear hell is quite … sultry."

Audrianna yanked on her forearms. "You mock God!?" she choked.

"God?" Lorna chuckled. "No, no. Audrianna, it's you I meant to mock." She kissed her on the temple and then slowly relaxed her grip.

Audrianna pulled out of her hands and shouted, "I hate you!" She began buttoning her completely dry blouse with shaky fingers, making minimal progress.

"Yes, I heard you," Lorna snapped, "and I've told you about the consequences of that choice." She stepped back and yanked open the curtain. "Go home and get some rest, Audrianna. I want you sober tonight. We have important things to discuss."

Audrianna whipped around and screamed, "I don't want to see you tonight!" She shook her head. "I mean—I don't know what the hell you're talking about!"

"Really?" Lorna replied coolly. "Perhaps you should ask for Dirk's counsel; he's very eager to offer you advice on the matter, I hear."

Audrianna grimaced in angry disbelief. Alcohol stoked her fire. "You hear *what*?" she spat. "From *whom*?"

Lorna smiled at her with thin lips. She gave her a once-over with the eyes and said, "In the future, you will not discuss our situation with either Niklas or Dirk. Is that understood? Dirk is a pessimist and Niklas is a romantic. Neither of them can keep it in the proper frame of reference at present. They both think with their dicks."

Audrianna's eyes widened. "The *proper frame of reference?*" she enunciated each word with a sharp, sarcastic edge. "What *is* the proper frame of reference, pray tell? Tell me so I'll know, too!" Dirk had obviously told Lorna about their dream conversation, and who knew what Niklas had said. Yes, she had talked with both of them about Lorna. How could they betray her trust that way?

Lorna narrowed her eyes. "I don't want our relationship discussed," she said. "Is that clear?"

"When we enter a *relationship*, I'll keep that in mind," Audrianna snarled. She stood up and fell against the wall, recovering with, "What are you so afraid of, Lorna? Are you afraid they'll know how much I want you? How much I love you?" She laughed at inhibition's effortless intervention. "There. It's said. Now what, Lorna?"

Lorna's features softened. "Fear is a luxury I cannot afford," she said. "Or is that your vengeance? Are you that clever? Do you secretly want me destroyed because of what happened to your mother?"

"Shut up about my mother! Shut up!" Audrianna threw her hands down. "I am so *sick* of talking in riddles with you, Lorna! Just say what you mean!"

Voices entered in the room, interrupting them. Lorna pulled the curtain and stepped back inside, placing her forefinger against her lips. In one smooth motion, she wrapped a trembling, disheveled Audrianna up with one arm and backed into the corner, holding her tight. "Shh," she whispered. "I don't have the power to make them forget if we're discovered in here."

Audrianna rolled her eyes. As if anyone had that kind of power. That type of grandiosity was exactly what carried Europe into the current world war. No wonder; it was her family.

"How can you be so brilliant and be so dense?" Lorna muttered to herself.

"I beg your problem—pardon," Audrianna corrected herself. The outside voices hushed and Lorna snapped her fingers lightly. Audrianna's voice was instantly suppressed.

"Did you see Countess Mehlinger on the far side of the room, Léonie?" A woman's voice nudged. Laughter arose.

"Don't be cruel, Julia," a softer, more matronly voice interjected, and the laugher petered off. "Who didn't notice Countess Mehlinger? She made quite a showy entrance in that gown. Was she lost?" Laughter again. "It isn't Léonie's fault in any case. She was completely seduced by Countess Mehlinger. Isn't that right, Léonie? She's done that to a number of aristocratic women across Europe. It's no secret. The important thing here is discretion."

"Who is the trollop she's dining with?" another woman's voice asked. "The one who came in with Niklas von Traugott? The homely looking one in rags."

Audrianna swayed and Lorna tightened her embrace. She wound her nose into Audrianna's hair and delivered soft little kisses to help ease the hurt from the insult. "Easy," she whispered.

"I think she's the American woman working at Baron von Traugott's hospital. She's a doctor, or at least, so they say."

"Well, she certainly isn't a lady. That much is obvious. What do you think the countess sees in her, Léonie? It's out of character for her to be associating with such a woman."

"Lorna Mehlinger does whatever she wants with whomever she wants," an angry voice replied. "I'm sure the American woman falls somewhere within her master plan. Poor little thing. She's clearly infatuated and can't see she's being used."

Nausea swept over Audrianna. Her body turned clammy. She placed her hand over her mouth to suppress the urge to vomit as stomach acid trickled into her throat.

"Perhaps she's meant as sacrifice to appease *the curse*!" Laughter erupted.

"Come with me, come with me," Lorna whispered, snapping her fingers repeatedly.

Audrianna fell appreciably numb. Darkness shaded her vision as she felt her body being slowly lowered to the floor. When she awoke, she felt buoyant. She opened her eyes to find herself being carried up stairs. She stirred.

"Wait a moment, my love. We're nearly there." It was Niklas voice. He juggled her with one arm whilst opening a door. Feet down first, he lowered her into a chair while he turned back her bed covers. Audrianna struggled to hold her head up. "Okay." Niklas swept her up and laid her down. "Here you are. Safe and sound. I should never have insisted you come. I'm sorry." He sat down on the side of the bed facing her. Audrianna opened her eyes.

"It's not your fault, Niklas," she said, taking his hand. "I know why you did—the celebration, I mean. Lorna told me."

"She had no right." He shook his head in angry disbelief.

"It's okay, Niklas," Audrianna said. "It was a bit of a surprise, but it made me very happy to hear."

Niklas softened. "It did?" he asked, eyes brightening.

"Of course it did, Niklas." Audrianna sat up and wrapped her arms around him, rubbing his back. "You'll make a wonderful husband and a wonderful father. I just know it." She lay back down and Niklas scooted closer to her head, taking her hand and kissing it.

"We should discuss the particulars, don't you think?" he said.

Audrianna pulled away and ground both fists into her burning eyes, yawning. "Yes, I'd love to hear your plans, Niklas, but maybe another day. I have a very early morning scheduled at the hospital and I need to get ... some ..." She drifted off.

"Right." Niklas said. He stood up and pulled the covers up to Audrianna's chin, tucking her in, kissing her on the forehead. "You're wonderful," he whispered. "Thank you for not being angry. I should not have included Lorna. I thought if she showed her support of the marriage, you'd be more amenable to the idea—but she always manages to make a mess of things."

Audrianna snorted herself awake. "I'm sorry. What?" she said. She heard him talking, but nothing of what he confessed.

Niklas scoffed lightly. "Nothing. I'll come see you at the hospital tomorrow night. We'll continue this then. Okay?"

"Sure," Audrianna breathed. She rolled over on her side and curled up with her pillow; her mattress recoiled; her bedroom door opened and closed. Sleep carried her away.

———— ·•◦•· ————

"I didn't want to see you tonight," Audrianna said without looking up. She had come to recognize Lorna's presence through extra sensory perception and could feel her distinct carnal energy whenever she was near. An incredibly stunning woman in any situation, Lorna's beauty was magnified in the dream world, and Audrianna braced herself to repel the acts of seduction that always seemed to accompany her. She needed explanations, not distractions.

"I can feel your conflict," Lorna said. "Your soul is uneasy. I can help you if you'll let me."

Audrianna laughed. Her anger from the day spilled into her dreams; she had no cause to check it. "Is that so?" she asked. "Help me what? Take my clothes off? Help me into bed?"

"Don't put words into my mouth, Audrianna," Lorna growled. "You know that's not what I mean. If that's what I wanted, I would've made my intentions very clear already. I have no reason to hide behind a mask of concern if it's sex I'm after."

Audrianna scoffed. "I'm sorry if I offended you, Lorna. I didn't think you *had* any other intentions for me." She turned away, desperate to free her mind.

"Please don't leave before we talk about this," whispered Lorna. She stood behind Audrianna, lowering her voice to a quiet croon. "Your investigation has the potential to place you in real danger. Abandon this obsession of yours now before you get caught up in something you can't escape. Please."

Audrianna shivered from the feel of Lorna's breath on her neck. "What danger, Lorna?" she cried. She tried to step away, intimidated by her own sexual inclinations, but Lorna's hands held her in place. "What right do you have to ask me to abandon anything? Do you honestly think that making love to me in a dream is all it takes to make us connected? If you want to help me, help me here." She pulled away from her and dredged the air with her fingers, siphoning an invisible force into her body. "Climb your emotional barricade and be at my side!"

Lorna wrapped her arms around Audrianna and said, "I know it's easy to condemn me, but don't mistake my caution for apathy. I am not the heartless creature you perceive, and someday the effects of our time together may prove that to you. I am here right now because I am incapable of being anywhere else, with anyone else. I can't seem to overcome you, and strangely, I don't want to anymore."

Lorna's words bent the bars of the protective cage Audrianna had erected around herself. She dropped her head against Lorna's shoulder and nuzzled the softness of her neck. "Help me, then," she whispered, braiding her fingers into Lorna's hands and guiding them inside the bust of her flimsy cotton gown. "I am in a very dangerous predicament." Her words were parsed; she touched her breasts with Lorna's fingers. "I'm in danger of falling more in love with you than I already am."

"Audrianna," Lorna moaned. "How can I follow through on good intentions? They become—immaterial when you offer yourself to me like this." She brushed a strap of the gown off one of Audrianna's shoulders. Her foot pushed one of Audrianna's out to the side. Her hand moved to Audrianna's thigh. "Stop me now if this isn't what you want."

Audrianna freed her hands and wrapped them behind Lorna's head, winding her fingers into her hair. "I couldn't even if I wanted to," she breathed.

A deep voice resounded: "But I can."

A subtly threatening presence drew the women apart. Dirk appeared at the hazy boundary. His long black hair was pulled back loosely with shorter strands falling softly around gray eyes. He was clean-shaven and charged with a new, different intensity.

"Son of a bitch!" Lorna spat, stepping protectively in front of Audrianna. "How dare you come here."

"I have as much right to be here as do you," Dirk replied.

Lorna bared her teeth at him and said, "Just because she trusts you enough to let you in doesn't mean you could take her from me. Are you sure you want to try?" It was a threat.

Dirk crossed the distance between them, incited by her challenge. "Listen to you!" he said, staring Lorna down with his graphite eyes. "When is this not going to be enough, Lorna? It's only a matter of time before you have to have it all! You forget that I know who and what you are! I won't let you do that to her! It ends here."

Lorna broadened her stance and encircled Audrianna's waist with one arm. "Only when she says so, Dirk. Not you. Ask Audrianna if she is ready to end it."

Dirk stepped around Lorna and grabbed Audrianna's arm. "Come with me, Audrianna. Don't let her torture you this way! You'll wake up in a little while and realize this is all you will ever have from her, these dreams. She is unavailable. The more you tempt her, the more dangerous this relationship becomes."

Audrianna staggered with their competing energies coursing through her. Enthralling, flattering. For a plain-looking girl to be wrestled over by the two most beautiful individuals she'd ever met. She pulled away from them both with a taunt. "Why *are* you here, Dirk? Were you afraid you were going to miss out on something?" Audrianna did not comprehend his motivations at all, and honestly, she did not care what they were. She only cared that his interest seemed to have sparked a hint of anger in Lorna, one that Audrianna enjoyed, and one she decided to leverage against Lorna to incite her jealousy. She reached up and pulled Dirk's face down to hers, kissing him with open lips—exaggerating more passion than she actually felt.

"Don't indulge this fantasy, Audrianna." Dirk pulled away. "You're playing with fire and have no means to extinguish it."

"Why would I want to extinguish it?" Audrianna laughed, her intoxication with power drowning his warning. Lorna had educated her on the rules of this domain. *Nothing to be afraid of, no risks, no consequences.* She pulled Dirk's hands forward and placed them around Lorna's waist. "Why can't we all partake in this pleasure?"

Lorna flicked her eyes to Dirk, then back to Audrianna. "Is that what you want?" she asked.

Audrianna nodded. She wrapped her arms around Lorna's neck, doling out soft kisses, encouraging her participation. "Help me understand ecstasy as I never have before," she murmured between kisses. "Let me watch your face as a man takes me for the first time."

Lorna seized her and pressed her mouth against her own. Audrianna reciprocated, devouring Lorna with equal tenacity. They tore at each other's clothes until each was naked, needing the other's flesh like air to breathe.

"You want to know what it feels like, Audrianna?" Lorna pressed her to the ground, forcing her legs apart. "To have a man fill you up like this?" She pushed her fingers inside, not gently, but salaciously and uncontrolled.

Audrianna cried out as Lorna stroked her, the roughness trounced by her expertise of motion. Ferocity removed emotion, and Audrianna reached the brink of orgasm faster than she wanted. She rolled on top of Lorna to stop herself from coming, straddled her pelvis, and began grinding her sweaty thighs around Lorna's hand without restraint, wanting her deeper inside of her than possible. Dirk knelt behind her and pressed his hand into her back, pushing her down on top of Lorna's bare chest. Erect nipples rubbed together as bodies rocked with lovemaking.

Lorna pulled her fingers out and flipped Audrianna onto her side. She heaved Audrianna's leg up and draped it over her own body to allow Dirk access to Audrianna's center. Dirk unbuttoned his pants and pulled his fly apart so only the most important part was exposed. He slid up behind Audrianna and she immediately felt him pressing into her. She looked back, suddenly afraid she might regret what was about to happen.

Lorna cupped Audrianna's face in her hands. "It's okay, my darling. Look at me. Do not give preconceived fears the power to invade this place. You are an exquisite woman. You deserve supreme bliss."

Lorna kissed her repeatedly, and Audrianna gave in with kisses of her own. She was right, her anxiety was foolish; this was not reality and she was not bound by the physics of the human body or by the rules of society. "I'm all right," she whispered, suckling Lorna's neck, wanting her nearness and grateful for her words. "I'm ready now."

Lorna reached down to spread Audrianna's juices in preparation for Dirk. Audrianna dropped her head against Lorna's chest, closing her eyes to the rhythm of her heartbeat. She felt Dirk probing gently at first, guided by Lorna's fingers as she continued to rub Audrianna with silky fingertips.

Audrianna felt herself become engorged with blood, heightening the sensation of his penetration. A gasp escaped from her lips as he slowly buried himself deeper and deeper inside. Lorna placed her free arm around Audrianna's shoulders, pulling her closer, comfortingly. She kissed Audrianna's steamy forehead and whispered directly into her ear. "Relax. Feel him inside you. When you're ready, move with him. Help him take you over the edge."

The voiced realization of the moment brought her instantly to climax. She rocked her hips and buttocks against Dirk's thrusts, clinging to Lorna's naked body as he drove himself into her. Her tempo slowed as she entered the paralytic phase of pre-orgasm. Dirk placed his hand on top of her thigh, gripping her pelvis to encourage movement. "Don't stop, Audrianna," he said. "It's so much better to move through it."

Audrianna cried out in passion as contractions electrocuted every nerve in her body. One after another after another they came without arrest, doubling her over with powerful spasms of pleasure.

"Dr. Foster?"

No! Another voice? Who was that?

"Dr. Foster, may I come in?"

CHAPTER 8

"Good morning, Dr. Foster. Did you find everything satisfactory on your rounds this morning?" Nurse Heilemann burst into Audrianna's office, and then immediately apologized, saying, "Oh, I'm terribly sorry." She turned away and fidgeted as Audrianna was plucked from the astral plane, returned to her cumbersome physical form. Air was stale and her neck stiff. Gravity reintroduced itself as she picked her head up and groaned.

"Should I come back?" Mrs. Heilemann peeped.

Audrianna squinted at her. She wiped the side of her mouth and then gradually sat up. "It's fine, Frau Heilemann," she croaked and then cleared her throat. "Please. I must've fallen asleep. Forgive me. I haven't been sleeping well since I've been here." She smoothed the front of her lab coat with her hands and asked, "What can I do for you?"

"I meant to inquire about your rounds, Dr. Foster," Nurse Heilemann repeated quietly. Do you have any concerns you would like to discuss?"

Audrianna took a few seconds to reorient herself and then said, "My rounds? Yes—since you ask, I do have some concerns about the quality of care some of the patients are receiving—from one nurse in particular." She adjusted the pins in her hair, and handed Nurse Heilemann a stack of charts she had set aside for further review. "Several of my orders have been overlooked, possibly even ignored. I have had to perform quite a few of my own dressing changes this week. I've spoken with the nurse, with no apparent resolution."

The portly old woman inspected the charts one by one, and then placed the lot of them back in front of Audrianna without comment. She reminded Audrianna of the strict head mistress at the Dana Hall Boarding School for Girls in Wellesley, Massachusetts where Audrianna received her childhood education. Nurse Heilemann's salt-and-pepper bun was wound so tightly behind her head that she appeared bald at first glance, and her duty uniform was so white and so crisp it could pass for a christening gown. Aside from her frigid exterior though, Urma Heilemann was a bona fide mother figure to everyone on the unit, including Audrianna, who appreciated the guidance the nurse had provided during her first month at the refugee hospital.

"I'm sorry, Frau Heilemann," Audrianna apologized. "I don't mean to make a fuss. It's not that I mind changing my own dressings, it's just that I've had a problem with this one nurse since I got here, and I'm not exactly sure why."

Nurse Heilemann stepped all the way into the room with painful, arthritic steps. "May I?" she asked, pointing to the seat in front of Audrianna's desk. Her robust frame was complicated by a height of at least five-foot-eight, making the anguish of maneuvering herself into a seated position excruciating to watch.

"Please," Audrianna replied. She sat back in her own chair, and waited for Nurse Heilemann to settle before continuing. "Am I expecting too much? Are the orders too complex? If they are, I can teach her."

"The nurse is Heidi Klaus, yes?" Nurse Heilemann offered.

"Yes," Audrianna answered.

The old lady shook her head. "She doesn't need to be taught, Dr. Foster. She's doing it to spite you."

Audrianna was taken aback. "But why?" she exclaimed. "I've never had a harsh word for that girl, even after I was sure she was neglectful of my patients."

"It's not what you have or haven't said," Nurse Heilemann said. "It's what she believes you have taken from her."

Audrianna's mouth slackened. "Taken—what I have taken from her?" She drew a sharp breath in through her nostrils. "That's absurd! I have never stolen anything in my life!"

Nurse Heilemann laughed. "Not stolen, Dr. Foster. And not some*thing*, but some*one*."

Audrianna blinked.

"I am not normally one to spread gossip, Dr. Foster," Nurse Heilemann continued, "but if I may, perhaps you would allow me to share some information with you that might help you understand the situation more clearly."

"Please." Audrianna offered her palm. "I'll admit I'm quite lost."

Nurse Heilemann nodded. "The other nurses tell me that Heidi had been enjoying the company of a very attractive, well-to-do young man for the past several months. Of course, with her beauty, she has never been in want of a suitor, but this one is different. He's a gentleman."

"Yes?" Audrianna's confusion showed. "What does that have to do with me?"

The older woman smiled without showing her teeth. "He's recently stopped seeing her, Dr. Foster. She thinks it's because of you."

"Because of me?" Audrianna said. "That's impossible. Who? I haven't—" She paused and reflected. *Niklas.*

"Dr. Foster," Nurse Heilemann continued, "anyone can see the two of you have developed quite a fondness for each other. I've seen it for myself. He lights up when you come around. It only makes sense that he would fall for you over someone like Heidi. You may not have Heidi's looks, but you are refined, educated and, if I might say so, quite intriguing. Heidi has no money, no class, and no chance to succeed in life except through marriage."

Audrianna felt sick to her stomach. Niklas was Heidi's beau and Audrianna's involvement with him, however innocent, had been misinterpreted. After the ordeal she and Niklas shared, it was only natural that they would grow close. Still, Heidi was wrong. Niklas' distance was not on account of his feelings for her, rather a boyish attempt at romance—a surprise offering of marriage. He tried to discuss his plans with Audrianna last night, only she was too drunk and too sleepy to listen.

Audrianna rose from her chair. "I'll go and speak with her now," she said. "Niklas and I are friends—nothing more. Whatever Nurse Klaus may or may not think, it is altogether unacceptable to withhold care from the patients for any reason. It is negligent, unethical, and I won't stand for it." She started out the door.

"But it isn't—" Nurse Heilemann called after her.

Audrianna did not stop. She did not care whether it was proper or not. "Good morning, ladies," Audrianna addressed the women at the nurses' station. The nurses rose from their chairs, as per custom—all but Nurse Klaus. She remained seated, eyes downcast.

Audrianna spoke to her, saying, "Nurse Klaus, I would like to talk to you privately before we get too far into this day. Do you have a moment?"

Nurse Klaus looked up; Audrianna leaned forward and said, "Follow me, please."

"As you wish," the nurse whispered. Audrianna headed for the labor room and waited. Nurse Klaus finally strolled in, and Audrianna shut the doors with the unpleasant sound of dead air.

"Nurse Klaus, you've made it very apparent you have no intention of hiding your disdain for me. You don't have to like me, but you do have to respect my position. It's one thing to treat me with a lack of civility, but it's another thing altogether to mistreat our patients by failing to complete my orders to the best of your ability. You will treat our patients properly, or you cannot remain here."

Audrianna softened her voice. "I understand you believe I have acted in some way that demands an apology from me. I assure you, I have not now, nor have I in the past, conducted myself or my affairs with any malicious intent toward you. If anything I have done has caused you unhappiness, I wish you would speak up." She risked stepping closer, and then touched her on the arm. "Heidi, tell me what this is all about, please. Perhaps I can explain. Or even make amends?"

Nurse Klaus snatched away from her, tears streaming down her face. "You've ruined my life," she shouted, "and you want to know what you can do to make amends?"

Audrianna held her hands out to her in an exaggerated defense of herself. "Ruined your life? I barely even know you! You barely know me! What is it you think I have done that warrants such a slanderous accusation?"

"You've stolen him from me!" Heidi screamed. "He was mine, and you've stolen him!"

"I haven't the first idea who or what you're talking about." Audrianna played dumb unconvincingly. Niklas made it abundantly clear how he felt about his news being delivered without his sanction. It was not her place to tell Heidi about his marriage proposal.

"The hell you don't!" Heidi continued in a rage. "He loved me! We were together until you came waltzing in, with your fancy title and your American accent. He would have married me if you had not come here."

Audrianna felt a hot flush creep into her face, partly from anger and partly from the guilt of withholding the truth. She was determined to keep her temper in check and to deal with the young lady in the kindest, most compassionate way she could. "Heidi, whatever troubles you are having in your personal life is your business, not mine. I am merely doing my work—as I expect you to do, by the way. Don't cast me in the role of a villainess seductress."

"No," Nurse Klaus shook her head with teary eyes and a malicious smile. "You seem much more like a common whore to me."

Audrianna reeled a step back as if punched in the chest. "How dare you!" she sputtered. "You—are relieved of your position here. You will turn your patients over to the head nurse and leave this property."

Nurse Klaus laughed. "You don't have the authority to dismiss me."

"Yes, I do," Audrianna said evenly. "I'll see to it personally that your unpaid wages are delivered to you. Now, unless you want Dr. von Traugott to know of your filthy mouth—"

Heidi slapped her across the face.

Audrianna brought a hand to her cheek, dazed by the woman's audacity and by the ferocity of her own words. She had not intended to reciprocate venom. Now what? Strike back?

The door swung open. A single, struggling orderly entered the room carrying the body of a young woman with a protruding belly. Blood stained the bottom third of her ragged blue dress. She was unconscious; her skin was waxen and bloodless.

"Jesus!" Audrianna exclaimed, rushing forward to assess the woman. "What happened here?!"

The orderly put the woman on the delivery table and raised his blood-soaked palms. "I found her collapsed on the front steps like this," he blubbered. "She was alone, out cold."

Audrianna felt along the woman's clammy arm for a pulse, starting at her wrist, then at the neck. "She's barely alive." She motioned for Nurse Klaus to come forward. "Quickly! Heidi, help me. Put her in the stirrups so I can examine her. We've got to see what is causing this bleeding."

Heidi hefted the woman's legs into the metal stirrups as Audrianna stepped forward to insert a cold, metal speculum. As soon as she did, a geyser of blood and reproductive tissue erupted from the woman's insides and showered both of them with a bath of crimson fluid. Nurse Klaus shrieked; Audrianna pushed her back to allow the remainder of the mess to fall onto the floor. When the flood had slowed to a trickle, Audrianna stepped back up to the speculum and peered inside from every angle. "Her cervix is only partially dilated and she's hemorrhaging from her uterus," she said as she pulled the instrument out. "We must do a Cesarean section to have any chance at saving the baby."

Heidi grabbed Audrianna's arm and screamed, "No—you'll kill her! Only a surgeon can perform Cesarean!"

Audrianna wrenched away from her without reply and began quickly gathering surgical instruments. The Cesarean section method was still being debated as an acceptable alternative to forceps delivery, or worse, craniotomy. But, in this case, neither of those options was plausible. Cesarean was the only way. Audrianna had undergone thorough training in her residency on how to perform the procedure and was not about to wait for a surgeon.

Heidi followed Audrianna around the room with renewed, fiery objections. Faces of other nurses peered in from the door. "It is immoral to sacrifice the mother for the child!" she screamed. "Craniotomy must be performed. I'm going to find Dr. von Traugott!"

"Nurse Klaus!" Audrianna exploded. "There is no time! The mother cannot be saved! She has lost too much blood and is now in a state of shock. I will not turn that baby's skull to mush just so it may lie in a coffin next to her. That, to me, is true immorality." She pushed a tray of instruments into the other woman's hands. "Now, help me before there's no hope for the child, either."

Nurse Klaus reluctantly accepted the tray, and Audrianna sopped up carbolic solution with a sponge, smearing it across the unconscious woman's distended abdomen. She lifted the scalpel with steady hands and cut midline from belly button to pelvis, first through flesh, then through muscle. Freshly oxygenated blood sprayed from the uterine artery.

"Clamp! Clamp!" she shouted, and slid one of her hands into the woman's pelvis. "The uterus is completely ruptured. The baby is drowning!"

Nurse Klaus placed a metal clamp into her free hand, but Audrianna lost her grip on it almost instantly. Blood congealed on her eyelashes; her vision was impaired. "Dammit!" she cursed as the instrument slipped through her fingers into a cavity of exposed organs.

"What are you doing?" Heidi yelled. "Get the baby out!"

Audrianna plunged her arms elbow deep into the mother's innards. "I'm trying!" she screamed, abandoning her attempt to clamp the artery. "I can't get a good hold on him. He's swimming in peritoneal fluid!"

The monsoon of blood from the incision slowed to a sprinkle, and the final ounce spilled into the woman's open womb. The mother's breathing stopped, and her bodily functions were relieved onto the table and floor.

"She's dead!" Nurse Klaus cried. "You've killed her!"

Audrianna ignored her ravings. She locked her fingers around the baby's tiny ankles and pulled it out into the air, feet first, like a naked chicken. She laid the little, lifeless boy-child on top of his mother's chest. "Give me the other clamps," she commanded, "and the bulb suction."

Nurse Klaus threw the items up onto the table and Audrianna clamped the baby's umbilical cord at both ends. She inserted the bulb syringe into the child's nasal passages, removing as much fluid as she possibly could. "Heidi! Don't just stand there," Audrianna said, exasperated. "Get me some blankets!"

Heidi tiptoed over to the linen cabinet, more concerned with avoiding the mess on the floor than completing the task. She carried two baby blankets to the labor table. "I don't know why you think you need these," she muttered, "that baby is dead, just like his mother. You've killed them both."

"*Nurse* Klaus!" Audrianna swiped away the blood and sweat on her own forehead with her sleeve, and severed the baby's umbilical cord. "Is your mission to crucify me that much stronger than your compassion for this child?"

Heidi opened the blanket to receive the infant as Audrianna handed him to her. "Don't think for a second you can ease your conscience by questioning my motives," Heidi said. "I voiced my opinion about your ability to perform this procedure before you butchered the lady. You've just killed two living souls. Now you have to live with it."

Audrianna snatched the bundle from Heidi and bent the baby forward and slapped it heartily on the butt several times. "Come on, little guy," she pleaded.

The baby did not respond.

Audrianna flipped him backward into the crook of her arm. She sealed her lips around his little nose and mouth, exhaling two shallow breaths into his lungs. But there was no life beyond the synthetic rise and fall of his chest. She repeated the maneuvers twice over, each time becoming more assertive and involved with the practice. She did not notice Dirk's presence until he spoke over her shoulder. "What happened here?" he asked.

Heidi jumped in front of him, taking him by the arm and pointing at the body on the table. "She's a murderess! See for yourself!"

"Quiet!" Dirk snapped. He turned to Audrianna holding the lifeless, bloody infant. "Tell me what happened here, Dr. Foster."

Audrianna trembled. "I … The woman was bleeding to death, Doctor." She stuttered through her explanation. "Her cervix wasn't dilated, and she was close to death. I opted for a Cesarean, so the baby might at least be saved. But, but her uterus was completely ruptured, and I couldn't get the uterine artery clamped." She stopped talking.

Dirk pulled the blanket away from the baby. "What have you done for the child?" he whispered, not looking at her.

"Physical stimulation and artificial respiration," Audrianna replied without expounding.

Dirk navigated his hands underneath the bundle and lifted him up and away from Audrianna. He bent forward and gave one long, exaggerated breath into the baby's mouth and nose, then smacked the infant smartly on the bottom. A strangled, garbled noise arose from the baby's throat, followed by a whimpering cry. Dirk smacked him once again and this time the little boy responded with a piercing scream. Within a few seconds, his arms and legs began to move deliberately and his cries became consistent and strong.

"I can't believe it," Heidi whispered. "He's alive."

Dirk handed the flailing child back to Audrianna and then started to leave the room. But he did not make it. He collapsed against the doorway, swaying as if to pass out.

"Dr. von Traugott!" Audrianna exclaimed, rushing to him as a nurse and orderly held him up.

Heidi brushed in front of Audrianna and wrapped her arms around his waist. "This is all your fault!" she screamed at Audrianna. "I wish you'd never come here!"

"Orderly!" Audrianna called out. "Hurry. Take Dr. von Traugott to the exam room so I may attend to him."

"No!" Heidi protested. "She'll kill him! Look at what has happened in here! Get Dr. Stuggart!"

"No!" Dirk resisted. He addressed the orderlies. "Just help me to my office. Heidi can handle taking care of me there. I'll be fine."

His words stung Audrianna's heart like a vicious jellyfish. He had openly undermined her dictates—to the orderlies and, more importantly, to Heidi.

"Dr. von Traugott, please," Audrianna implored, pushing her hurt feelings aside. "You're ill. Let me examine you."

Dirk stood up with the assistance of orderlies. "I'll be fine," he repeated. "I just need—"

Audrianna approached, but he turned to her in anger, his eyes darkened into muted black pearls. "Dr. Foster! I said I'm fine. Take care of your patient. Now!"

"Take him," Heidi said to the orderlies. "I'll follow in a moment." She turned to Audrianna as they left. "Wait until I tell him how you've treated me; he'll insist upon *your* dismissal." She leaned forward and whispered into Audrianna's ear. "I'll see to it personally that your unpaid wages are delivered to you by tomorrow."

Audrianna clutched the still-screaming baby to her chest as if to shield it from Heidi's acid. She also felt strangely frightened, and remembered her dream. Could something from that world manifest in consequences here?

"Are you all right, Dr. Foster?" Nurse Heilemann placed her hand on Audrianna's back consolingly. It was twelve hours later, the end of a long day.

"I'm not sure," Audrianna replied. "I have a surreal feeling that I've been asleep for a month and can't quit a horrible dream." She slipped a finger into the newborn's palm, arousing a squeeze. Audrianna had left him only long enough to take care of her own basic necessities.

"You charmed a miracle today from the angel of death," said Urma, picking up the infant from the crib for his feeding, and lowering herself painfully into a rocking chair. "There is nothing horrible about that. Why don't you get some rest?"

"I didn't charm a miracle from anyone. Dr. von Traugott saved that baby, not me," Audrianna said. She looked around the room to bestow the compliment, but Dirk had not been there at all that day. Nor had Nurse Klaus. "I think he may be angry with me for performing that Cesarean without him. And now I wonder myself whether I did the right thing."

"Of course you did the right thing!" said Urma. "If you had waited for him, this little boy would be dead—I've no doubt about that. Dr. von Traugott trusts you to make decisions without his approval, when necessary. What makes you think he would be angry with you?"

Audrianna shrugged, not certain how much to share. "When he fell ill so suddenly this morning, he refused my help and he … he left the delivery room with Nurse Klaus. He never returned to check on me—on the baby, that is." Urma gave Audrianna a knowing glance. She pulled the bottle from the child's mouth and patted him on the back for a burp. The maternal silence was calming. Audrianna continued. "What I really mean to say is that I am troubled as to why he would refuse my help?"

"Dr. Foster, you're so tired you're not thinking straight," Urma said. She rose from the rocking chair with some difficulty, placed the infant into a crib, and picked up the next hungry baby with another bottle. "Why do you think he refused your help?"

"I'm not sure," Audrianna looked back down at the newborn. "Perhaps he really believes me incompetent."

"Well, that's not it!" Urma laughed. She sat back down in the rocking chair and continued, "Dr. von Traugott wanted that baby to survive. What kind of chance would the baby have if you were tending to the doctor and not the child?"

Audrianna had not thought about it that way. She could easily believe that Dirk's demeanor in the delivery room was a direct result of his concern for the newborn baby, but was less convinced that he had not made time to make it over to the ward today to check on his patients. She needed to see him now, to know he was okay.

"I think you may be right." Audrianna left the cribside and gathered her things. "I need to get some sleep. I'll see you in the morning. Thank you, Urma."

"Goodnight, Dr. Foster," said Urma, returning her attention to the little one she was feeding, humming softly and rocking along in cadence. Audrianna slipped out of the ward to look for Dirk, making inquiries and eventually realizing that no one had seen him since that morning. He had postponed his scheduled surgeries and passed his patients off to the general hospital physician. Not only was this unusual practice, it was completely out of character for Dirk. He was a hands-on clinician, obsessive in his belief that good physicians must at least speak with their patients on a daily basis in order to help them heal.

Panicked, Audrianna sped around the corner to the administrative wing and smacked right into Niklas. "Ahh!" she shrieked. She tossed her belongings into the air and bounced against the wall, clutching her chest.

"Wait! Wait! It's just me!" Niklas grabbed her by the wrists, shaking her gently. "Calm down. It's just me." He turned her loose.

Audrianna dropped her hands and blinked hard. "Oh my God, Niklas," she said, blowing out her breath, and then laughing once. "You startled me! Are you looking for Dirk, too?" Her expression turned concerned.

"No," Niklas replied. He scooped up Audrianna's coat and bag and added, "Dirk is in his office. I was looking for you."

Audrianna rolled her eyes a little. She pushed herself off the wall and ran her hand through her hair. "Okay, yes," she nodded. "Good. I need to talk to you, too, but first—let me go and see Dirk for a minute. Okay?"

Niklas caught Audrianna by the arm as she started off. "Wait, Audrianna," he half-whispered with a sneaky grin. "Dirk is busy."

Audrianna snapped her head back and raised one eyebrow. "Busy?" she asked.

Niklas nodded. "He's, uh, entertaining."

Audrianna took a step back, chewing angrily on her lip. "I see, well—" she forced a laugh, "I guess he's feeling just fine, then. He doesn't happen to be entertaining Lorna, does he?"

Niklas shrugged. "I didn't knock on the door and ask," he said.

Audrianna exhaled. She relaxed her posture and shook her head, embarrassed by her own impertinence. "I'm sorry, Niklas," she said. "That's none of my business, either. Let's go talk in my office, okay?"

"Okay," Niklas replied. He started into what he wanted to say the instant they were there. "I came to tell you that I've just received my transfer to the artillery corps, and I have to leave first thing tomorrow afternoon. I'd like to be married before then."

Audrianna leaned against her desk and stared at him. "Artillery corps? What?" She shook her head. "It's too early for you to return to active duty, Niklas. But if you must go, I feel compelled to tell you that your choice of wife—"

"I have to go back, Audrianna," he said, taking a step closer. "If I don't go now, I'm not sure I will ever be able to leave you."

Audrianna narrowed her eyes. "Leave me?"

"I love you," Niklas said, his voice cracking. "I've loved you since the first time I opened my eyes and saw you standing there in France. I invited you out last night to ask you to marry me. I thought you already knew that: Lorna."

Audrianna staggered. This was another dream—it had to be. She pulled her hands to her temples and closed her eyes, remembering Lorna's far-away words: *This isn't a prison. All you have to do is open your eyes.* Audrianna opened her eyes; Niklas was still there. "Oh, God," she whispered. "Lorna told me you wanted to be married, but she didn't say you wanted to marry me!"

"It doesn't matter," he continued with a laugh. "All that really matters is this." He pulled a velvet box from his jacket pocket and sprung the lid. Inside sat a magnificent black diamond set in prongs of muted white gold and surrounded by a cluster of smaller diamonds.

Audrianna clutched her throat as if she had swallowed it, stammering, "I—I mean, we're friends, Niklas, good friends. If I've given you the impression of something more, I'm sorry."

Niklas flinched. "We are friends, Audrianna," he fussed. "That's what makes the situation ideal. We like each other enough to make marriage a success. We have fun together. I thought you loved the idea of us getting married. You said so last night."

"I loved the idea of *you* getting married, Niklas!" Audrianna exclaimed. "Didn't you just hear what I said? I had no idea you were going to propose marriage to me!" She covered her face with her hands, scanning her memories for missed clues.

"Why not?" Niklas persisted.

"Because I'm not ready to get married, Niklas," she stalled. "I haven't finished my mission here. I haven't completed my father's work."

"You wouldn't have to leave, my love," he reasoned. "I'll be on the front lines; that's no place for a woman. You would stay here with Dirk, of course, until the war is over—even after, if you like. We can go wherever you like. Just say you'll be my bride."

Audrianna threw her hands down, completely panicked. "I don't love you, Niklas! Okay? I don't love you!" She squeezed her eyes shut and laid her hand against her breastbone; her voice lost power. "I mean, I don't love you in that way. I'm sorry."

Niklas pulled Audrianna closer even as she squirmed to move away. "Don't think I'm ignorant of your interest in Lorna," he whispered gruffly. "I know how you've suffered for those emotions you were tricked into feeling. Please don't let the fantasy of what can never be dissuade you from achieving lasting happiness and true stability. You may not think you love me now, Audrianna, but give yourself time to get used to the idea. I love and admire you for all you are. I think we have a lot in common and I know I can provide for you and a family."

Audrianna stared at him with her mouth hanging open, aghast at his knowledge of her feelings for Lorna, unable to think of anything but her own embarrassment.

"I've caught you off guard," Niklas chuckled. He set the box upon the desk and took a couple steps back. "Keep this with you and I'll wait. My new duty station is close by; I can be here within two days of your call. Once you've had time to think it over, I know you'll see how perfect it would be."

Audrianna did not speak. She did eventually nod, not knowing what she was agreeing to, but wanting to be away from him so badly she didn't really care.

Niklas hugged her. "Goodbye, for now," he whispered, and he left.

The chime clock on the wall struck 1:00 a.m. The witching hour prodded Audrianna's conscience with a guilty poker. It didn't matter, though. She could never love Niklas, and she hated herself for the reasons why. "Lorna." She whispered her name out loud, just to feel it as it passed through her lips. "Will you ever let me go?"

The next day Dirk caught Audrianna alone in her office just as she was about to leave for the day. "I heard you've taken the afternoon off," he said as he popped his head in the door. "May we speak before you leave?"

Audrianna looked down and away from Dirk as soon as she saw him, unable to look him in the eyes with ease. "I'm glad to see you're feeling better, Dr. von Traugott," she said sarcastically. "Forgive me, but I have an appointment for which I am already running late. Perhaps in the morning?" She fumbled with some of the papers she had extracted from her father's journal, stuffing them into her bag without any sense of order. She needed to be out of there in a hurry, away from Dirk before her ill temper got the better of her.

"Audrianna, please." Dirk blocked her escape by stepping quickly into her office and closing the door. Audrianna longed to push by him, but she didn't. In some abject, tortured way, she needed to hear what he had to say. "I can just imagine what you must think of me after the way I treated you yesterday," he started. "I should have come around to check on you and the newborn, but I was, preoccupied, I guess you could say."

Audrianna turned around to hide her reddening face. "Preoccupied?" she snorted. "That *is* a different way to put it. Romance isn't your strong suit, either. No wonder you and Lorna get on so well together."

"I'm sorry?" Dirk said, his tone confused.

Anger and jealousy overtook Audrianna, and she became cold. "Don't worry yourself, Dr. von Traugott," she said. "You owe me no apologies. I am your employee and nothing more."

"You know you're more than that to me, Audrianna," Dirk quietly replied.

"And because I am only that," Audrianna continued, "your insincere apologies are unnecessary. Now, if you'll excuse me, I have other business to attend to." She wheeled around and charged for the door, needing to break away in the full force of her anger before she succumbed to an all-out emotional scramble. He had hurt her with his actions. He had hurt her with his words. And he had hurt her with his blatant dishonesty. Did he really think she was just going to hand him her heart now like a foolish, infatuated child?

"Audrianna, wait." He blocked the door with his body. He stopped her with his hands and forced her to look at him. "I know you're neither foolish nor infatuated—not with me, anyway. What is it you think I've been dishonest about? I simply could not have seen you yesterday. It would've killed me. Please try to understand."

"*Killed you*? Really, Dirk—" Audrianna stopped her vocalization mid-thought. She jerked her head back and stared at him.

She had not said any of that out loud, but even that frightening thought was not what spooked her. It was his eyes. Their color had changed, not from light gray to dark gray as was their tendency, but to a completely different color. They were emeald green, just like Lorna's.

"Your eyes," Audrianna whispered, pointing to his face. "They're …"

"I know." Dirk turned away. He released his hold on her and stepped away from the door.

Audrianna did not leave. Her legs would not move and her brain would not force them to carry her. She had treated a number of patients with cirrhosis, a liver disease in which the whites of the eyes actually turned yellow, but this was not the same thing. In this case, the irises themselves changed color. The profundity of the change made Audrianna momentarily question her version of the previous night. "Dirk, I want desperately to understand what's going on here," she started.

Dirk scoffed. He cut his bright eyes toward her in unmistakable amusement. "That's funny. You say you want to understand, but you don't really want to know. How do you expect me to explain it to you with those kinds of limitations?"

Audrianna shook her head. Another thing he had in common with Lorna: they both loved riddles. Must everything be symbolic or ambiguous?

"You couldn't possibly understand, Audrianna, because nothing is symbolic or ambiguous for you. You think in absolutes! This," he said, pointing at his eyes, "is not a medical condition! It's a stigma!" He ran his hands over his face in frustration, his usual calm character now antsy and annoyed.

Audrianna looked him up and down.

"Can't you see?" he asked, pacing. "Your simple, beautiful innocence has built a fortification around you with walls so high and so insurmountable that the only thing that exists there is fantasy. You deny yourself the truth. But I'm here to tell you that life outside your walls is ugly, Audrianna. And whether you wish to hear it or not, depravity looms at your heart's door, plotting and scheming to enter into your world."

Audrianna exploded. "I am perfectly capable of recognizing and dealing with any kind of circumstance that comes my way! I'm working here, aren't I? Despite my misgivings! Since you seem to imply that wickedness may be enjoying my confidence, though, I'll have you know I am fully aware of the oddities that surround you, Lorna, and your creepy religious cult. In your hasty appraisal of my naïveté, did you even bother to consider that the reason I affix a logical explanation to everything is that I do not wish to believe that I have spent the last month in your employ, or worse still, in your close company, with you having misled me all the while?"

Dirk shook his head. "You think I am the enemy?" he asked. "Well—I guess I've trampled heavily on your feelings yesterday and today. Perhaps I've inflicted wounds so deeply on your pride that you judge me unworthy of your trust. *Everything* I have done, including having you come here and work for me, has been to safeguard you. Are you blind? Or are you just so fearless you have absolutely no sense of danger?" He stared into Audrianna's face with his strange green eyes. "I am tortured by my inability to reach you. I cannot protect you if you are immune to my warnings! My words are not powerful enough to pierce your bubble of perfect denial and I will die before I move you otherwise."

Audrianna stomped her foot. "Protect me from what, Dirk?" she cried. "Stop talking in circles and just tell me! Explain it to me in terms free of puzzles and imagery. Trust me, please. I can stand under the weight of your menacing secret—whatever it is."

Dirk pulled Audrianna into his arms. He placed his cheek on top of her head and rocked back and forth, comforting her, or maybe comforting himself, Audrianna was not sure which. A weak impulse of refusal passed in and out of her mind, but she was exhausted from fighting battles with this group. She did not care who had won, if anyone had.

"I will tell you everything, Audrianna," he said. "I promise." He nudged her away from him, just enough so he could look into her eyes. "But not here, not now." He opened his pocket watch and glanced at the time. "I want you to go to my house and wait for me there. I have a surgery scheduled for this afternoon that I really can't delay, but I'll join you as soon as I can."

"My appointment," Audrianna started.

"Can wait," Dirk finished.

Audrianna nodded, although the idea of sitting alone in his big house was unnerving. It would make more sense to carry on as she had already planned to do. She had been able to locate an address for the mother of one of the patients, Amalie Kaltenbach, mentioned in her father's journal. She had arranged a meeting with her that afternoon.

"No, Audrianna!" Dirk exclaimed, shaking her slender arms. "Please do not go and see that woman! Nothing good will come of it!"

Audrianna gaped at him; Dirk relaxed his grip on her and softened his features. "Trust me, please," he whispered. "I will explain everything in a little while. Go to my house and wait for me."

"Dr. von Traugott! Dr. von Traugott!" Nurse Heilemann's frantic wails sounded clearly through the door, followed by an urgent, persistent knocking. "Help! Please!"

Dirk threw open the door. "What it is? One of the patients?"

"No! Oh, Dr. von Traugott!" Urma cried. "It's just terrible! You have to come quickly."

Dirk stepped into the hallway and placed his arm around the shaking woman. "Calm down, Urma. Tell me. What's wrong?"

"It's Heidi. Nurse Klaus, sir," Urma sobbed, dabbing at her tears with a handkerchief. "When she didn't turn up for work, I had one of the orderlies go out to her house and check on her." Urma looked from Dirk to Audrianna and back. "They've gotten her, sir—The Children of Gavrilek."

Audrianna felt her breath stop.

"Don't be ridiculous!" Dirk chided. "That wives' tale will not be entertained in this house of healing, understand?" He withdrew his arm and turned away, pacing off a few steps.

Astonished at his defensive outcry and his lack of compassion, Audrianna took his place at Urma's side. "Calm down, Urma," she soothed her. "I'm sure everything is going to be all right. Where is she now?"

"In the main hospital ward," Urma sniffed.

"Oh, for Christ's sake!" Dirk cursed, throwing his hands up in the air. "If the staff can't keep this in the proper scientific perspective, what makes you think the patients can? We'll have a blasted mob on our hands!"

He did not wait for rebuttal, just sped down the hall toward the main ward. Audrianna followed, walking at a snail's pace to accompany Urma. Her mind raced in alternating condemnations and defenses of Dirk's behavior.

They reached the main ward just as Dirk was shoving his way through the gathering crowd. "You people get back to your beds and stay there!" he bellowed, scaring the onlookers and causing them to scatter. Audrianna and Urma followed him toward a tattered brown cloth stretcher on the floor where Nurse Heidi Klaus lay, her body stiff and hyperextended, her fingers and toes stretched and locked into place at every joint. Her skin was transparent, fluoresced by a highway of purple veins. Her eyes were infinite black holes.

"Oh!" Audrianna breathed. She crouched down next to Dirk who was already kneeling over the girl. "I've never seen anything like this," she said, although she recognized the signs as similar to those reported in lyovitalis. She placed her hand lightly on Nurse Klaus's chest to determine if she was, in fact, still breathing. "Heidi?" she called, pressing her hand deeper into the unconscious woman's sternum. "Heidi, can you hear me?"

Heidi's respirations were not detectable, and she was unresponsive in every way; she did not move or speak. She did not even blink. Her eyelids were stuck open as if sewn into place by invisible thread. Audrianna shuddered at the thought of her own mother like this.

"I think she's dead," Audrianna said, not certain but unsure of how else to describe Heidi's state.

"No," Dirk replied. "She's not dead. Not yet." He stood up and shouted for one of the orderlies. "Get the university hospital on the telephone and have the ambulance pull up out front." He was coarse, anxious, and acting in complete contrast to his generally compassionate disposition. When he directed the orderlies to take Heidi's body outside and place her in the back of the ambulance, Audrianna rose to confront him.

"What are you doing?" she demanded.

"I'm sending her elsewhere to die," he answered coolly. "She's caused quite enough trouble around here, don't you think?"

Audrianna shook her head, speechless, flabbergasted even. His callousness sickened her, and if it were not for the fact that their interaction was being closely observed, she would have told him so in those exact terms. "Dir—Dr. von Traugott," she said in a forced hush, "how can you be so cold?"

"How can you be so concerned after the way she treated you yesterday?" Dirk countered. "Are you not relieved to have to deal with her no longer?"

"Relieved?" Audrianna sputtered, struggling to remain calm. "Yes, she and I have had our personal and professional contretemps, but I could never, ever wish illness or pain on anyone!" She placed her palm against her forehead, frustrated with him and unable to hide it any longer. "The girl is dying, for God's sake, and you're behaving as though it's nothing!"

Dirk stared at her without speaking, his face an inscrutable mask.

Audrianna glared back. "It's not nothing! It's a young woman's life. And not just any young woman." She lowered her voice. "What about Niklas?"

Dirk darted his eyes to the spectators and then back to Audrianna. "Niklas?" he replied with a succession of incredulous blinks.

"Yes, Niklas," Audrianna snapped. "Or don't you care how he'll feel when he finds out the girl he once wanted to marry has died?" She laughed. "Oh, yes. I know all about it. But she probably wasn't good enough for your family, was she, Dr. von Traugott? Come to think of it, I'm probably not good enough either!"

"That's enough, Dr. Foster," Dirk said brusquely. "We'll discuss this in private later, after I deal with this issue."

"This is not an 'issue'; this is a patient!" she shouted. Her words echoed off the ceiling; the room went completely silent. Dirk reached for her arm but Audrianna backed away, screaming, "Here's another 'issue' for you to deal with, Doctor von Traugott! I quit!"

———◈———

"I've been expecting you for some time now," said Frau Kaltenbach. She opened the door and welcomed Audrianna inside, showing her to a sitting room off the kitchen. A cast-iron kettle dangled over the dying embers of the fire, swinging to and fro with the excitation of the steam.

"I'm sorry," Audrianna apologized. "I had hoped to be here earlier, but something came up at the hospital."

"Your work must keep you very busy," Frau Kaltenbach said. She brought forth a rugged old serving cart with a pair of cups and a clear glass bottle with no label. "Care for a taste of schnapps?"

Audrianna hesitated, not wanting to be rude. "I'm not sure I should."

"Dear, there is nothing wrong with taking a little now and again," Frau Kaltenbach reassured her, pouring a splash of yellow liquid into both cups and topping it off with hot water from the kettle. "Sugar?"

"Yes, thank you," Audrianna replied. She had no intention of drinking.

Frau Kaltenbach added a lump of brown granules to both cups, then handed one to Audrianna. She settled herself into the chair directly across from Audrianna with a cup of her own and turned her attention to her guest.

"Now then," she said graciously, "what brings you by?"

Audrianna pretended to take a sip of the schnapps. Afterwards, she set her glass down and cleared her throat. "I want to ask you some questions about your daughter, Amalie. You spoke with my father after her death last year, but I've been unable to locate a complete account of your discussion." She cleared her throat again.

"Your father?" Frau Kaltenbach reached into a linen box on a table beside her chair and handed Audrianna a folded handkerchief.

"Oh, thank you," said Audrianna, blotting her face with the cloth. "I'm sorry, Frau Kaltenbach. My father, Dr. Britton Foster, was one of the lead researchers on the university's study of lyovitalis. You may remember him."

"Ah yes, I see. I remember him quite well," said Frau Kaltenbach with a warm smile. "But you're mistaken. I only knew your father when Amalie was alive." She shook her head. "I never saw him again after she died. It was the other one," she bobbed her forefinger up and down, "Dr. Adler. He's the one I saw in the days following Amalie's death."

"Oh, really?" Audrianna replied, wiping her face again. The air in the room was sweltering and stale, and she, overheated and uncomfortable. "I was under the impression all the work done on the study was done postmortem. Uh—" She squinted her eyes and quickly added, "after death. I mean after death." She opened her eyes.

"No," Frau Kaltenbach replied. "Your father examined Amalie on several occasions in the months leading up to her death. He was very kind. No one outside my own people ever really cared about those monsters killing off our girls before he came along."

"Monsters?" Audrianna choked into the handkerchief.

"The Children of Gavrilek," Frau Kaltenbach went on. "I assumed that was why you were here?"

Audrianna smiled to hide her confusion. She had come to Zurich to investigate a disease, not a myth, but somehow the two had become interconnected. "Yes. It's just that—" she started and stopped, looking inward and then continuing as gently as possible. "My father wasn't overly *descriptive* in his depiction of the connection between your daughter's illness and the Children of Gavrilek. I apologize for reopening old wounds. But would you share the account with me again?"

Frau Kaltenbach smiled uneasily, perhaps to stave off tears. Her eyes connected with a memory, like a picture film that only she could see. "Amalie wasn't a bad girl," she began. "I'm convinced her beauty was her downfall. She was sweet and irresistible. Too young to understand what men really wanted from her."

Audrianna took out paper and pencil from her bag and began to write. Heat made her hands pudgy; concentration in the stuffy room was much more difficult than she would have liked. Her rate of perspiration intensified; she found it necessary to keep the handkerchief pressed to her forehead in order to keep sweat from dripping into her eyes. "Amalie had many, how do you say, gentlemen callers?" she asked.

Frau Kaltenbach shook her head. "She had many *suitors*, most no better class than she, so I never gave it a second thought when she told me she'd met someone new. But things started to change."

Audrianna scribbled a shorthand notation as the woman spoke, afraid she might miss an important detail. She would study it later when she had her wits about her: alone, cool, and unruffled.

"She started bringing new things home," Frau Kaltenbach continued. "Nearly every day. Small tokens were usual from her other callers, but not like this: dresses, fancy hats, jewelry. This man could afford the very best. He gave things to Amalie like a husband would his wife."

Or a married lover his mistress, thought Audrianna. "What else changed?" she probed. "Did anything else make this situation different?"

"She became very secretive and defiant," Frau Kaltenbach answered her. "Up until the last few months of her life, she was in her bed each night by nine o'clock. After she met this man, she started coming home later and later—some nights not at all." Frau Kaltenbach stared at her schnapps glass, shaking her head at the memory. "And when she did come home, she was beyond exhausted—tired, withdrawn, and empty. I tried to punish her, to keep her locked up inside the house, but she would simply sneak out after I had fallen asleep. It was like she was possessed from the want of this man and no amount of reasoning could deter her from going to him."

A sexually transmitted disease, Audrianna considered. Her father's notes had mentioned the possibility that gonorrhea or syphilis could be involved. "Did you ever meet him?" she asked.

"Goodness no!" Frau Kaltenbach exclaimed. "It wouldn't do for a gentleman like that to be seen with the likes of us. I never even knew what part of town she was going to until I followed her out that last night." She swallowed the rest of her schnapps, allowing the rim to linger on her lips until the final drop slid into her mouth. She set the cup down and said, "You don't believe in the Children of Gavrilek, do you, Dr. Foster?"

Audrianna stopped writing. Had she come off as condescending? "What makes you say that?" She blotted away more perspiration, fanning herself afterwards.

Frau Kaltenbach smiled without mirth. "I don't think Dr. Adler believed me either. It wasn't until after I showed him the watch, with the monster's emblem, that he realized I was telling the truth."

"I am sorry, Frau Kaltenbach," said Audrianna. "I must admit, I know so little about the story that I don't know what to believe. What is the 'monster's emblem'?"

Frau Kaltenbach sighed. "Do you have children, Dr. Foster?"

Audrianna shook her head. "I can only imagine how difficult it must be for a mother."

"I could see her growing ill before my eyes. I thought if I followed her, I could prevail on the gentleman's sensibilities. Her behavior had become so erratic. She was sleeping all day, barely eating. Then she would wander the streets, wrapped up in one of those fancy furs he'd given her. Ask her what she was doing, and she'd just laugh or stare blankly into space."

Steeling herself to go on, Frau Kaltenbach poured another two inches of schnapps and held the bottle up in offering to Audrianna who shook her head. Frau Kaltenbach added water and sugar, and continued. "I pretended to fall asleep early, and when she slipped out I followed her. Down dark, dirty streets, nowhere a decent person would travel. She disappeared inside a run-down shack, hidden way off the main street."

"Do you think she met this man there before that night?" Audrianna dabbed her face again with the handkerchief. Her nose began to run; the cloth was completely dampened.

"Does it matter where they met?" Frau Kaltenbach came back with a whiff of annoyance. "She was under his control. He was directing her movements with his thoughts, bringing her to him like a rabbit to a trap, only the bait he used was love."

"What are you saying?" Audrianna lifted her voice and made a twisted face. "Are you telling me you think he cast some kind of spell on her?"

"He did!" cried Frau Kaltenbach. "That's what they do. They pry into your mind, manipulate your thoughts. They seduce you and make you fall in love until you willingly surrender your soul to them. Soul thieves! That's what they are. You doctors call it anything you want, but the common people know what it really is. It's the Children of Gavrilek."

Audrianna bit her lip. A thought of Lorna fleeted through her mind. She focused. Having never grown up around superstition, she was not sure how to react to it being taken literally. Furthermore, she was confounded by her father's inclination to accept this tale. There had to be something more. Something she was not seeing. Amalie's change in mentation could be related to cerebral deterioration—consistent with an aggressive form of syphilis or gonorrhea. That would certainly weaken Dirk's diagnosis of Landry's paralysis and place lyovitalis into the realm of cerebropathy or cerebropsychosis. Was that where her father had been going with this? She wished she could think about it more clearly. Why was the room spinning?

"Are you all right, Dr. Foster?" Frau Kaltenbach asked with concern.

Audrianna leaned forward on her elbows to steady herself. She placed her head into her hands and dropped the handkerchief on the floor. Something was wrong. "I am not shertain," she said, trying in vain to enunciate clearly. "It would sheem I am ecksheptionally, inek—splikably inebriated." She laughed uneasily because she had not drank a drop.

Frau Kaltenbach sat unaffected—a habitual drinker, Audrianna considered. But then another idea suddenly occurred to her. She looked at the handkerchief where it had fallen. "Frau Kaltenbach, have you put anyshing on that cloth—silver polish or, or perhapsh another cleaning sholution?"

Frau Kaltenbach looked shocked. "Nothing!" She lifted the lid of the box and looked at the remaining cloths. "Those handkerchiefs belonged to Amalie! I would never use them for cleaning!"

Audrianna rubbed her eyes. "Has anything, um, shpilled inshide the box?"

Frau Kaltenbach peered into the box. "I don't think so." She dug to the bottom of the box with her hands, her fingernails skidding along the wood as she explored the contents. "Wait! Something has!" She held up a small vial. The cork had slipped below the lip of the bottle, creating a gap. Only a minute amount of fluid remained inside. She held it to her nose and said, "It's Amalie's perfume. You're quite right. It has spilled all over these handkerchiefs! What a mess!"

Frau Kaltenbach placed the vial on the serving cart and began pulling out each of the soiled cloths to examine the saturation. Audrianna picked up the little bottle and sniffed the contents deeply. Frozen fumes seared her skull. "Oh my God!" she gasped, letting the vial drop to the floor next to the handkerchief. "Where did she get that?"

"A gift from that cursed man, I'd venture. Sweet smelling stuff, must be expensive," Frau Kaltenbach replied. "It was with the rest of her belongings when she … After I found it, I put it into this box with her handkerchiefs." She stopped sorting through the handkerchiefs and leaned back in the chair. "Oh my," she whispered, "I don't feel at all well."

Audrianna seized the handkerchiefs from her, throwing all of them, and the one on the floor, back into the linen box. She scooped up the vial and raced for the front of the room, holding her breath.

"Dr. Foster? What's wrong?" Frau Kaltenbach called after her.

Audrianna opened the door and set the box on the ground. She inhaled the cold, clear air for a few moments, then closed the door and returned to the sitting room. She opened a small window inside the room and let the chilling breeze blow in. After her head cleared, Audrianna said, "Frau Kaltenbach, that *wasn't* perfume. It was a very powerful anesthetic called chloroform."

No wonder Amalie's behavior had been so bizarre. She had unknowingly been drugging herself with chloroform. Audrianna could think of no reason—no respectable reason—why a man would purposely drug a woman. She steeled herself with her growing hypothesis. The wind that chased the dangerous vapors from the room caused the fire to flare briefly, and then died down quickly. Smoldering coals dwindled into heatless ash, leaving only coldness and smokiness, and many, many unanswered questions.

"Frau Kaltenbach, you told me Dr. Adler didn't believe you until you showed him this—'monster's emblem.' What did you mean?"

Frau Kaltenbach shook her head. For a moment, Audrianna thought she had been frightened into silence. But then the words came, rapid and unbridled. "After Amalie disappeared into the building, I walked back home. I didn't feel safe there. I wished I had waited. I should have waited. Or I should have knocked on the door and made my presence known. But I didn't. She didn't come home for four days, and I went back to that garbage-strewn shack to look for her. She was already dead."

Darkness announced an ending to the sun's creep across the sky. A chill pierced Audrianna's bones with phantom bayonets. She began to tremble.

"On the floor inside that shack, under the bed," Frau Kaltenbach continued, "I found a solid silver watch. It was etched with the monster's emblem. A snake," said Frau Kaltenbach. "A snake slithering up a wizard's staff."

Audrianna took a sharp breath. Combined images of serpent and staff were associated with the healing arts. Amalie's gentleman suitor was either a doctor or an apothecary; Audrianna's father must have suspected it, too—he saw Amalie using the perfume, or perhaps *she* told him. "Gavrilek" in his journal was not an endorsement of myth, but an acknowledgement of a medical conspiracy. It would be very easy in this town to conduct unauthorized medical experiments or test new drug therapies under the façade of researching a legitimate disease process. If the patient population could be frightened into believing the illness was of supernatural origin, the disastrous outcomes would go unpunished.

Audrianna took a chance on a hunch. "Did the watch have any writing on it?" she asked. "A name or initials, perhaps?"

"It did, under the lid," said Frau Kaltenbach. "But with these old eyes, I couldn't make it out and Dr. Adler never said." She lowered her head.

Audrianna patted her hand. "Don't distress yourself. May I take a look?" she asked.

"I sold it to Dr. Adler," Frau Kaltenbach replied. "He paid me very well for it."

I bet he did, Audrianna thought. Rage coursed through her veins. Dr. Adler had recognized the name on the watch and purchased it to protect the owner. Or maybe *he* was Amalie's mystery lover. Before Audrianna's father had an opportunity to expose him, Dr. Adler sent him packing as an unreliable schizophrenic. What a miserable, deceitful man.

Audrianna interlocked her fingers on top of her head, thinking. What was she going to do? What would her father want her to do? He wanted her to be safe, whatever she did—he had told her that.

Safe. *Safe!* She flashed back to his final moments.

"Safe ... my child ..."

Of course she would be safe ... He seemed to be trying to speak, but had exhausted his energy. His hands moved up to his neck where he fished a leather pouch from beneath his undershirt. Finally, he unearthed a metal key and offered it to her.

The key swung to the tremor of his hand and Audrianna took it, momentarily transfixed.

"Father, what is this to?"

She shook his shoulders gently, but nothing. She had a sudden awareness of emptiness in the room ...

"Father!"

He was not telling her to be safe. He was giving her the key to get into a safe. Dr. Adler's safe! By God, that was exactly what she intended to do.

———◦———

"Dammit!" Audrianna mumbled. She watched as the bulky flashlight she had borrowed from Mr. Brindle's workshop slipped from her hand and plummeted to the ground. Impact extinguished the light. Her arms and fingers were like jelly after her climb up the huge sycamore outside the school of medicine; she readjusted her hold on the tree. It was only after she found all the doors padlocked that she saw the partially open window at the back of Dr. Adler's office. The idea was remotely desperate, but not so much that it kept her from scampering up the branches like a monkey—as close to scampering as she could manage in a long skirt.

Audrianna looked at the crescent moon, considering whether or not to continue. She was tired. If she climbed down to retrieve the light, she might not make it back up. She took in the light from the street lamps, combined with moonlight, and decided it should be enough to at least feel her way to Dr. Adler's safe—if it was still there. Hoisting herself forward, she held onto a limb above her head and tottered toward the window like a tightrope walker. The wood began to bend and crack beneath her weight, and she jumped for the stone ledge. Her fingers instinctively grabbed at seams in the bricks like a spider on a web. She caught her breath and convinced herself that looking down was the worst thing she could possibly do.

The window sash was wedged in place, making it necessary for her to snake herself, feet-first, through the narrow opening. After inching her chin under the window, she dropped forward to her knees with a clumsy thud, tumbling forward onto her elbows. Instantly, she regretted her decision to break in. She listened intently for signs she had been detected, letting her eyes adjust to the gloom. She had not really thought about what she would say if someone caught her. If her suspicions about Dr. Adler were true, he would be unlikely to intercede on her behalf. She realized jail or deportation was a realistic possibility.

Danger twisted a knife in Audrianna's gut, inducing her to a quadrupedal scamper across the floor to the niche underneath Dr. Adler's desk. Darkness teased her eyes. Even the safe, which sat directly in front of her, danced wickedly inside its own dark shadow. Slamming doors and voices began to sound inside the building. Audrianna's courage became fueled by anger; there was no way she was leaving without seeing inside that safe.

She crept out from under the desk on tender knees to explore the metal casing of the lockbox. There was no keyhole immediately apparent, but as she continued her sweep around the entire frame, she discovered a small, unnoticeable crevice on the lateral edge of the door. With frantic fingers, she removed the key from around her neck, inserted it into the hole, and turned it counterclockwise. Her anxiety transformed into excitement as the bolt disengaged and sprung the door open. She reached inside the safe with the curiosity of a thousand cats and pulled out a stack of loose papers, a book, and a watch—a heavy, silver pocket watch ornately decorated with the rod of Asclepius: The emblem of the monster.

Audrianna tilted the watch in the moonlight but could not make out the engraving. The rhythm of rattling keys bounced with the beat of footsteps, crescendoing nearer. She heard Dr. Adler's voice debating someone unknown to her. "A woman you say? Crawling into my office? It's that Foster girl, I know it! Go secure the building while I investigate inside. Now, man! Before she gets away!"

Audrianna plunged both arms into the bowels of the safe one last time. She latched onto a small metallic box. She should have recognized it as a surgeon's kit, but did not make the connection until after she opened the lid and sliced her finger with the scalpel.

"Damn!" she cried, the box spilling to the floor. Sticky liquid gummed her fingernails and tips. She wiped her forefinger across her blouse and jammed the finger into her mouth. A shadow appeared behind the pebbled glass separating the outer room. She stuffed the papers, the book and the watch in her bag and forced herself back through the window. She had just pulled her feet through and edged to the side of the window when the light switched on.

"What is this?" Dr. Adler exclaimed, no doubt spotting the droplets of blood leading from the safe to the windowsill. "My safe! I've been robbed!" Footsteps clomped toward the window. She saw fingers wrap under the window and lift, unable to budge the pane. Light from the room was blocked—a face pressed against the glass, examining the outside. The face disappeared; the footsteps fell back.

Audrianna had few options. A leap to the branch would be seen. She crept along the ledge toward the next office to check the window there. Again, she heard Dr. Adler's voice, this time from a darkened room. "*Hallo! Ja!*" he spoke in German. "My safe has just been looted! Everything was taken. You'd better come here as quickly as you can!" He slammed the phone down and pattered away.

Audrianna wondered if he called the police or a co-conspirator? Either way, she did not have much time before she was captured by the security officer. She edged along the ledge until she came to another tree and climbed onto a broad limb, lowering herself to hang from it. Audrianna dropped to the slope of grass behind the building, scanned for witnesses, and headed for the street. She found a horse-drawn carriage parked and roused the sleeping driver. "Ausleiden Boarding House," she whispered, her voice scratchy from her time in the cold night air.

The driver rubbed his eyes and looked at her bloody hand and clothing. "Are you sure you don't need a doctor first?"

"No, I'm fine. Please hurry," Audrianna told him. The driver switched the horses into a trot and Audrianna sat forward on tenterhooks. After a few minutes, the taxi stopped in front of her house. She paid the driver and stumbled in through the front door, catching Mrs. Brindle off guard as she came out of the kitchen.

"Bloody hell!" Mrs. Brindle screamed.

Audrianna threw out her hands and shushed her. "No. No. Mrs. Brindle, please," she quietly begged. "Look, it's my finger. I cut myself. I'm all right." She held up her injured finger and tracked sideways up the staircase, holding strong eye contact, and adding, "I'll just go get cleaned up, okay?" She broke away and charged into her room. She adjusted the lamplight as high as it would go and dove into her bag. She pulled out the pocket watch. Fumbling fingers sprung the lid; trembling lips read the inscription: *Dr. Britton Foster.*

"God!" Audrianna collapsed to her knees and turned her face upward, clutching the watch in her fist. She searched inward for several long minutes and finally said to herself, "How can this be?" Her voice turned desperate. "Father, how can this be?"

Audrianna snatched the book from her bag, *The Children of Gavrilek.* Its cover was faded and frayed as though it had been in and out of a thousand hands since the time of its creation.

She opened the cover and read the introduction.

The Children of Gavrilek

In the early period of time known as the Middle Ages, when all of Europe sought prosperity through war, there erupted divisions of social class that exist to this day. In that time of frequent wars, when husbands were gone for years at a time, a secret sport of hunt arose amongst women of rank and nobility.

Under cover of darkness and shrouded in mystery, these ladies met in furtive household covens for the purpose of entertainment. At these gatherings, a paid huntsman produced a creature of sexual myth and fantasy, the incubus, for them to enjoy as they pleased. Once completely exhausted of its sexual wiles, the beast was then slaughtered and burned over a raging fire for the women to watch and enjoy.

Born without a soul and with an inability to reproduce on its own, the incubus was extinct by the age of the Renaissance. Their magical lineage survives now only through the Children of Gavrilek. These unfortunate hybrids, spawned through the unions of captured creatures and their mistresses, are human in appearance but possess unearthly abilities of mind control and subliminal manipulation. Aided by their beauty, their powers, and their sexuality, the Children of Gavrilek purge human hosts of their souls in order to survive, rendering them lifeless and unrecognizable to God.

They hide behind the inherited titles of their mothers and puppeteer the human race for enjoyment, vying the covens of old against each other for domination of the world. Their only real weakness is love, the influence of which is lethal.

Audrianna closed the book. She dumped the mess of loose papers on the floor and read her father's handwriting on the first page: *In order to save the soul, one must destroy the mind.* She gurgled; her hand cupped her mouth. Audrianna flipped to the next page, and the next, and the next—each with the same opening line, followed by individual medical histories and progress notes of the patients that *he* was conducting mind-altering experiments on—including Amalie Kaltenbach. He *was* insane; Dr. Adler was telling the truth.

Audrianna lay down on the floor with her eyes closed, heart pounding beneath her ribcage. Time ran away with her mind. She was ruined. The Women's Medical College of Pennsylvania already had scruples about issuing a medical diploma to someone with a bipolar disorder. This folly would do her in. The state medical board would pull her license; she would be barred from practice. Her distrust, her stubbornness, her relentless pursuit of her father's illusion had cost her career and had quite probably paved the way for an extended stay in prison.

A knock came at the door. "Dr. Foster," Mrs. Brindle said in a tremulous voice, "the Kantonspolizei are here, dear. They want you to come down."

"I'm sure they do," Audrianna half-whispered. "I've made a terrible, terrible mistake."

Mrs. Brindle came in uninvited and helped Audrianna up from the floor, saying, "Now, now. It can't be as bad as all that." She brushed the dust off Audrianna's dress, and then handed her a handkerchief. "You didn't kill anyone, did you?"

Audrianna blew her nose and then sniveled. "No. I stole these things from someone's private safe." She gestured toward the watch and the papers scattered across the floor. "And the funny thing is, the person I stole from was obviously trying to protect my father's dignity by keeping these things hidden."

Mrs. Brindle patted her arm and said, "Come on then, dear. If he's as generous as all that, he won't leave you to hang on the yardarm. Right?"

Audrianna gave her a fleeting, sad smile. Maybe so. Maybe she and Dr. Adler could talk this out without any ensuing criminal charges. They walked together down the stairs where three policemen stood waiting for her by the door. They wore stiff uniforms and stiff expressions; their hands rested on their guns.

"Audrianna Foster?" One of the men called her name loudly, even though she was only three feet away.

"Yes," Audrianna replied, gulping down a breath. Mrs. Brindle wrapped her arm around her for support.

"You are being placed under arrest by the district magistrate of Zurich," the policeman continued, "for the murder of Dr. Gustav Adler."

CHAPTER 9

"All right! Yes! I was there!" Audrianna admitted. "But I didn't kill him. He was alive when I left!"

A small piece of plaster fell from the crumbling ceiling and landed in her hair. The room was damp and confined, with one door, no windows and exposed bricks dribbling a hundred years worth of sludge onto the concrete floor. The conditions were enough to rattle the most hardened criminal, much less Audrianna who had never even seen the inside of a police station before now.

"I am Inspektor Bättig," said the man, folding his hands before him on the desk. He convicted her with prolonged silence, sentenced her with his stare. His light skin and light hair disguised his age with as much precision as the mulch of coarse hair over his lip disguised his expression. "This part of the building is very old, yet it will remain standing—provided you can manage to contain further outbursts, Fräulein."

"I'm sorry," Audrianna said, aware of her precarious position. "Really, I am. I just. I just don't understand what is happening here. Honestly, Inspector. Do I look like a killer?" It was a stupid question. Audrianna knew that. But surely he could see the absurdity of the accusation. She was a woman and a doctor, both traditional contradictions of the idea.

Bättig did not reply. Instead, he took a draw on his malodorous cigar and puffed it out. "You look … bloody," he said.

Audrianna laid her hand on the detective's desk and flicked her finger. "I cut myself. Rather badly. As a matter of fact, if you have a first aid kit anywhere—"

He cut her off. "You said you left him alive. What time was that?" he asked.

Audrianna focused her scattered energy. "Probably around ten o'clock or so," she stammered.

"I see," Inspektor Bättig nodded. "2200 hours. And how is it that you came to be in Dr. Adler's dark, locked office at that time of night, Fräulein?"

Audrianna thought quickly. If he knew her to be capable of breaking and entering, he might think her capable of murder as well. On the other hand, if she were caught in a mistruth, she would lose all credibility. What she needed was a nice mix of the two, a half-truth that would easily allow her to follow one direction or the other if pressed.

"It's Dr.—Dr. Foster. I've been working on a medical research project that Dr. Adler was well acquainted with. Knowing he was leaving the university very soon, and having no idea where he might live, I went to his office hoping to share with him some important information I had acquired during the course of the day."

"And?"

"And he wasn't there, so I left," Audrianna concluded.

Bättig made a tent with his hands and regarded her over them with a smile. "That's interesting, *Fräulein Foster*," he said, emphasizing the civilian address. "You have told me both that he 'was alive when you left' and that 'he wasn't there.' How do you know he was alive without having seen him?" He took another puff from his cigar in an exaggerated fashion and leaned forward to meet Audrianna's eyes. "Fräulein, when exactly, and under what circumstances *did* you see Dr. Adler? Before or after you went climbing in the trees outside his office? Before or after his throat was cut? Perhaps *as* it was cut—by you?"

"What!" Audrianna cried. Several small chunks fell from the ceiling again, this time thumping the detective in the head and lodging in his mustache. He shot her an aggravated look and picked the fragments out of his mustache.

Audrianna apologized profusely. She rose to brush the white dust from his jacket, but he motioned her back into her chair with a stern look. "Sit. Please."

Audrianna obeyed, but she could barely sit still in that vindictive little chair. Its unyielding hardness laughed at her crisis and mocked her shame. It tortured her with her own lies and mistakes. It concealed from her its verdict—freedom or incarceration? She bounced her leg; her father's voice resonated in her inner ear, echoing like a phonograph stuck on a phrase. *Promise me you will continue my work.* Audrianna had continued it, all right. She had allowed it to possess her, to take control of her sanity. She had written this ending.

"Fräulein, did you or did you not see Dr. Adler last night, alive or otherwise?" the detective asked.

Audrianna bowed her head and replied, "Yes, I saw Dr. Adler alive. Or rather, I heard him. We did not speak, and I do not know if he saw me."

"Go on."

Audrianna continued, "I was hiding on the ledge outside his office when I heard his voice. He sounded perfectly healthy when I left."

"On the ledge?"

"That's right," Audrianna hunched her shoulders. "I snuck into his office through a broken window, and then opened his safe with a key my father, his former research partner, had given me."

"Why?"

"I believed Dr. Adler was hiding information from me, as well as evidence of some kind of medical conspiracy. Yes, I stole things from his safe, but I didn't kill him," Audrianna finished. "I have no idea who might've wanted him dead."

The Swiss officer got up from his desk and walked around to where she sat. His body was short and thick; he had a slight wobble in his legs. The half-smoked cigar dangled from his lips like a permanent attachment. "Forgive me if I don't believe you, Fräulein," he said, perching on the desk. "The campus security guard tells me Dr. Adler accused you straight off of breaking into his office, accused you by name, and then sent him to lock the building down. I have a driver who reports picking up a passenger of your description right outside the university and dropping her off at your boarding house. He said the woman was covered in blood."

Audrianna looked down at the dried, crusty streakings of blood that covered her hands and arms, her dress and shoes. "But that's from my finger, see?" She held up her index finger once more. "I cut it on a scalpel in Dr. Adler's surgical kit. And I didn't have anything to wrap it up with."

"A scalpel. How interesting," said Bättig. "I have a university physician lying dead in his office. His throat is sliced open with his own scalpel."

"His own scalpel?" Audrianna whispered. She pulled her hands to her throat.

"Yes," Bättig drew the word out on another puff of smoke, and then added, "Tell me, Fräulein, have you ever heard of fingerprint analysis?"

Audrianna shook her head.

"Our fingerprints uniquely identify us," said Bättig, closely regarding his own fingertips. "Fingerprint analysis is a new science in which we are able to compare fingerprints left at the scene of a crime to those of a suspect. It is supposed to be error-proof, because no two sets of fingerprints are identical." He leaned in closer to her. "We found dozens of bloody fingerprints in that office, Fräulein Foster. Now, is there something more you would like to tell me?"

The door swung open in a swoosh, pounding the wall and precipitating another flurry of plaster from above. "Don't say another word, Audrianna," Lorna said, looking like she stepped off the cover of a fashion magazine.

Audrianna jumped to her feet. "Lorna," she breathed. "Thank God. Help me, please! They think I killed Dr. Adler." Audrianna fidgeted with her hands for a moment, then gave into her longing. She flung her arms around Lorna and clung. Audrianna stifled the flare of desire she felt as she touched Lorna, recognizing her displacement of emotions.

Lorna held Audrianna tightly against her body in a protective embrace and spoke over her shoulder to Bättig. "On whose authority do you hold this woman?" she asked.

Bättig rolled his eyes and replied, "I act on behalf of the district prosecutor of Zurich. Who are *you*?"

"I am Countess Lorna Mehlinger, great niece of Kaiser Wilhelm II," Lorna informed him.

Inspektor Bättig laughed. "Impressive title," he said. "Too bad we're not in Germany."

"Insolent fool," Lorna snapped. "This lady is not only a close friend of mine, but of Dr. von Traugott's as well. She is also an American citizen. You will release her at once."

The inspector casually flipped the remaining dust from his hair and then reached into one of the desk drawers to remove a pair of handcuffs. "Neither you nor Dr. von Traugott have enough influence or money to get your friend out of this," he said, pulling a clinging Audrianna away from Lorna and fastening metal cuffs to her wrists. "I believe we have more than enough evidence to detain her for the murder of Dr. Gustav Adler."

Audrianna began to cry. She did not want to but could not help it. Lorna took her face between gloved hands and wiped her tears away. "Don't cry, darling," she said. "I won't let them do this to you. Give me one day, two at the most. I'll get Dirk and be back. Okay?"

Audrianna nodded her head, trying to control her sobs.

"And you," said Lorna, addressing Bättig. "When you and your family have nowhere else to go but the poorhouse, you'll regret the day when you underestimated my influence."

"Perhaps," Bättig replied, leading Audrianna out the door. "But it will come too late to keep your friend from the guillotine."

———•◦•———

"Jailor! Open this door at once!"

Audrianna looked up at Dirk and Lorna where they stood partially visible through the metal bars of her cell. Dirk wore a black tailored suit and Lorna a creamy-blue afternoon dress with a matching coat and hat. They both looked as flawless as mannequins, taking her in with matching green eyes, glowering as if they could not believe the sight of her.

"This woman's condition is an outrage!" Dirk shouted at the jailor. "When I spoke with the Kommandant, he assured me she would be treated in a manner befitting a lady of her class. Who is responsible for this insult?"

The jailor inserted a key into the latched iron plate on the door. "This isn't a hotel, sir. She was kept apart from the others, and given extra blankets and extra portions of food. I can't help if she won't eat."

Audrianna diverted her eyes to the untouched breakfast tray on the table. The thought of eating was disgusting to her, sickening to the point of nausea. She was confused, exhausted, and depressed, conditions that excluded anything but the tendency to perpetuate more of the same.

Dirk stepped inside while Lorna hovered at the gate. He pulled up the only chair and faced her alongside her cot. He touched her tenderly on the arm. "Why aren't you eating, Audrianna?" he asked.

Audrianna looked away, ashamed of how she must appear to him, to both of them. She wore the same dress she had worn the night of the murder, stained with the blood from her injuries. Her hair was filthy and matted, and her face was spotted with patches of makeup she had not cried away yet.

"I didn't kill him, Dirk," Audrianna whispered, ignoring his question. "Please tell me you know I'm not a killer."

Dirk took both of her hands in his. "Audrianna, look at me."

She flashed her eyes toward him, but did not turn her head.

"Will you look at me?" he asked again, placing his fingers against the side of her face and turning her his way. "I know you didn't kill anyone, but we're going to have a hard time convincing everyone else of that."

Audrianna nodded her head in acknowledgment.

"The Kantonspolizei found your bloody fingerprints all over that room," Dirk continued. "They were on Dr. Adler's empty safe as well as the scalpel."

"I told them I was in there!" Audrianna cried. She bounced her hands off her thighs and held up her finger. "I cut myself on that scalpel when I was snooping through his stuff. It's my blood! Not his."

Dirk shook his head and said, "There is no way to prove whose blood it was, Audrianna. Dr. Adler was a well-known figure in this community and the public is clamoring for a speedy conviction. You can imagine how easy it is going to be for them to—what's the American phrase? Throw the book at a foreigner."

"But I didn't do it!" Audrianna whined. "I thought Dr. Adler was participating in some kind of medical malfeasance." She put one hand on her forehead and gesticulated with the other. "There's this, this crazy local folklore surrounding lyovitalis." She snapped her fingers. "The Children of Gavrilek, remember? What Frau Heilemann was saying about Heidi. I thought Dr. Adler was exploiting peoples' beliefs in order to conduct unethical experiments on the young women in the community. So, yes, I broke into his office to see if I could find any evidence!" Her posture crumpled. "The only evidence I found was against my own father." Audrianna started to cry.

Lorna moved in from the doorway and Dirk turned to look at her. She reached into her handbag and retrieved a golden cigarette case, flicking it open with her thumb and placing a thin stick of tobacco in her mouth. She lit it with a matching lighter and inhaled as deeply as she could, breaking eye contact with Dirk only long enough to blow off the smoke.

"Lorna, Dirk, please," Audrianna pleaded between sobs. "I am guilty of many things, but not murder!" She wiped away her tears with the backs of her hands. "Please help me. I have nowhere else to turn."

"We're *here* to help you," Dirk said gently as he pulled her into his arms. His touch felt genuine, solid, and protectoral. Audrianna snuggled against his chest and closed her eyes. "Your preliminary inquiry was held earlier today," he continued. "The district magistrate has decided enough evidence exists to authorize a jury trial."

"Why wasn't I there?" Audrianna sniffed. "Don't I have the right of publicity? To defend myself? To have counsel and witnesses?"

"The laws here are not the same as in America," Dirk quietly answered. He rubbed her back. "Preliminary proceedings for criminal charges are performed in secret in Europe, which really is fortunate in your case because the public is not on your side."

Audrianna sat quietly, unsure of what else to do or say.

Dirk pushed her back to arms length; Audrianna opened her glistening eyes and looked at him. "Lorna and I have used every bit of influence we have to secure your release from this pre-trial confinement," he said. "All of your belongings are being packed up and moved from your boarding house to my estate as we speak. Lorna has gotten the German government to agree to offer you sanctuary there—since you are the wife of a German officer."

Audrianna gaped. "Since I'm—what?"

Dirk pulled a small velvet box from his inside pocket and placed it in her hand, lowering his voice. "I found this in your office. You may want to put it on. Niklas has taken leave from his post, and will meet us tomorrow night just inside the border, so you may be married."

"Married! But I, I ..." Audrianna stammered.

"But what, Audrianna?" Lorna asked, coming in close to speak for the first time. Her voice was low and controlled, although irritability was detectable. Audrianna looked at her. Lorna understood all her reasons for not wanting to marry Niklas, and yet here she was, pressing her to voice an explanation.

"Dirk, would you leave us alone for a few minutes?" Lorna asked him, dropping her cigarette on the floor and crushing it with her foot. "We'll meet you in the hallway in a few minutes. There's a mob outside. See if you can't arrange for a guard or two to take us out."

Dirk glanced between the two of them, nodded and left.

Audrianna stood up and walked toward Lorna. "I want to feel your arms around me," she said. The words flew from her mouth quickly and without remorse.

"I know," Lorna whispered. She stood her ground, too stiffly. "I can feel your thoughts. They hunt me down like a rabid dog and maul me until the pain makes me crazy."

Audrianna raised her arms toward her, but Lorna stepped back. "No—not a good idea," she said. "I don't want you to be confused about what we're doing here."

Audrianna shook her head. "I'm not the one who's confused. It's you and Dirk who think that you can make decisions about my life without my consent, despite how I feel, or don't feel."

"Audrianna," Lorna snapped. "They are going to cut—off— your—head! Do you understand that?"

Audrianna laughed, bitterly. "So I die instantly, or I die slowly over a lifetime with a man I don't love, being his wife, bearing his children, dreaming all the time of someone else. Loving someone else. The first option seems far less painful to me."

Lorna held her palms out and tried to reason with her. "Listen to me," she said. "After you are married and away from this mess, all the things you have felt for me will mean nothing. I will mean nothing to you. Do you hear me? Don't make a foolish choice based on this ill-conceived infatuation of something we both know can never be."

"*Infatuation*," Audrianna sneered. "Damn you," she spat. "What gives you the right to tell me how I will feel and when I will feel it? You know perfectly well I fell in love with you the day we met! I loved you even after I discovered all of your lies, and God forgive me, I love you now. Don't think for one instant that you can wish it away just because it's inconvenient for you."

Lorna grabbed her arms and Audrianna felt instantly incapacitated, unable to move or speak. Her concentration slowed to a crawl as a familiar intoxication began to slur her thoughts.

"It's more than inconvenient for me," Lorna hissed. "You've made me weak and vulnerable. The harder I try to let you go, the more difficult you are to overcome. More importantly, it's *inconvenient* for you, you and your unrealistic fantasies. You mock me with your proclamations of love while you act the martyr. If you spent half as much time examining the truth of our relationship versus what you would like it to be, you would see that I'm the one who is making the sacrifice, not you!"

Lorna took the small black box from Audrianna's hand, opened it and placed the ring on her finger. "I am saving you from yourself. You will marry Niklas, live a long, happy life and forget you ever knew me. Now let's go," she said, dragging her into the hall and passing her arm off to Dirk. "No guard?" she asked him.

"No guard. We're on our own," Dirk replied.

"Well—nothing new there," Lorna said. She reached into her silk handbag and pulled a .38 special. The latch released; the cylinder spun; the hammer cocked. Lorna put the gun back into her bag and pet Audrianna's head, whispering, "I know you're prone to dramatic outbursts, darling. But do step out of character for once and stay calm. I'm not ever going to let anyone hurt you—not ever."

Audrianna swallowed hard. Her bladder felt loose.

Dirk escorted Audrianna out the door of the building and down the stairs as Lorna followed. When they emerged on the public side of the wall, a crowd of reporters attacked them.

"Did you kill Dr. Adler over discovery rights, Fräulein?" a man in the front shouted. "Did your father develop a cure for lyovitalis?"

A cameraman squeezed in and captured Audrianna's picture, then another, then another.

"Step aside," Dirk barked at them. He nudged through the crowd with a prominent elbow, protecting Audrianna from the front while Lorna came closer and guarded her from behind.

"Dr. von Traugott, did you bankroll the lyovitalis research project to negate the curse associated with your hospital?" yelled a reporter as the three pushed through the crowd with Dirk leading the way.

Audrianna felt a pain in her throat. She glanced back at Lorna. Dirk pushed more aggressively through the swarm.

"Fräulein Foster, were you aware Dr. von Traugott was a silent partner in your father's research? Were you aware that all documented cases of lyovitalis in the city were women who were employed at one time or another at the refugee hospital?"

Audrianna's eyes stretched open. Her legs weakened; she stumbled with her heart pounding in her ears. Dirk swept her up into his arms, kicking forward with one of his legs to keep the people away.

Lorna darted in front of Dirk. She pulled her weapon and pointed it straight ahead, finger to trigger. The crowd stopped charging, but they did not stop asking questions.

"Dr. von Traugott, it is a matter of public record that a telephone call was made from Dr. Adler's office to your estate in the hour preceding his death. Would you care to comment on the nature of that phone call?"

Audrianna choked as the hypothesis she had resisted came forcing itself on her. Breathing became difficult. She tried to scream, but she couldn't.

Lorna glanced over her shoulder and calmly said, "Dirk, she knows. Shut her down now before we draw any more attention this way."

Dirk hedged.

"Christ!" Lorna cursed. "I'll do it." She reached back and swiped her cold fingertips across Audrianna's forehead.

All went black.

"Oh, Dr. Foster. You're awake!"

Audrianna opened her sleepy eyes to the face of an unfamiliar person in the waning light of evening. She sat up too quickly and felt her head begin to spin.

"Dr. von Traugott will be so happy to see you up. He's been terribly worried about you."

Audrianna collapsed back down into the fluff of the bed, remembering everything. "Who are you?" she asked.

The young lady smiled with concern. Her skin was pock marked across her cheeks and forehead where chickenpox had played havoc as a child. Her hair was short and brittle, and her teeth were broken. The sight of her should have been startling, but Audrianna was not startled. She was relieved—relieved that she was not dead, at least not yet.

"Don't be frightened, Dr. Foster," the girl said sweetly. "You're safe here in Dr. von Traugott's home. Not in that awful jail anymore."

Audrianna closed her eyes. Her hair was damp and stuck to her face like wet straw. She smelled and felt clean, like she had just been bathed with lavender soap. Her bloody clothes were gone and in their place she wore a soft cotton gown that buttoned to her neck and covered her to the ankles.

"What happened to my clothes?" Audrianna whispered.

"I gave them to the laundress after your bath," the girl replied. "I'm not surprised you don't remember. You were quite ill and in such a daze. I was afraid you weren't going to snap out of it—we all were. Countess Mehlinger wouldn't leave your side until after you'd fallen asleep."

Audrianna unbuttoned the gown to her sternum and fanned herself. She was trapped in the house with a sociopath, a pathological liar, and in her estimation—a killer. She could not be sure of Lorna's involvement, but honesty had never been her forte in the past.

"Shall I bring your dinner tray up, Dr. Foster?"

Audrianna shook her head. "I don't think I can eat just yet," she said, masking her terror. "Maybe I could just sleep for a little longer."

The girl nodded. "I understand. You must be exhausted. Is there anything else you need?"

Audrianna thought quickly. The girl would report her condition to Dirk. Knowing Audrianna was awake, he might want to come and "persuade" her of a different story than the one she had been piecing together. Who knew how far he would go to prove his point.

"No, thank you," Audrianna said. "I just need some more rest. Please tell Dr. von Traugott I'm fine, just sleeping through the night."

"Certainly. If you change your mind or need me for any reason," the girl told her, "just ring the servant's bell over there on the wall." She pointed to a call bell system mounted beside the bed, a gadget of the wealthy.

"Thank you," Audrianna said. The girl closed the door and left Audrianna in a shroud of semi-darkness. Audrianna waited until the patter of footsteps disappeared down the hallway and then climbed out of bed. She had to get out of there. Surely she was less safe now than in the jail. Dirk could let her meet the same fate she would have faced in court and never give her the opportunity to expose her discoveries to a jury.

Flickers of firelight danced around the small apartment, illuminating the room just enough to see. Two Queen Anne armchairs faced the flames, hiding the fireplace from total view, but the heat was palpable all the same. Audrianna searched through empty drawers for clothes and her personal belongings. She would take only what she could not do without.

"Looking for something?" Lorna rose from one of the chairs, dressed in a fresh riding suit and boots. She held a crop in her hand.

Audrianna swallowed her heart. She pulled her hands out of the drawer and stood slowly to face Lorna, scared and sure that it showed. Adrenaline squeezed her voice box. "I was looking for," she cleared her throat, "something to read. I couldn't sleep."

Lorna grinned at her, mischief sparkling in her eyes. "If it's bedtime entertainment you crave, we could certainly amuse each other," she said. She moved out from around the chair in Audrianna's direction, draining a glass of red wine she held in her hand.

Audrianna lurched away. Lorna laughed.

"What's the matter, darling?" Lorna feigned sympathy. "This morning you pledge me your undying love, and now you tremble at my advance." She held out her arms in mocking fashion. "Don't you want me to hold you anymore?"

Audrianna did not answer her. She looked down at the floor. They had done a good job, Lorna and Dirk—tricking her, manipulating her, trapping her there like the little naïve child they had always claimed she was. Well, she guessed she had proven them right—this time; a mistake that would not be repeated if she could find a way out of this bind.

Lorna refilled her wine from a cut decanter next to the fire. The red liquid poured as thickly as blood, splattering the insides of the crystal like a spurting artery. She offered it to Audrianna, watching as the light reflected through the glass. "Would you like some? It might help you relax."

Audrianna shook her head.

"I hope you don't mind," Lorna said. "But I'm having another." She put the glass to her mouth and drank the entire amount before Audrianna could reply.

"No. Go right ahead. I don't care," Audrianna whispered. Her words were dry and cracked from the heat. She licked her lips to help lubricate their flow.

Lorna looked up with seeming concern. She stared at Audrianna's freshly moistened lips for a moment before emptying the rest of the decanter into her glass. Her hush escalated into an unbearable, blaring silence. Finally, she spoke, "The Swiss government has frozen your bank account, confiscated the cash you had at your boarding house, and seized your travel documents. How far do you think you'll be able to run?"

"I wasn't planning—"

"Audrianna," Lorna cut her off, her tone somber and threatening. "I am not a fool. Please don't treat me like one." She scrubbed her fingers across her forehead as if trying to wipe something off her skin. "Your thoughts are so loud they give me a headache. So why don't you just say aloud what it is you're so convinced you've figured out?"

Audrianna stayed quiet, kicking herself internally. Everything about Lorna suddenly seemed so dark and sinister.

"You don't trust me," Lorna said simply. "Then let me tell you what I hear you thinking." She placed her thumb and forefinger underneath her chin in a parody of thoughtfulness. "Hmm, let's see here. You believe you've caught Dirk in some questionable medical practices, and now he most certainly wants you dead, through a legal execution if possible, or through other means if necessary. Does that about sum it up?"

"Lorna, please. I never said—"

"Of course, there are lots of details fluttering around in there that are quite muddled, like Amalie Kaltenbach, the murder, and of course, that pesky folk tale that started it all," said Lorna, rubbing her forehead again. "But I really see no point in getting into all of that. You explained it well enough in your jail cell this morning. Remember, darling?"

"Lorna, I don't want to quarrel with you."

"Well, you're wrong," Lorna dropped her hand and continued. "In fact, your suppositions are a bit daft." She took another gulp of wine. "Dirk is no more capable of premeditated murder than are you. You and he are two of a kind. I guess that's why I've had such a hard time with you, getting you, or getting over you." She laughed at her own words.

Audrianna began to shake. She did not understand.

"No, Dr. Adler was being paid to keep this whole mess under wraps," Lorna said, pacing off a few steps. "I do have other functions in our group, but my primary mission is to make sure Dirk survives. If this scandal had come to light, the pain for him would have been unbearable. The refugee hospital—everything he believes in might have been lost. It likely would have destroyed him." She casually leaned against the back of the chair as if she were discussing the latest social events. Her tone was flat, her form relaxed. "When Dr. Adler telephoned that night to tell me he how clumsy he had been, I decided to silence him."

Audrianna's lips began to quiver. "You?" she whispered. "*You* killed Dr. Adler?"

Lorna folded her arms across her chest and gestured with one of her hands, her tone annoyed. "He was a *pawn*, Audrianna. The fact that the police believed you responsible was a glitch—not my intention at all. I hope you believe that. You should've left it all alone as I asked, and then none of this would be happening."

Audrianna began backing toward the door, clutching her gown closed at the throat. Lorna did not follow, just continued talking as if nothing were amiss. "Oh," Lorna snapped her fingers and said, "and there's one more part of your theory that's complete fantasy. Dirk would never dream of conducting unsanctioned medical experiments. He's far too honorable. It's your father who was drugging the girls. Dirk was simply trying to sustain himself."

"Sustain himself?" Audrianna squeaked.

"Yes, darling." Lorna drummed her fingertips against her arm. "There is no such thing as lyovitalis. The word is the medical community's attempt to try and explain a supernatural condition in scientific terms." She drew a breath and continued, "Dirk and I are not like you. Our humanity is limited to our physical bodies. We have hearts that beat, lungs that breathe. If you cut us, we bleed. Beyond that, we possess no traits that link us to your world. We survive on the energy of the human soul. Not our own souls—we have none—but the souls of humans who are either too weak, too deluded, or too careless to resist us."

Audrianna recalled the opening paragraphs of *The Children of Gavrilek*. She shook the memory from her mind. "I don't understand a word of what you're saying," she stammered. "You're making this all up—this vampire story."

"No, darling. I wish I were," sighed Lorna. "Nurse Heidi Klaus? Dirk's famishment brought about her death. Yes, she's dead now."

"She was Niklas' girlfriend!" Audrianna cried.

"No. You *thought* she was Niklas' girlfriend," Lorna replied. "It was Dirk she wanted, and Dirk eventually gave in to her—to excess. There are ways of acquiring the energy we need without taking things as far as he did. But he waits too long—this time until he was almost dead, until he had no resistance left in him, and then he lost control. You see, he gets reckless because he's depressed. He's tired of playing the game and he's tired of living. Because we don't really live, you see. None of us do. We just … exist."

Audrianna twisted frantically at the doorknob, but found it locked.

"No, Audrianna," Lorna said. She swallowed the last of her wine and hurled the glass into the open fire, precipitating an explosion of flames. "I'm not finished yet. I'm not finished with you. Come here."

Audrianna didn't move. She tightened her grip on the door handle. Lorna glared more intently each second Audrianna didn't comply. Lorna threw out her arm, palm open wide, adopting a stance of power and speaking in an almost unrecognizable voice. "Audrianna! *Come to me!*"

Audrianna felt her body creep back into the center of the room, under no control of her own; her legs dragged beneath her. She used hands to grab at anything to slow her advance, but things only toppled onto the floor.

"Audrianna, what are you scared of?" Lorna growled, wrapping her long cold fingers around Audrianna's arm and easing her closer. Her grip was firm but not cruel. "If I wanted to hurt you, I could have a thousand times before now."

Audrianna choked on her words, and Lorna continued without waiting for her to settle down. "You're afraid I'll touch you."

"Yes," Audrianna whispered, gulping little breaths of air.

"You're afraid you'll want to touch me back."

"Yes."

"You're afraid to want me," said Lorna.

"Yes."

"But are you afraid to love me?"

Audrianna looked around in a panic one last time for a way to escape. There was none. She lifted her head with all that was left of her courage and said, "Yes." Her breath fell into pants as she listened to her own voice surrender to the will of another woman, a professed killer, and whatever else she was claiming to be. "Do whatever you want to me," she whispered. "Nothing can possibly hurt worse than this ache I have endured for you."

"It's time for the torture to end," Lorna said. "For both of us." She grabbed the lapels of Audrianna's gown in both hands and ripped the flimsy cotton down to her belly button. With ruthless, superhuman strength, she flung Audrianna onto the bed and ripped off her own shirt, sending the buttons flying. Audrianna, shaky but now aroused, reached up and started unbuttoning Lorna's pants. She had rehearsed this so many times in her dreams.

She slipped her hands down the back of Lorna's pants and rested them on bare buttocks, pulling her forward to nuzzle her navel with tiny kisses. Lorna wound the fingers of one of her hands into Audrianna's hair and reached down with the other to fondle one of her nipples. She rolled it between her thumb and forefinger, mingling pain with pleasure.

Audrianna gasped as Lorna stood and slowly, deliberately removed the last of her own clothing. Her jutting hipbones sloped inward to a flat belly; rising up were two perfectly proportioned breasts. She positioned herself in between Audrianna's legs, jackknifing her body so she could grind their clitorises together. They moved, and watched one another, not diverting their eyes for a moment as their bodies danced sinuously toward climax;

slipping, sliding, gyrating on each other's wetness. The mutuality of movement heightened the sensation, and Audrianna shrieked out in ecstasy, climbing to orgasm by Lorna's relentless, aggressive lovemaking. She began to contract and let it come, indomitable, strong. But, as she did, Lorna let out a spine-chilling scream, much shriller than her own. Lorna pulled from their entanglement as though she had caught fire and curled into a ball at Audrianna's feet.

"Your soul overtakes me," she whimpered. "This is even more calamitous than I expected. My fortitude cannot withstand your seduction."

Audrianna moved to comfort her, but Lorna shrugged her off, sitting up on the side of the bed instead and burying her face in her hands. "As much as I want to, I cannot be with you like this in the physical world," she said. "I cannot sustain myself. My energy supply burns too quickly. And if you continue to allow me free access to your soul as you just did, you are taking a terrible, terrible risk. You saw what Dirk did to that girl, Heidi. I don't want that to happen to you. I could do that. I am strong, but I am not infallible, Audrianna. Don't tempt me too much."

"You told me Dirk didn't have to go that far," Audrianna said as she wrapped Lorna up in her arms; this time, Lorna did not resist. "You could take just a little," Audrianna continued, not caring what she was agreeing to. "Just enough to keep you going. Then we could be together!"

"I don't know if I could stop without having it all," Lorna calmly replied. She looked up and said, "I won't do it." Her eyes were red.

Audrianna gasped. She took a long fifteen seconds to recover from the shock and then she whispered, "You won't do it because you love me." There was no inquiry in her voice.

"I told you. For me to love is suicide," Lorna growled. "I don't have the choice. If I love you, I die."

But Audrianna knew Lorna loved her. She would not have gone to such pains to stop their coupling otherwise. Audrianna fought tears. She felt something she had never felt before and hoped never to feel again. It was not the bliss of a hard-fought, requited love. It was the devastation of suffocated hope. Audrianna knew if she wanted to spare both of them more of the same, or worse, she had to leave Lorna alone.

They found each other's hands and intertwined their fingers, speaking in a language that required no words. "Tomorrow, you must leave with Niklas. After that, you and I can never meet again," Lorna said finally. "Do you understand why?"

Audrianna nodded. She pulled her torn nightgown up around her and walked to the door. This time it opened easily, yet Audrianna found it much more difficult to leave. She turned and looked at Lorna, hoping something might be different, that she would call her back. But she did not. When it became clear she was not going to, Audrianna left the room.

She navigated the house without thinking, lost in her own grief. Her course had already been decided for her, and Lorna had reconfirmed it just a few seconds ago. Tomorrow she would be smuggled across the German border, somehow, and married off to Niklas. Until then, she might find a closet somewhere to hide in like she had when she was a little girl. The confined space and darkness had always made her feel safe. And that's how she wanted to feel right then, even if it was a false sense of safety.

"Audrianna! What's wrong? What's happened to you?"

In her bemused state, Audrianna collided with Dirk. She stumbled backward, shocked by the sight of him, by his voice and body. Into her heartache swirled terror. It tore through her chest like a howling banshee. "Oh my God! Leave me alone!" she cried out, clutching her torn gown closed and floundering around the banister at the top of some stairs.

Dirk followed. "Why are you frightened of me?"

"I know who you are, what you've done! How dare you try to manipulate me?" Audrianna shouted.

Dirk spoke calmly. "I don't know what you think you know, Audrianna. But I can show you the truth now, if you're ready."

Audrianna glared at him. "Show me how?" she spat. "By paralyzing me and dragging me off to your bedroom? How about some chloroform, or did you use it all on Heidi?"

Dirk held out his hand and softly said, "No. You'll come with me of your own free will, or not at all. I'll not force you."

Audrianna opened her mouth to refuse, but then closed it. She was an accused murderess, about to be married as a means of escape. If the truth killed her, at least she would be free. She inched her hand forward and whispered, "Yes, Dr. von Traugott, show me your truth."

CHAPTER 10

"Fine. What is Gavrilek?" Audrianna asked Dirk, once in his room.

Dirk gave her a plush lounging robe to put around her shoulders. Audrianna had forgotten her current state of undress until reminded by his gentlemanly conduct. She wrapped herself up and tied it closed, too defeated to bother with feeling embarrassed.

"I think you mean where," Dirk answered.

"I beg your pardon."

"*Where.* Gavrilek is a place."

Audrianna flashed a perturbed look. "All right, then. *Where* is Gavrilek?"

Dirk poured himself a crystal tumbler of bourbon and sat down on the sofa in front of the fire. "I'm sorry, Audrianna," he apologized, jumping right back up again. He made a broad, sweeping gesture with his hand, inviting her to be seated on any of the parlor suite pieces in the room. "Please," he said. "May I pour you a drink?"

"Whatever you're having," Audrianna replied, risking the side effects, wanting the numbness. She moved around the side of the couch and took a seat in a rocking chair as Dirk prepared a second glass of bourbon.

"Gavrilek is the second dimensional mirror of the planet Earth," he said, handing her the drink and then reseating himself. "It's in the biverse."

"I'm sorry. What?" Audrianna replied, blinking.

"The infinite cosmos is laid out in triplicate dimensions, superimposed on top of each other," Dirk continued. "The first dimension is the universe, the second is the biverse, and the third is the antiverse. Each cosmic body in the first dimension has a second mirror in the biverse, and a third in the antiverse. In the case of the planet Earth, the second mirror is Gavrilek, the third mirror is Tawn."

Audrianna took a large gulp of the bourbon, hoping just one unladylike guzzle would be all it took to generate an immediate state of drunkenness. She had changed her mind. She did not want to be numb. She wanted to be *drunk,* needed to be drunk, to be able to take what he was saying seriously. "Let's pretend I believe what you're telling me," Audrianna said quickly. "What does any of that have to do with you or Lorna, or lyovitalis?"

"Lorna and I, and all the other soul-less entities on this planet, come from Gavrilek," Dirk explained. "We've been stranded here."

"Soul-less entities?" Audrianna winced as she gulped more bourbon.

Dirk nodded. "Witches, werewolves, vampires, goblins, trolls, mermaids, the list goes on."

Audrianna grimaced. Eventually, she managed a question. "And which of those are you?"

"I am a cambion," Dirk replied. "Third generation Gavrilekian."

"And Lorna?"

"The same," said Dirk. "Although she is second generation."

Audrianna put her glass down and leaned back in the rocking chair with her eyes closed. She gripped its arms and closed her eyes. The only reason she did not burst out laughing was because Dirk was dead serious. There was no mistaking that. "All right. And what *is* a cambion? A generational Gavrilekian?" she asked with her eyes still closed.

"A cambion is the offspring of an incubus and a human woman. The term 'generational Gavrilekian' refers to how much biverse energy, or strength of incantation the creature carries—based solely on the number of human crossbreedings—the more human we are, the more susceptible to the devastating effects of emotion."

Audrianna picked her glass back up and choked down another mouthful of liquor. His answers came so quickly and with too much certitude to be apocryphal. He at least believed what he was saying and that intrigued her. "Okay, Dirk," she said, "tell me more."

"I'll tell you what I know." Dirk savored his bourbon in small, controlled sips. "But you're still likely to have questions." He reached into a side table, pulled out a cigar, and lit it. "Even I still have questions. I won't be able to answer them all because my memories are a quarter of what my grandfather's were when he incarnated here five thousand years ago. The number of subsequent procreations has eradicated a lot of the knowledge he carried with him."

"Meaning—?" Audrianna lifted her eyebrows.

"Every memory my grandfather brought here from Gavrilek, every bit of understanding, and every special ability, was embedded in the energy of the biverse. So when he was hunted and forced to cross with a human being, only half his biverse energy passed to his offspring, my father. And when my father made the decision to breed with another human being, he left me with just one quarter of the original biverse energy. Did you get a chance to read *The Children of Gavrilek* before you were arrested?"

Audrianna felt her lip curl. She hardened her eyes; Dirk did not seem to notice. "Of course, there is some mistruth there," he continued, "put there for dramatic effect."

"What part, Dirk?" Audrianna said sarcastically. "It all sounds completely implausible to me."

Dirk grinned but it did not reflect in his eyes. "I'm sure it does," he said, tilting his head. "And some of it is. Mind control, for instance. As far as I know, there is no such thing. What we are doing is distorting the flow of energy, tinkering with it, so that the body interprets the signals differently from what they were intended. Your thoughts, also electrical currents, are released from the brain and easily translatable if you have an understanding of how energy works."

"Is that so?" Audrianna retorted. "And how is it that you and Lorna have this understanding, but no one else I know does?"

"Because of the biverse."

"Of course, the biverse. I forgot."

Dirk took another sip of his drink and then set it down on the table. "I can see my words are making no headway with you. Perhaps I can change your mind through another of your senses."

"What are you talking about?" Audrianna asked him with suspicion.

"Wait. Watch. Listen. I need your mind still so I can accomplish this feat. It's not an easy one with the limited amount of power I possess. I'm not as strong as Lorna."

"But—"

An unexplained gust of wind blew the fire out. The smoke from the cinders poured out of the fireplace toward them, but then stopped; stopped in the space that was between Audrianna, Dirk, and the mantel. Ash began to rotate, spinning up an invisible pole until it formed one long column from ceiling to floor

"Audrianna."

She heard her father's voice and turned her head to look for him.

"Audrianna. I am here."

The column of smoke took the shape of a human, forming a head first, then arms and legs. Within a few seconds, facial features were discernible: a mustache, a full scalp of silver hair, genetically etched wrinkles down the sides of an all-too-familiar mouth.

"Father!" Audrianna called out. "Father, where are you?" She fell to her knees at the base of the specter, trying to grasp him, but coming up with only fists of ash.

"I am here, Audrianna. In Heaven," the specter said.

Audrianna knelt in front of her father's image, weeping. "But where is mother? I want to see her, too!"

"Your mother isn't here, child," her father replied.

"I cannot hold him here, Audrianna," Dirk said. "His vibrations are too powerful for me to anchor in tangent."

Audrianna let out a tortured scream. "No! Tell me where mother is! Why isn't she in Heaven?" She tumbled forward onto her elbows, wrapping her arms around the vaporous ankles of the phantom. "Tell me!" The smoky figure collapsed, showering her with a rain of soot. She sat back on her haunches and watched as the dust particles retracted into the fireplace and disappeared up the chimney, the fire spontaneously reigniting on its own.

Audrianna wiped the ash from her face with her hands; she remained on the floor. It seemed appropriate in her current state of mind: lowly, filthy, and worn. She wanted to fade into it, like one of the cracks in the long boards. "All right, Dirk," she croaked. "You've got my attention. How did you make my father appear like that?"

"I didn't make him appear," Dirk replied. "He was already here. I simply slowed his vibrations enough for you to be able to see him with your eyes. Your God has designed this place to be your Heaven—Earth, that is. Just because you can't see the entirety of the creation doesn't mean it doesn't exist. It is here. You are the one who has chosen to exteriorize your spiritual form into a physical body, a state that is far less real and far less eternal than Heaven. Your God does not require it from you."

"God!" Audrianna half-cried, half-laughed, shaking her fists in the air, frustrated. "If that is true, why would anybody do it?"

Dirk stamped out his cigar. "I'm not exactly sure," he said. "I have never met your God, but I suspect the intention was to give humans a way to experience adventure. Physical incarnation must be rewarding in some manner, although, when weighed against the potential dangers, I can't say it makes much sense to me."

"Dangers?" Audrianna laughed.

"Yes. There is no guarantee that you'll make it back to Heaven once you leave. Your God has erected a protective fortress around your soul and equipped you with the armaments to protect yourself from foraging entities—"

"Like you?" Audrianna snapped.

Dirk nodded. "Yes, I'm ashamed to say like me. Your God, however, made no provision to protect human beings from themselves. He gave you free will. If you choose to destroy your own soul with negative emotions, your God will not intercede. You may willingly give yourself to another, even if that other is a pilfering being, hungry for your soul. I think you are following me. If you're absent a soul—for whatever reason, you will be turned away from Heaven when you try and return."

Audrianna's tears began to roll. "Is that what happened to my mother?" she cried. "She gave her soul to someone?"

"I'm afraid so."

"But how is that possible?" Audrianna carried on. "She was happy with my father. They were happy together—I think." She folded her arms over her stomach and reflected on the memory of her parents' relationship. She did not know if they were happy or not, but could not see her mother as an adulteress. "I just don't understand how that could've happened," she added, shaking her head.

"It's easier than you might think, Audrianna," Dirk told her. "It sounds like her disposition was such that it lent her to love easily. It likely wasn't a conscious decision on her part. Your mother's lover took advantage of a state of vulnerability. Maybe he felt himself falling in love, too, and had to end it permanently before it destroyed him." He paused and allowed Audrianna to process what he said.

After a short period of silence, Dirk redirected the conversation. "Do you know what lyovitalis means, literally interpreted?"

Audrianna wiped her face on her sleeve and said, "Dissolving?" She shrugged and then frowned. "No, I don't suppose I do."

"It means dissolution of the soul," Dirk quickly told her. He adjusted his seat forward and continued, "Your father went on to call it the disease of love. He lost his wife, your mother, to lyovitalis. He was hell bent on finding out why. He did something a lot of physicians don't do, he set aside his preconceived notions and *listened* to patients' families; he *listened* to the community. Unlike other educated professionals, he took the legend of Gavrilek seriously. When he did that, he found me," Dirk snorted. "Not that I was so very hard to find. I think deep down, I wanted him to find me. He acknowledged my existence with kindness; he proposed a medicinal intervention that might benefit both our species—a love antidote. I *was* his silent partner. I *did* bankroll the study. Initially, Dr. Adler had no involvement, nor did the university."

"Heavens, a love antidote." Audrianna turned her eyes down and fluttered her wet lashes, embarrassed, but not sure why. She noticed the initial buzz of alcohol. "That is … different," she stammered. "To what benefit?"

"It was a fairly complex concept," Dirk began. "Simplified, it went something like this: Love is the key to the soul; consciousness is the lock on the door. Your father wanted to study the effects of low-dose anesthetics on my human hosts. He hypothesized that the variance of consciousness associated with the drugs would result in my inability to siphon the soul. He was right. The drug obscured emotion—love in particular."

Audrianna cringed. She thought of her mother and felt sick first, then angry. "So we're reduced to animals just to stave off the likes of you?" she snarled. "Our consciousness sets us apart from other living things—our ability to love makes us special."

"Also your arrogance," Dirk replied, mildly irritated. "The only thing that sets your consciousness apart from *any*thing on this planet is that body you're in, specifically the larger, more complex brain. The only way you know to qualify consciousness is by demonstration, through words, or through action. You have arms and legs and a mouth—how fortunate for you. Imagine yourself trapped in a pine needle, navigating life without a voice, then consider who is really set apart."

Audrianna's mouth went slack; her body began to sweat.

"As far as love goes," Dirk continued with a laugh. "Well, humans don't have the monopoly on that, either." He paused and Audrianna continued to stare. "The benefit of a love antidote is the same as any antidote, to decrease the mortality rate associated with poisoning. Love is a toxin. It kills humans; it destroys us."

After a moment Audrianna whispered, "So, what happened? It obviously didn't work … the 'antidote' I mean." She looked down and played with her hands. "They died—Amalie Kaltenbach and," she cleared her throat, "Heidi Klaus."

"The treatment did work when the girls were compliant with the application of the drug," Dirk countered. "Which was only half of the time. Your father overlooked the addictive qualities of the chloroform when formulating his theory, and frankly, so did I. Amalie Kaltenbach overdosed her prior to my ever having arrived to see her that night."

Audrianna touched her fingers to her lips, staring intently.

"Your father and I performed artificial breathing and chest compressions on her," Dirk continued, "but we never got her back. It was probably during our efforts to save her that your father's watch fell out of his pocket." He paused. "Mrs. Kaltenbach found the watch in the days following and began to stir the story into the community, calling for an official inquiry into Amalie's death. To avoid an investigation, Dr. Adler was brought in as the cleanup man. His name legitimized the project; his professional reputation diverted scrutiny from your father, and thereby me. For this, he was handsomely paid. The study fell entirely into the hands of the university; your father fell ill and went home. Dr. Adler was in the final weeks of squashing the project completely when you showed up asking questions."

Dirk dropped his head. "That's what happened with Amalie. I didn't give Heidi any chloroform," he confessed. "After giving some of my energy to that baby, the one you so courageously worked to save, I simply had nothing left. I knew she loved me. So I took what she was offering. I despised her narcissism and resented her cruelty toward you. I am not proud of who I am or what I have done, and I'm sick to death of this existence. Having to live off the souls of others is no life at all."

"Heidi." Audrianna said absently. "The way she protected you that day. I should've known." She slowly shook the glaze out of her eyes and continued, "Is this soul-siphoning process, is that the game? Is that what Lorna was talking about when she said you're 'tired of playing the game'?"

"The game, no," Dirk scoffed. "Soul siphoning is simply our process of refueling—what we have to do to survive. The energy generated by the human soul seems to be the only acceptable fuel exchange for our biverse energy." He quickly followed with,

"I'm not sure why. If my grandfather knew, unfortunately, it isn't a memory I have ingrained."

Audrianna squinted. "What do you mean ingrained? How could your grandfather's memories be ingrained in you?"

"I have some of my grandfather's memories because I have inherited some of his biverse energy," Dirk replied. He got up from his chair and knelt with Audrianna on the floor, then continued, "I'm sure you're acquainted with Mendel's genetic theory, right?"

Audrianna nodded, although acquainted was a bit of a stretch. She had heard of it—studied it long enough to take an exam. It was a subject of controversy, a scientific description of how hereditary characteristics were passed from parents to their offspring.

"One of the genetic factors that is passed in the energy of the biverse is memory," Dirk said.

"But if you have your grandfather's memories, wouldn't that," Audrianna nibbled on her tingling lips, "wouldn't that make you him?"

"Not exactly—no," Dirk laughed. "Identities can change and do so all the time. Memories are permanent stamps on the space-time continuum of the soul, or biverse energy, in my case. Because my biverse energy is only a small portion of the original amount my grandfather had, my memories are quite fragmented. Such is the case of anyone from Gavrilek who has been cross-bred with a human."

Audrianna lifted her hand to her forehead and squeezed her eyelids tightly shut. She wished she had not guzzled that liquor.

"I'll explain another way," Dirk offered. "Have you ever gone somewhere you've never been to before and found it already familiar? The smells? The sounds? The way the place looks?"

"Like déjà vu?" Audrianna said, nodding. She opened her lazy eyelids.

"Exactly." Dirk snapped his fingers. "And although modern science tries to pass it off as some kind of false impression or psychopathology, the recognition is really an imprint—a memory you've been able to awaken from the library of knowledge that belongs to your being, stored there by one of your previous identities in one of your previous lifetimes. You haven't always been Audrianna Foster, you know."

Thank God, Audrianna thought. Silence forced her to talk before she was ready to. "How did you ... get here?" she asked.

Dirk replied, "We fell. The entire planet fell from the biverse during a storm. I remember falling. I remember that feeling because it hit me in the middle, like being ripped apart. There was fire all around, and I remember hitting a solid surface, causing unimaginable pain. We all scampered around like a frenzy of locusts—up in the air, down on the ground, all of us trying to find creatures to hide in—creatures without souls. My grandfather and Lorna's father stuck together, helped each other. After several days, they invaded a pair of incubi. That was during the Roman Empire."

"That's, um, good." Audrianna closed her eyes again and pinched the bridge of her nose. She could not remember the point of the conversation.

Dirk chuckled at her. "You initially asked me about the game," he said. "That's how it started."

"That's right," Audrianna croaked. She opened her eyes and shook her head, embarrassed.

"To answer your question," Dirk went on, "'the game' is the race to restore Gavrilek to the biverse and re-inhabit the planet. The outcome of the competition determines which of us will rule once we're home. To that end, we stifle each other's efforts by manipulating political and social unrest amongst humans. Wars are the largest conveyors of sabotage; if a group loses a war, they are generally out of the game for a very long time."

Considering the implications of Dirk's explanation, alongside the war going on in nearby countries, gave Audriana pause. She blinked hard and forced herself to focus. "Are you telling me that you, you ..." She heaved a sigh and scrubbed her fingers across her forehead. "I'm sorry, what do you call yourselves? Aliens or creatures or people or what?"

Dirk hesitated. "I've never given it any thought."

"All right, just forget it," Audrianna waved him off with a little aggravated headshake. "Are you telling me that you *people* incite conflict on this planet in order to improve your odds of winning a game?"

"Yes," Dirk quietly replied.

"Why, in God's name?" Audrianna demanded. "It's one thing if you all want to fight amongst yourselves, but why involve us? What did we do to deserve such horrific manipulation and abuse?"

"Nothing," Dirk replied in earnest. "But you have to remember, Audrianna, we don't *feel* empathy like humans do. Many, many of the masters have no perspective of emotion whatsoever. They don't care what kind of devastation they inflict upon *anyone*." He forced a laugh. "Including members of their own team! I've been killed a number of times by my master when I've proven hurtful to his cause."

Audrianna grimaced. "I'm sorry. What?"

"Audrianna, that's what you happened upon that day in my office," Dirk told her. "Oskar was there to kill my physical body. Had you not come along, he would've put a hole in my skull and my biverse energy would've instantly transferred right into an unoccupied human baby somewhere on the planet at the moment it drew its very first breath. Babies are born somewhere nearly every moment, so there's almost no chance we would not be incarnated should our human bodies meet with an untimely demise. My master would've tracked me down and put me right back into play with another identity. It's a vicious, vicious cycle and I'm not going to do it anymore."

"Yes, but ..." Audrianna put both palms on the floor to steady herself. "I'm sorry, I'm having a very hard time keeping up with what you're telling me." In truth, she heard only half of what he said and understood less than that. "Who are these captors—masters?" she shook her head and asked.

"Master Gavrilekians," Dirk clarified. "Creatures who have never been crossbred with a human—the incubus, in our case."

"I thought they were extinct."

Dirk shook his head. "A few survived the hunt; they rule the rest of us."

Audrianna reached forward and wrapped her arms around him. She did not know why. She felt sorry for him, despite everything that had happened. She could at least hope things would get better for her. From what she had been able to ascertain, Dirk and Lorna were destined to eternally miserable circumstances.

"But—I'm through with it, Audrianna," Dirk stated.

Audrianna pressed her lips together and inhaled deeply. She spoke as she exhaled. "What do you mean 'through with it'?" she asked.

"I've decided—to love you," Dirk replied. "That is my choice."

Audrianna's eyes flew open; she felt awkward. "But, you can't," she finally managed. "You'll die."

Dirk blinked softly and responded with warmth. "Allowing myself to love you is the only opportunity I'll have to *feel* alive." He leaned forward on his knuckles and, with only a slight hesitation, kissed her. Burgeoning whiskers scuffed her face. Audrianna drew back in a startle. "Sorry—" Dirk apologized. "I didn't mean to scare you."

Audrianna shook her head and got up from the floor, stumbling around. "I just ... I don't know." She held onto the mantel. "I'm not sure what I'm supposed to do here. I mean, what do you want me to say? Or how should I feel?"

Dirk followed Audrianna to her place by the fire. "I'm not expecting you to reciprocate the feeling, if that is your conflict," he said. "I'm well aware of where your heart lies, and I can't say I blame you. Lorna is a remarkable woman, Audrianna, and in any other world, well worth your anguish. But not here. Not now. She is emotionally unavailable. I am not."

Dirk waited until she looked up at him. He took her look as assent and drew her into him by the folds of his robe she wore. He pulled her neck directly in to his nose and lips, and Audrianna gasped a short, staccato gasp, startled by this sensual display. "I'm carrying something in my biverse energy that is important to the survival of my *people*," he whispered, his tone prophetic. "I'll entrust it to you."

Audrianna had no idea what he was saying. She plied already sweaty palms along the wood of the mantel, wringing her fingers around it nervously. The room was spinning. The fire was hot, but she was cold, everywhere but, oh ...

He turned her, placed his hands around her hips and bent her away from him like a V, rubbing his pelvis into her backside until she felt him hard through their clothing. She should feel ashamed, appalled—*frightened*—but she did not. She could not have Lorna and she did not want Niklas. She did not want Dirk, either, but her desire for life had slipped along with her grasp on reality. She was going to let him do whatever he wanted to do to her. And if she did not end up in Heaven—maybe at least she would see her mother again.

Dirk pulled loose the tie on the robe and stripped it from her shoulders so it hung momentarily off her hips. Audrianna reached to bunch the hem of her nightgown up until it rested on her lower back, exposing her bare buttocks as permission to continue. She heard him fiddling with the buttons on his pants, and braced herself against the mantel, nestling her fingers into the carvings for grip.

The bones of his hips were against her before his penis swung up and touched her between the thighs. His skin was so hot, compared to her skin, and hard. Audrianna had not imagined it that hard. She instinctively shimmied her feet wider, stretching her opening to be penetrated by him. He teased her. Using his hand to guide himself, he spread her wetness around her with gentle pressure, enough to arouse her evolutionary desire.

Audrianna moaned. He slipped inside her—halfway. She wrenched with her mouth hanging open, shocked at her first sensation of intercourse. Like having a decayed tooth pulled: warm, bloody. Tissues being severed while others clung together. Nerve receptors screaming pain, others pleasure. Every thought filled with desire: the desire to complete the task overthrowing the desire to halt everything.

Dirk slowly moved in and out, slightly farther with each thrust. He turned loose of her hips and gripped her breasts. Their entirety lifted in his hands; Audrianna felt herself throbbing below.

"Let go. Let go." Dirk panted as he lifted both her legs off the floor with one arm and held her torso against him with the other. "Let go of the mantel. I want you on the bed."

Audrianna let him carry her to the bed, keeping inside her the entire time. He set her on the mattress, knees first, so she hunched into an egg-like shape.

"You're so tight," Dirk murmured, instantly resuming his movements in and out of her. "So unbelievably wonderful. I'm not going to be able to hold on much longer. Put your head down and close your eyes, Audrianna. Your retinas will not tolerate the flash." He leaned into her and pushed her head down so her face pressed uncomfortably into the blanket. She began to squirm. "I'm sorry," he told her. "But it has to end. I. Can't. Do. This. Anymore. I love you, Audrianna."

A fluorescent green explosion lit up the room as he orgasmed, knocking pictures from the walls and books off shelves. Audrianna screamed and covered her face, holding her breath for whatever was to come. And then there was darkness, pure and simple—gravity that would not allow the escape of sight or sound. It was over.

———•◦•———

"Audrianna! What have you done?"

Lorna's distressed voice perforated the silence of sleep, prodding Audrianna from a solid state of unconsciousness. Nausea slammed into her body like a tsunami as she tried to sit up. Her vision blurred; she did not immediately recognize the place.

"Dirk!" Lorna screamed. "Dirk!" She rushed forward to the bed and pulled Dirk's naked body into her arms. His lifeless arms flopped as she sobbed on his chest.

Audrianna bobbled her head from side to side, bewildered by what she was seeing. "Dirk?" she whispered, confused. "What's happened? What's wrong?"

"He's dead, Audrianna! Dead!" Lorna shouted at her. She let Dirk's lifeless body fall back down on the mattress. Audrianna shot up and out of the bed. *Oh my God! Oh my God!* She squeezed her eyelids shut, trying to debar the nightmare. It had to be a dream! It had to be a dream! He could not be dead!

A charring slap across her cheek pulled her back.

"You bitch!" Lorna shrieked, drawing back as if to strike her again. Audrianna shielded her face from the blows, and when she did, Lorna clamped down on her arms like vice grips, shaking her brutally until she was barely able to stand. "I ripped the heart from my chest and let you leave with it last night, nearly killing myself in the process, and you, you make a beeline straight to Dirk's bed! Couldn't you see how vulnerable he was? Couldn't you see he was struggling with his feelings for you? God damn you!"

"Lorna, please," Audrianna stammered, trying without much force to break free of her hold. "I don't understand what has happened here, but I can't help him if you don't let me go."

Lorna shoved Audrianna backward and laughed. "Help him? Yes, *doctor*," she said bitterly, wiping at tears falling from her shining red eyes. "Bring back the dead, why don't you?"

Audrianna charged to Dirk on the bed, grimacing at his already cold body. She pressed an ear to his chest; she felt for a pulse, and then pried his eyes open. They were black. He was indeed dead. If she had to assign a medical cause, she would have to conclude it to be—lyovitalis: The disease of love.

"I—" Audrianna grabbed her head and quickly thought how to explain. "We made love," she said. "That's it, I promise. He told me he loved me and that he wanted to feel alive—"

"Shut up!" Lorna screamed. Then she broke down. "Just shut up. I know exactly what happened. I don't need the sordid details." She shook her head slowly back and forth and Audrianna became scared, silently watching Lorna. She suddenly wondered how many years—how many lifetimes—she and Dirk had been companions.

"It was supposed to have been me, Lorna," Audrianna said, wincing. She lifted and dropped her palms. "I thought I was the one who was going to die!"

Lorna stared at her through watery eyes, piercing Audrianna's spirit with the blistering poker of dashed hopes. The revelation flittered through the air, settling back on Audrianna's heart as a blanket of ugly, unremovable disgust.

"Should I feel better?" Lorna bit. She rounded the bed toward Audrianna, and Audrianna cringed, wanting to run but too frightened to move. Lorna moved in forcefully, stopping her advance deep inside the perimeter of Audrianna's personal space. Her tone changed to vindictive. "Last night I jeopardized my total existence just to spare your soul. Do you understand that? I've never done that for anyone. And you fuck someone else, excusing it by saying you thought it would *kill* you? 'It was supposed to have been me.' Audrianna, you didn't even love him. If you were so intent on dying, why couldn't it have been with me? We could have died together."

Audrianna hung her head. She tried to turn away but Lorna kept her still and steady with nothing more than her eyes and breath. The explanations she conjured carried no weight, not even within herself. She wanted to blame the alcohol, but it seemed an irresponsible, insufficient excuse. How was it that she was responsible for Dirk's death?

"He killed himself, you fool," Lorna spat out a response to Audrianna's thoughts. "He was just looking for a way to give up, and falling in love with you was it! Unrequited love is suicide for us. Requited love—murder-suicide. God! Your naïveté never ceases to amaze me!"

Audrianna exploded. "Lorna, if I am naïve in this regard, it is because you have made me that way!" she shrieked, throwing down her hands. "The only thing you ever gave me to formulate an intelligent theory about who and what you both were was a whisper here and there, an allusion to some illusive, religious cult, and lie after lie after lie. By the time I realized my absolute trust in your word was misplaced, I was far too caught up in disentangling your fingers from my heart to worry with any of the rest of it!"

Lorna laughed out loud. "I didn't come close to touching you, Audrianna. Believe me. If I had, Dirk would still be alive. You wouldn't have had the strength to walk away from me last night. If I had let my power wash over you, there wouldn't have been a clear thought in your head for over a month. Your heart would literally beat to my memory; your body would starve for the scent of my skin."

"How dare you pass judgment on my feelings for you!" Audrianna came completely unglued. She threw a punch in the air and screamed, "You have no clue how I've wanted you, how I've yearned for you—sometimes so badly I couldn't take a breath of air without feeling the texture of you inside of me." She stared deeply into Lorna's eyes, jabbing a finger in her face. "You want me, Lorna?" Audrianna took a step back, opened her arms and tilted her head backward, simulating crucifixion. "Here I am. Take me. Sacrifice me on your altar. Spill the blood of my soul on your wounds—but don't you *ever* belittle the depth of emotion I have carried for you!"

"Emotion. Ha!" Lorna scoffed at the boorish exhibition. "You should be careful. Your offer is almost too enticing. But it's much too late for that. I couldn't have you now, even if I wanted you. You've seen to that, haven't you, Dirk?" She turned away from Audrianna, walked back to Dirk's body, and ran her fingers through his silky black locks, whispering to him, "How could you leave me?"

Abandoned on her cross, Audrianna relaxed her position. "What do you mean, 'too late'?" she quietly asked.

Lorna shook her head, hesitating. Finally she spoke, in a controlled, listless tone. "I mean your life will never be the same again, Audrianna. Whether you wanted it or not, you are about to become intimately acquainted with the curse I've been trying to protect you from. Dirk has transferred the remnants of his biverse energy into you. You now carry a fourth-generation descendant of the Children of Gavrilek inside your womb."

"Where are we going?" Audrianna asked Lorna for the third time as the car bounced on pockmarked roads.

Lorna rubbed her own face, clenching her jaw. She kept her eyes closed, facial features fixed as if she had placed herself into some sort of trance—concentrating, no doubt, on pictures in her head that Audrianna could not see.

"You can't ignore me forever, Lorna!" Audrianna snapped.

Lorna broke from her stoic posture. "Do you have *any* understanding of what's going on here?" she asked, hanging her head and sighing. She kept her eyelids purposely closed, hiding her eyes from Audrianna's view. "Do you comprehend the danger you're in?"

"No," Audrianna replied. She touched Lorna's arm in an attempt to draw her full attention. "I haven't the first clue what's going on."

"Clearly you don't," Lorna said, "otherwise, you wouldn't be distracting me." She opened her eyes and turned sideways in her seat, allowing Audrianna to see her face. Audrianna inhaled sharply through her nostrils. "What's the matter, Dr. Foster?" Lorna asked, her tone sarcastic. "You seem alarmed."

Audrianna looked away as a reflex but then sneaked a troubled glance at Lorna's turbid eyes. The more she saw this look, the more she understood. Dirk looked the same way after giving the baby some of his life.

"What can I do?" Audrianna asked.

Lorna turned away from her, resuming her trancelike state before answering. "Close your eyes and your mind, Audrianna."

Audrianna shook her head, and Lorna felt her fight.

"I am using an enormous amount of my energy to block the searchers the master has hunting for you," she said. "It helps that you don't know where we're going, but you're looking out the window and seeing landmarks. Your anxiety is magnifying those thoughts—exactly what the searchers are looking for. I am a player, not a blocker. It won't be long before they break through the screen I am creating and they will find us. They will imprison you until after the baby is born, and then will kill you. Now turn your mind off and think about nothing."

Audrianna bit at her lips. Why was this master searching for her?

"He wants your child, of course. Dirk's child," Lorna answered.

Audrianna's palms began to dampen. She wiped them on her dress. This was all too much to be real, she mused, escaping to the reasonable part of her mind for logic. Surely, any minute now she would wake up and see it had all been a dream. She began to pinch the skin on her arms, hoping the pain would drive her from the captivity of such a deep, deep coma.

"Audrianna." Lorna's tone teetered on desperation. "Stop it! I don't have the strength to deal with your panic. If your mind cannot be still, think of calm, happy thoughts: your home, your mother. Feel her spirit inside you and let it carry you to repose."

At the mention of her mother, Audrianna *wanted* to stop her mind. To die without a soul: Panic again. Audrianna sat back and closed her eyes and slowed her breathing. She conjured her mother's face as best she could and daydreamed of a time when safety was not in question. The imaginary hum of soft gospel swayed her into a restless meditation, breeched after some time by the jolt of the stopping car.

Audrianna looked out the window at an enormous, slate-colored château, set apart overlooking a snow-sprinkled field. "I know this place," she whispered, not quite placing it.

"Audrianna, for God's sake," Lorna mumbled, her voice muffled like she was speaking from behind a closed door. "Detach yourself—your life may very well depend upon it. There is a treasure entombed here. It is embedded in the Earth's rare elements and you'll need Dirk's—Dirk's child to sanction its release. If I don't come out with it, please remember what I've said."

Jakob turned around from behind the steering wheel and questioned Lorna in German. Lorna shook her head. "No. Stay here with Dr. Foster. I will go inside. In three minutes, drive this car to the rendezvous point—with or without me. Niklas should be waiting."

"Wait!" Audrianna grabbed her. "Why wouldn't you be back?"

Lorna drew a deep breath and released it. "For once, darling, please," she said, tenderly this time. "Just do as I am telling you. Stay in this car." She climbed out into the wintry evening without looking back, fighting snow flurries up to the château. The place seemed abandoned; Lorna managed the heavy, wooden door on her own.

"Jakob," Audrianna said. "Something isn't right. Shouldn't there be someone here, a housekeeper, someone? Maybe you should go with her."

Jakob considered the suggestion, staring at the half-opened door. Nighttime fell in full force. It smothered the last of the sun's rays and added an ominous twist to the scene. "I think maybe you're right," he said finally. He reached underneath his seat and pulled out a shiny maple box with the Colt factory banner emblazoned on its lid.

Audrianna pulled herself forward and poked her head into the front compartment. "A gun? What are you thinking?"

Jakob removed the first of two matching .45 caliber pistols. "I hope I don't need this. If I do, I hope that it's enough," he said, cocking the sculpted slide and introducing a bullet into the chamber. He sheathed the weapon and repeated the same preparatory sequence on the second gun. "Do you know how to use this?" he asked Audrianna, placing the maple-eyed grip into her hand.

"No!" Audrianna cried.

"Let us pray that you won't need this first lesson, then," he said solemnly. He reviewed the features of the gun, how to clear a jammed bullet, how to avoid misfires. All Audrianna remembered was how to aim and how to shoot. "Lock the car doors when I leave," he continued. "Anybody you encounter, other than us, will not be here for friendly reasons." He disappeared into the house and she locked the doors, left alone to glaciate on the unpliable, leather seat.

The windows steamed quickly from the condensation of her breath. It congealed against the windshield, forming bubbles that popped and rolled down the glass to form networks of water slides. Audrianna shivered inside her lamb's-wool coat, and her teeth chattered in her head so badly her entire body seemed to vibrate. Cold or fright? Dread? Panic? Panic at the idea of Jakob believing he needed a gun? Or worse, that she might? She sat for ten minutes. Could she drive this thing if it came to that? But where was the rendezvous point?

Soon, Audrianna could no longer think of anything *but* where they were. She knew this place from somewhere. Why did it seem so familiar? Why did the recognition of it warm her to the core of her body even as she sat trembling in the cold?

"Come with me. I want to show you something," Audrianna heard Lorna say from inside the subconscious closet of her mind. *"It's the first snow of the season,"* the memory said. *"This is a section of the Bavarian Alps that my family has owned since the reign of the first Hapsburgs over seven hundred years ago."* It was coming back to her now. *"Every year since I can remember,"* said Lorna, *"I've come back here to watch the first snow of the season. It doesn't matter where I am or what I'm doing. I stop. I stop, and I return home to witness the same beautiful spectacle that you're seeing now. I tilt my head up like this, just as you're doing now, and I rejoice in the awe of Mother Nature's grace. I know it sounds like a crazy ritual, but until now, it's all I've known of God. Until I met you."*

"You brought me here," Audrianna said out loud. "You brought me here and made love to me in your bed. You brought me here because you needed to feel safe. You were *already* risking so much by loving me. Everything you've done for me has been a risk for you. I am such a fool!"

An explosive series of gunshots startled Audrianna. Her heart beat stronger, stirring her courage like a meringue, thickening until it was stiff enough to stand on its own. Lorna was in trouble. She had gone into that house knowing full well that catastrophe awaited her inside. It had been a stall, one meant to last long enough for Audrianna to get away. Jakob was meant to stay outside and drive off with Audrianna when Lorna did not return. Another risk. Another sacrifice.

"Well, not this time, Lorna!" Audrianna cried out. She opened the car door and raced through the snow with pistol drawn.

———•◦•———

"You disappoint me, Lorna."

Audrianna followed a man's voice up the stairs, slithering like a snake. She hugged the wall with scales of steel, brushing each step just long enough to propel her from one to the next. Orange candlelight reflected off the balcony banister over her head like a series of lighthouses on a treacherous coast.

"You've been my best player for hundreds of years—now look at how you've turned up. You should've let Oskar kill Dirk when he had a chance—at least his biverse energy would not have been lost. And now look—trying to steal the child away from me, Lorna. I can scarcely believe it."

Audrianna sunk to her knees short of the opening at the doorway and pressed the pistol against her cheek. She leaned into the frame, surveying the scene with only the movement of her eyes. Lorna was bound by ropes against a large pillar in the center of the room. Her legs had buckled and her head hung forward, hiding her face. Two men with glowing green eyes encircled her—Oskar and an older man. The older man had a diamond-shaped face, balding with a horseshoe fringe of fine blonde hair; his skin fell down his neck in folds.

Audrianna spotted a motionless body at the periphery. Jakob lay face down in a pool of red. His arms stretched toward claw marks of blood, showing his several attempts to reach Lorna before death took him. He had loved her, too.

Anger coursed through Audrianna. Heartless, compassion-less creatures! He was just a boy. She had to act now before they sensed her thoughts and killed her, too. But what to do? If she pulled the trigger at this distance, she would likely miss. What she really needed to do was get closer to them. Or get them to come closer to her. That would be easier and far more effective.

Audrianna scanned the immediate vicinity for something to throw, something large enough to cause alarm and draw them out of the room. She spotted a dagger-like letter opener on the hall table. She crept and snatched it into her pocket, returning to her previous position.

"I am intrigued," the older man said to Oskar. "A human capable of inflicting this much damage to our team should be rec-ognized. I shall enjoy adding her to my line once the child is born."

Lorna stirred. "Don't you touch her," she snarled, struggling to raise her head. Her eyes were black now, like onyx, with lips red and out of place against her pallid skin. She was ancient, desiccated, and deathly ill.

The older man chuckled. "What are we going to do with you, Lorna? Fallen under the influence of love. After all this time?" He cupped Lorna's chin to keep her face on him. "I'd rather not lose you, but cannot help it if you sacrifice yourself—to a worthless cause. But, to sacrifice the future of our planet—my future?" He shook his head at her. "Did you honestly believe you would be able to block her mind from me? And look at how it has drained you. You're nearly dead. Was it worth it?"

Lorna defiantly jerked her head out of his hand.

"What a foolish thing to do," the man continued. "You could've had her back after the child was born. A reward for your centuries of service. But what now, Lorna? How could I trust you now?" He patted her on the head and then turned his back to her and toward his younger colleague. "What do you think I should do with her, Oskar?"

Oskar smiled wickedly. "I think you should give her to me. I'll see she never causes you any more vexation."

The old man laughed. "Of course! Would you like that, Lorna?" He bent down on his haunches to face her where she half-hung, half-stood. "You'll have to keep her chained, though. If she gets away from you and regains her power, she'll kill you."

Oskar approached Lorna's slumped body. He ran his beefy, calloused hands through her sweaty hair, smoothing it back against her skull before tilting her face up. "I'll keep her chained, all right."

Lorna reared back and spat in his face. "Bitch!" Oskar shouted, raising his hand high to strike her. The old man seized his wrist and stopped him. "Enough! Oskar," he growled. "Let her be. Go get *that woman* out of the car so I can experience this phenomenon for myself. She must be some kind of sorceress to have caused such trouble."

Oskar wiped the foreign saliva from his face with his sleeve, shifting his weight in anger. Audrianna backed down the hall to the center of the stairway. She would not have to bait them after all. She hoped Lorna was still blocking her thoughts from them—and the effort would not kill her.

Aim and shoot, aim and shoot. Her arms shook so badly she had to brace her elbow against the wall just to steady her hand.

It was now or never, and never simply was not an option. The darkness had hidden the shadow of her for a second, but that second had passed, and now he was upon her. She held her breath and pulled back on the inflexible metal trigger.

Boom! The gunpowder exploded, sending Audrianna reeling backward down a couple stairs and dropping Oskar to his knees clutching his stomach. Oh, God! She hadn't killed him! Her aim had been too low!

"Dammit!" Audrianna recovered her footing and charged back up the staircase to where he wobbled back and forth. She pressed the barrel of the gun to his forehead and pulled the trigger one more time. *Boom!* The gun went off, splattering brain matter all over the shiny white marble. "I didn't aim low that time, you son of a bitch."

Audrianna stepped over his body, careful not to slip on his innards. She ran to where Lorna was being held. Both hands on the smoking weapon, she pivoted on her feet into the opening of the room. "If you move, I'll kill you!" she screamed at the old man. He did not appear to have been caught off guard at all. He had known Oskar's fate in advance. His disregard for life made Audrianna furious.

"I don't think so," the man said calmly. He pulled a cigar out of his coat pocket and snipped off the end with a cutter. "Put the gun down on the table there and come sit," he said with a genteel voice that contradicted the bloody hostage next to him. "I'm interested in getting to know you. After all, we'll spend quite some time together over the next nine months."

"Like hell we will!" Audrianna spat. "I'm tired of you already!" She took a couple paces forward, pointing the gun at his head, not intending to make the same mistake twice.

"There is certainly no reason to be rude," he remarked, smiling. "Is that how they are raising their young people in America these days?" An invisible force pried Audrianna's fingers from the handgrip of the gun. The weapon flew from her hand. She watched in astonishment as it came to rest gently on the table where the old man had asked her to place it. "Thank you," he said. "Now please, sit."

The end of his cigar burst into flame without a tangible catalyst. He puffed and pulled it from his mouth to blow out the flame, gesturing Audrianna to a chair across from where he stood. Reluctantly, she obeyed. She was dealing with a force far greater than any she had encountered before. She was careful not to let these thoughts traverse beyond the border of her senses.

"Do you know who I am?" the man asked.

"Your name? No. But you must be one of the Children of Gavrilek, perhaps even one of the so-called masters," Audrianna replied levelly. "Your eyes give you away. If I've learned nothing else all this time, I've learned about those eyes." She looked over at Lorna who had not moved at all since Audrianna had entered. There was no way to tell if Lorna was still alive or not.

"That bothers you, doesn't it? Not knowing?" he asked. Audrianna did not respond. Any emotion would be a gateway to her mind, an opening he would use to his advantage.

The old man snapped his fingers, causing the ropes holding Lorna to loosen and drop to the floor. Three smoke rings he blew toward Lorna expanded in size, encircled her body, and levitated her in an invisible cradle. As the fumes dissipated, Lorna was lowered to the floor at Audrianna's feet. "There now," he said, drawing up a chair for himself and settling down with the cigar, "No more distractions. You humans have such a hard time focusing on anything when sentiment is in play."

Audrianna flipped her eyes down. Lorna was breathing, but barely. Time was running out, and she was really no closer to saving her. Just then, Audrianna saw her opening; she was careful not to betray it with her eyes. "Are you going to tell me who you are?" she stalled, channeling her intentions through her mind, not her heart. She could not afford to feel. She could not embrace fear, or worse still, hope. She must use only logic or else he would see into her mind. And Lorna would die.

"I am the Lord of Berburg and Zerbst," he said, "and yes, I am a master. One of the few, as far as the incubus is concerned."

Audrianna nodded. She poked her tongue lightly in her cheek and said, "I heard you tell your buffoon that I'm going to be heading to your line at some point. What exactly does that mean?"

The man laughed cordially, but his reply was sinister. "The line is my closet," he said, "where I keep my human casings: physical bodies that have had their souls removed. I wear them when I have to go out into public, like now."

"Delightful." Audrianna refused to allow herself to be disgusted. "Do you mind if I pour myself a glass of whiskey?" She pointed to the glass carafe on a nearby side table. "I'm chilled. And frightened, of course. I need something to take the edge off."

"Certainly you may," he said with a smile. "Pour me one as well." *Gladly.*

Audrianna rose from her chair and opened the container. She poured a generous amount of whiskey into the two glasses with now-steady hands. She observed the liberation to do without anticipation, to act without considering meaning. It was easier to achieve than she had imagined.

"I must admit I have underestimated your understanding of the Children of Gavrilek," Lord Berburg said. "You know I cannot dominate you until you engage emotion. You do well to keep your feelings safely guarded. I'm amazed you have that much control over your innate human weaknesses. Lorna has been a good teacher." He took another long draw on his half-smoked cigar, admiring its red smoldering end deliciously. "Still, I detect the quintessential energy of a strategy. Soon, you will not have Lorna's assistance to hide behind."

Audrianna smiled coldly. "Yes, Lord Berburg. You have underestimated me," she said as she stepped casually forward as if to hand him his drink. "You've underestimated my knowledge of open flames and combustible liquids." She splashed the contents of both glasses into his face and lap, surprising him so much he dropped his cigar. The alcohol ignited into a brilliant blue flambé.

Audrianna lunged for the gun on the table as the old man swatted to extinguish the fire. She aimed for flame, pulling the trigger in rapid succession until the chamber was empty. The body stumbled forward to its knees, landing face down on the carpet, missing Lorna by a few feet. "So much for my innate human weaknesses!" Audrianna screamed. "I guess you underestimated those, too!"

The fire spread from his chair and body to the thick carpets and then to the heavy drapes, inextinguishable. Audrianna rushed to Lorna's inert form, pulling her up so her upper body rested against Audrianna's chest. "Lorna. Wake up!" She patted her face. "We have to get out of here!"

"The fire was out of control the last time we were here together, too," Lorna whispered without opening her eyes. "But we did put it out. Do you remember, darling?"

Audrianna shook her head. "Lorna, please. You're talking crazy. I have to get you out of here." She made an effort to rise from the floor with Lorna in her arms but collapsed, unable to lift the dead weight. "Lorna, you have to help. I can't lift you up."

"I made love to you in this place, this wonderful place," Lorna continued, in another world. "Tell me you remember."

"I remember. I remember, darling," Audrianna replied, wincing at the climbing heat. "But please! We really must get out of here before we're burned alive. If you don't help me, I'll have to drag you down the stairs. Have you ever been dragged down stairs before? I don't think it's going to be very pleasant!"

"You're going to have to shoot me, Audrianna," Lorna said.

Audrianna kissed her on the cheek and smoothed her hair back from her forehead. "I'm just teasing, Lorna. I'm not going to drag you down the stairs. I was just trying to motivate you. But we do need to hurry. Come on, now! Put your arms around my neck."

"Audrianna, no. No." Lorna resisted Audrianna's efforts to move her. "I won't make it to the car. You have to shoot me now, free my energy from this body. It's the only way I can—survive."

Audrianna began to choke. "You, you can't be serious. Oh my God! You *are* serious! I'm not going to shoot you!"

Lorna swallowed hard and the flames made their desires plain on Audrianna's bare skin. "There is a child ready to draw its first breath. I need the velocity of a physical death. If I take my last breath without it, I will end. Do you understand? No Heaven, no hereafter. Forever."

"I … I … No!" Audrianna burst into tears. "I don't understand! Where will you go? How will you get by?"

Lorna shook her head. "Wherever I'm born, I'll find you. I'll be nurtured by the soul of my mother until I can make it on my own, then will grow and find you. Please, Audrianna. If you love me—kill me."

Audrianna pulled her close. "Oh my God. I do love you. But I can't do this! Please don't ask me to do this!" she sobbed, closing her eyes and bowing her face into Lorna's hair. "This can't be the end! If I can just get you to the car—"

"There isn't time, darling," Lorna whispered. "Where is the gun? Please hurry. I can't hold on much longer."

Audrianna wiped her eyes with the backs of her hands, knowing the gun was all out of bullets. She kept her mind calm to avoid letting Lorna know. She sat quietly, and it came to her. The letter opener was still in her pocket.

Lorna opened her eyes. "I'm blind, Audrianna," Lorna said. Her voice was completely empty and still. "I have but a few seconds."

Audrianna sniffed and pulled the letter opener out of her pocket. She tilted her head up to the ceiling invoking the strength of a higher power. *God! Give me your mercy on the day of my judgment. I act on love and love alone.* She raised the blade overhead with both her hands and plunged it into Lorna's chest with all her might.

The body sprung forward from the impact of trauma, then fell back down, mouth agape. Audrianna drew her arm back again, and plunged again and again. She stabbed through flesh and muscle she had once nuzzled and felt perspire. Soon there was but a pool of mush where a living, beating heart used to be. When she was certain it was finished, she dropped the knife to the floor. "You're safe now, Lorna," she cried. "Goodbye, my love."

EPILOGUE

"Push, Baroness! Push! Once more!"

Audrianna felt her skin rip apart down below as she pushed the baby from her womb. It hurt, which she wanted. She wanted physical scars to match the mental and emotional ones she carried.

It had been nine months since Niklas had rescued her from Lorna's burning manor, from the threat of execution, and so far from any other Children of Gavrilek. It was only right that the new Baron, elevated after Dirk's death, believe the child she was bearing was his own.

They now resided at the von Traugott family estate in Austria, though Niklas very rarely stayed there. Audrianna did not care.

"Here you are, Madame," the doctor said, presenting the bloody bundle of whimpers and wiggles. "The next Baron von Traugott. Will you be naming him after his father?"

She shook her head. "His name will be Devon."

She held the baby and looked through sweating glass to colors of fall on the Austrian countryside.

She imagined, could almost see, the child's life to come.

She tried to make out which birthday it was that she saw, when her child would invite a new friend. A friend who had taken her own child under its wing, a child she knew she would also love. She closed her eyes to better picture that friend's face. It was beautiful, with those shining green eyes.

www.ingramcontent.com/pod-product-compliance
Lightning Source LLC
Chambersburg PA
CBHW021509240626
47154CB00002B/559